FILE M FOR MURDER

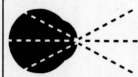

A CAT IN THE STACKS MYSTERY

FILE M FOR MURDER

MIRANDA JAMES

WHEELER PUBLISHING
A part of Gale, Cengage Learning

GALE
CENGAGE Learning

Detroit • New York • San Francisco • New Haven, Conn • Waterville, Maine • London

GALE
CENGAGE Learning·

LIBRARY OF CONGRESS CATALOGING-IN-PUBLICATION DATA

James, Miranda.
    File M for murder : a cat in the stacks mystery / by Miranda James. —
Large print ed.
        p. cm. — (Wheeler Publishing large print cozy mystery)
        ISBN 978-1-4104-4934-4 (pbk.) — ISBN 1-4104-4934-3 (pbk.) 1.
Librarians—Fiction. 2. Cats—Fiction. 3. Murder—Investigation—Fiction. 4.
Mississippi—Fiction. 5. Large type books. I. Title.
PS3610.A43F55 2012
813'.6—dc23   2012019516

Published in 2012 by arrangement with The Berkley Publishing Group,
a member of Penguin Group (USA) Inc.

Printed in the United States of America
    1 2 3 4 5   16 15 14 13 12
FD244

For David

ACKNOWLEDGMENTS

As always, I must thank my Tuesday night critique partners: Amy, Bob, Heather, Kay, Laura, Leanne, and Millie. Their critical input makes a huge difference, and I owe them a great debt of gratitude. Thanks also to the Hairston-Soparkar clan, both two- and four-legged, for sharing their beautiful home with us every Tuesday and allowing us to work.

My editor, Michelle Vega, and my agent, Nancy Yost, have assisted me in so many important ways, and I am incredibly grateful for their support. The same goes for my bookstore family, McKenna, Brenda, Anne, and John. Thanks for selling my books so well and for making the time I spend with them so memorable. Copyeditor Andy Ball did a super job on the manuscript, for which I thank him profusely.

Finally, three friends continue to sustain me and encourage me: Terry Farmer, my

Maine coon expert and fellow voracious reader; Julie Herman, fellow writer and the best non-biological sister anyone could have; and Patricia R. Orr, fellow survivor of graduate school and immeasurably dear friend.

ONE

Connor Lawton made an abysmal first impression on his initial visit to the Athena Public Library.

Now, four weeks later, I'd seen enough of the tattooed playwright to know he didn't improve on further acquaintance.

This afternoon, I wanted to curse my luck as I watched him amble toward the reference desk, where I waited to help library patrons.

From around my feet I heard an interrogative warble, and I glanced down at Diesel, my three-year-old Maine coon cat. He always seemed to sense when something, or someone, caused me stress or anxiety, and I had to smile. "It's okay, boy. Nothing to worry about."

Diesel warbled again and stretched, reassured.

"Talking to your feet?" Connor Lawton gave me a sour smile. He looked more like a prize fighter than a playwright, with his broken nose, buzzed haircut, and muscular frame. Today he wore a sleeveless shirt that revealed the colorful ink on his upper arms. The tattoos, Japanese in style, offered a stark contrast to his tanned skin and white shirt. A diamond stud glittered in his left ear.

"No, I was speaking to my cat. Remember him?"

Lawton grimaced. "Unfortunately. Never seen such an unfriendly animal."

Now I wanted to laugh. Diesel likes almost everybody he meets. He's a very sociable, easygoing cat — a lot like me, actually. But there are some people who rub him the wrong way, and that's what Lawton did the first time he saw Diesel. The man immediately stuck his hand under the cat's belly and started to scratch, and Diesel was offended by the improper first greeting. He growled, Lawton jerked his hand back, and Diesel turned and stalked off.

Since then Diesel had no use for Lawton, and evidently it still rankled the man.

"I'm surprised they let you bring the beast to the library," Lawton said. He exaggerated his drawl when he continued, "But at least Ellie Mae ain't in here with all her critters."

I suppressed a heavy sigh while I felt Diesel place a paw on my knee. If he stood on his hind legs, he would be able to peer over the counter at the playwright. "What can I do for you today, Mr. Lawton?"

"Old newspapers." Lawton frowned, and for a moment he appeared troubled by something. "Research for the play I'm writing."

Ah, yes, the play. Lawton mentioned it frequently. By now every person in Athena knew that the brilliant young playwright Connor Lawton, the toast of Broadway and Hollywood, was in Athena for two semesters as writer-in-residence at the college. The fall semester started in ten days, but Lawton arrived in Athena early to settle in and "immerse the Muse in the fecund atmosphere of the literary South, the home of immortals like William Faulkner, Eudora Welty, and Flannery O'Connor."

The man's pretentiousness evidently knew no bounds. He even told me he was named for Flannery O'Connor, but that he had dropped the *O'* from his name because it sounded too artsy-fartsy.

"Are you looking for old issues of the local paper? We have access to a number of newspaper archives online, but the *Athena Daily Register* hasn't been digitized yet. At

11

least, not prior to 1998."

"Local, at least for now." Lawton stared at me and frowned.

"If you'll follow me, then," I said as I headed around the desk to the open space in front, "I'll show you where the microfilm is."

"Whatever." Lawton moved closer and pointed to a spot behind me. "Does the cat have to come with us?"

"Yes, he does," I said as I glanced back at Diesel. "If he wants to, that is."

Diesel, his gaze intent on my face, chirped a couple of times before he turned and walked back behind the desk to sit with Lizzie Hayes, one of the circulation staffers. *Good choice, Diesel. Lizzie is much nicer.*

"Follow me," I repeated as I turned and walked away. I heard Lawton mutter something from close behind me.

We walked down a hall near the desk, and I showed the playwright into a small room with filing cabinets, a couple of small tables, and two microfilm-reading machines.

I paused by the cabinets. "The films for the *Athena Daily Register* are here. The dates are on the cards on each drawer. When you finish with a roll, please put it in that basket on top of the cabinet." I stopped a moment to clear my throat. "Have you used microfilm readers like these before?"

Lawton nodded as he approached me. I moved aside to let him peer at the labels on the drawers. He squatted, pulled out one of the drawers, and examined its contents.

"Then, if there's nothing else, I'll head back to the desk."

"Yeah, thanks," Lawton said.

"You're welcome," I said, surprised. This was the first time he had uttered the word *thanks* in my hearing, despite the other times I had helped him.

I glanced at my watch on the way back to the reference-circulation desk. A quarter to three. Only fifteen minutes more on the desk, and then Diesel and I could go home. I looked forward to some quiet time. This had been a long, hot week, and a brief nap before I cooked dinner sounded appealing.

As I mulled possible menus, I resumed my seat behind the desk. Diesel left Lizzie and came back to me. I scratched his head as he rubbed against my right leg. He was an affectionate creature and didn't often stray far from my side — except to spend time with one of his many human friends. He was popular with the library's patrons, and he enjoyed them — as long as they didn't have small hands that wanted to pull cat hair, that is.

I helped two more people with their reference questions, and when I consulted my watch again, the quarter hour was down to three minutes.

The library's newest employee, Bronwyn Forster, offered a sweet smile as she neared me, ready to take my place. "Afternoon, Charlie. Has it been busy?"

"About the usual," I said. "When school starts next week, things will pick up."

Bronwyn nodded as she rubbed Diesel's head. She cooed at him for a moment, and Diesel warbled back at her. I knew Diesel would agree with me that Bronwyn, with never an unkind word for anyone, made a pleasant change from Anita Milhaus, the obnoxious woman she replaced two months ago.

I waited until Bronwyn finished petting the cat, and then Diesel and I bade her and Lizzie good-bye. I retrieved my briefcase from the office I shared with one of the full-time librarians on the Fridays that I volunteered. I put Diesel into his harness, attached the leash, and we were ready.

The hot August air slapped us both as Diesel and I left the library for my car. I opened the doors to let the heat out, then got in to crank the car and get the air conditioner going. In the meantime, Diesel

14

hopped onto the floorboard on the front passenger side of the car. I detached his leash and stuck it in my briefcase.

On the way home, I thought longingly about a cool shower. I felt sticky from the heat despite the cold blast of air from the car vents.

I pulled into the driveway and hit the garage door opener. As the door rose, I saw Sean's car in its slot. I smiled, glad he was home from whatever mysterious errand he said he had to run today. I pulled my car in beside my son's, and I thought about the change in our relationship over the past five months. We were getting along much better now, and I enjoyed having him with me.

Diesel hopped out of the car and made it to the kitchen door ahead of me. I watched, grinning, as he opened the door. Earlier in the year he had learned how to do it by twisting the knob with his front paws, and I still got a kick out of watching him. I suspected my boarder, Justin Wardlaw, taught him the trick, although Diesel was smart enough to have figured it out for himself.

I followed my cat into the kitchen and closed the door behind us. Diesel loped off to the utility room, home to his litter box and food and water bowls. I followed his example and poured myself a glass of water. As I drank I heard laughter from the direction of the living room. I recognized the baritone rumble of Sean's voice, but there was a second voice. A female voice, and it sounded oddly familiar.

"It can't be," I said as I shook my head. My heart beat faster, and I set the glass on the counter.

Moments later I paused in the living room doorway and stared at the two people on the couch — my son, Sean, and my daughter, Laura.

She caught sight of me and jumped up. "Surprise, Dad!" She grinned as she ran to give me a hug.

I threw my arms around her and held her tight. "What a wonderful surprise." I glanced over at Sean, still on the sofa. He grinned broadly.

"Look at my movie star daughter." I released Laura and stepped back. I hadn't seen her since Christmas, and I was thrilled to have her here. Her visits home were all too infrequent. "You and Sean really put one over on me."

"Not a movie star yet, Dad, but I'm working on it." Laura laughed as she posed for me. Even dressed in jeans and an old linen man's shirt she was still beautiful and looked several years younger than her age, twenty-four. Like her brother she had curly black hair and expressive eyes. She had the gamine grace of Audrey Hepburn despite the fact that she was five-ten in her bare feet.

"I had a hard time not telling you on Wednesday when you called me." Laura laughed again. "I knew Sean would kill me, though, because we wanted it to be a real surprise." She took my hand and led me to the couch.

I sat with a child on either side of me. "So your mysterious errand was going to the airport in Memphis." I smiled at Sean, and he grinned.

I turned back to Laura. "How long can you stay? At least a week, I hope."

Laura exchanged a sly glance with her brother. "Actually, I can stay longer than that, if you can stand having me."

"Of course," I said, delighted.

"I'll be here through Christmas." Laura giggled at my stunned expression.

"That's wonderful," I said, somewhat bewildered. "But can you afford to be away from Los Angeles that long? Career-wise, I mean?"

Laura shrugged. "I guess I'll find out. But

in the meantime I've got a pretty good gig here."

"What kind of gig do you have in Athena?" I couldn't imagine what kind of acting job she had found here that would last several months.

Before Laura could respond, my thirty-six-pound cat jumped into her lap, startling all of us.

"Diesel. You rascal." Laura hugged the cat as he warbled at her. Diesel adored my daughter, and the feeling was mutual. Last Christmas Laura threatened to catnap Diesel and take him back to California with her.

After a minute or so of loving attention to the cat, Laura focused again on me and Sean. "I'm going to be filling in at the college for a professor on maternity leave this fall. The person who was originally hired to do it got a full-time job and backed out, and I'm the last-minute replacement."

"That's wonderful," I said. "So you'll teach acting?"

Laura nodded. "A couple of basic courses, plus I'll be helping with the fall productions of the Theater Department. Should be fun."

A cell phone ring interrupted our conversation. Laura frowned as she pulled the phone from the pocket of her shirt. "Sorry about that." She glanced at the display, then stuck the phone back in her pocket. "I am *so* not in the mood for *him* right now." She grimaced.

"Him who?" I had to ask. Was some guy bothering her?

A guilty expression flashed across her face. "Oh, it's just my former boyfriend. He's always having some kind of crisis. But what can you expect from a playwright?" She wrinkled her nose and frowned.

Playwright? Dismay hit me. *No, surely not. Not him.*

TWO

"I thought you dumped him," Sean said. "For what, the third time now?" He quirked an eyebrow at his sister.

Laura grimaced. "Second time. But I've got to put up with him this semester. He helped me get the gig, after all."

"Are you talking about Connor Lawton?" I tried to keep my distaste for the man from coloring my voice.

Laura nodded. "Have you met him?"

"Several times," I said. "He's been in the library every Friday that I've worked the past month." I paused. "I don't remember you mentioning him before, although it sounds like you told Sean about him. Have you known him long?"

"Eight months, I guess." Laura glanced down at Diesel, still lying across her lap. She stroked his head, and he purred in response. His tail flopped up and down across my legs. "I met him right after

Christmas when I was cast in one of his plays. I told you about that. You know, the one where I played the waitress who thought Elvis had possessed her husband's body?"

Sean snorted with laughter, and I had to smile. Laura was a huge Elvis fan, and I imagined she had had great fun with the part.

"I remember that much, but you neglected to tell me you were dating the playwright." *Or anything about him,* I added to myself.

"Sorry about that, Dad." Laura shrugged. "The only reason Sean knew about him was because he spent a weekend in LA with me and saw the play back in February. I wasn't dating Connor then, though he'd already asked me out a few times."

"He came to Laura's dressing room after the play." Sean met my gaze as I turned to look at him. "He seemed okay, though he sure has a healthy opinion of himself. He spent probably fifteen minutes quoting reviews of his plays." Sean shook his head in obvious amusement.

Laura snickered. "That's Connor. *Self-absorbed* ought to be his middle name. I told him that once, and he took it as a compliment."

"Why would you date someone like that?" I asked, puzzled by what I was learning

21

about my daughter. "I can't see the attraction myself." *Not for someone as independent and strong-minded as you,* I added silently.

"He can be charming and sweet when he makes an effort. And he really is an awesome writer. His plays are amazing." Laura ran a hand through her curls. Diesel warbled, and she rubbed his head again. "But he's also exhausting. *High maintenance* could be his other middle name."

"Are you together now?" Sean asked.

"No, just friends at the moment," Laura said. "And that's all we'll ever be, trust me."

"I hope it stays that way," I said. I didn't fancy the idea of Connor Lawton as a potential son-in-law. "You can do a lot better, no matter how gifted he is."

"You don't think anyone's good enough for me." Laura poked my arm with a finger. "Admit it."

"True," I said, treating her to a mock-severe frown. Then I grinned. "Probably no one ever will be, though I'm willing to be convinced at some point."

"Maybe there's a prince somewhere willing to marry a commoner." Sean smirked. "Dad can recruit him for you, little sister."

"And maybe he'll have a sister for my *big brother,*" Laura said in a sweet tone. "That is, if she's willing to kiss a frog." She stuck her tongue out at Sean.

I laughed but decided to shift the conversation back to Connor Lawton. "Will it be awkward for you, having to be around him all semester?"

Laura shrugged. "I'm going to be way too busy to think much about him. Besides, we get along fine as friends."

"The less you have to be around him, the better," I said.

Laura shook her head at me. "Dad, don't worry. I've dealt with bigger pains than Connor, believe me."

I was probably better off not following up on that statement, I decided. I worried enough about Laura on her own in Hollywood as it was. "I'll try. What say we go to the kitchen and figure out something for dinner?"

"Sounds good to me," Laura said. "I'm starving. All I had for lunch was a few pretzels on the plane." Diesel hopped from her lap to the floor and rubbed his head against her leg.

I smiled down at the cat. "Diesel is hoping you'll drop him some tidbits like you did the last time you were here. Just don't overdo it."

Laura and Diesel came with me to the kitchen. Sean disappeared upstairs, saying he'd be down later.

In the kitchen I found a note stuck to the refrigerator door with a cat magnet. I recognized Stewart Delacorte's handwriting. Stewart, a professor of chemistry at Athena College, moved in five months ago after his great-uncle was murdered in the Delacorte family home. His stay was supposed to last only until he found a permanent place to live. Somehow he didn't seem to be able to find a place he liked, so he was still here, occupying a large bedroom on the third floor.

The note informed me that Stewart had prepared a chicken and mushroom risotto and left it in the refrigerator. The note included instructions on heating it for supper. He concluded by stating that he would probably be late tonight and not to wait for him.

"Looks like I don't have to cook after all," I said as I handed the note to Laura.

She skimmed the contents and handed it back to me. "Sounds yummy. You told me he's an awesome cook."

"He is," I said. "Between him and Azalea, Sean and I have been eating better than ever." I patted my waistline ruefully. "I need to be getting more exercise. I miss seeing my feet."

Laura laughed. "Oh, Dad, stop exaggerating." She cocked her head to one side as she regarded me. "But if you want to get up and run with me in the morning, I'd love it."

"Thanks, honey," I said. "I'll stick to walking, if you don't mind. Besides, Diesel likes to go with me, and he doesn't get motivated to run unless there's a squirrel involved."

At the sound of his name, Diesel chirped several times, and Laura reached over to scratch his head. "Yeah, big boy, I bet you'd run with me, wouldn't you? We'd have fun."

I laughed at the expression on the cat's face. I would have sworn he understood Laura and didn't like the notion of running any better than I did. He moved away from Laura and closer to me.

"I guess not," Laura said with a wry grin.

"I'll make a salad to go with the risotto," I said and opened the fridge door to find the salad makings.

Laura set a large bowl on the counter by the sink and pulled a knife from the drawer. "Do you have any plans for tomorrow night, Dad?"

I placed lettuce, onions, and red bell peppers in the sink. "Helen Louise and I talked about having dinner." Helen Louise Brady, owner of a local Parisian-style bakery, was a good friend, and lately we'd been spending more time together. We'd known each other since childhood, and she had also been a friend of my late wife's. "Was there something you wanted to do?"

"I don't want to interfere with your plans." Laura began to tear the lettuce and drop it into the bowl. "There's a cocktail party tomorrow night, kind of a reception for the faculty and the grad students in the Theater Department. I was hoping you'd go with me."

"I don't think Helen Louise would mind skipping dinner when I explain," I said. "I'll invite her for Sunday dinner instead. She'd like to see you again."

"Thanks, Dad. I appreciate it." Laura found the chopping board, then started cutting up the peppers. "Do you know any of the Theater Department faculty?"

"Not well," I said as I tried to remember names.

"The host of the party is the chair of the department," Laura said. "His name is Montana Johnston."

I snickered. "His real name is Ralph. I do know him. He decided a few years ago when he started writing a play that he needed a more artistic-sounding name, and he came up with *Montana*."

26

"I thought it sounded odd." Laura dropped slices of pepper into the bowl.

"Pretentious is more like it," I said. Unpleasant memories of the man's play came back to me. "I actually went to a performance of his play, and it was dreadful. The man just isn't the best writer."

"Then he'd better not ever ask Connor to read anything of his," Laura said. "Connor is brutal to less-talented writers."

"Like water off a duck's back with ol' Montana," I said as I shredded the last of the lettuce. I picked up the onion and started to peel it. "Ralph has the thickest skin of any person I've ever known. He's as convinced of his own worth as your friend Connor. It might be interesting to see the two of them trying to dent each other's hides."

"Count me out," Laura said with an exaggerated shudder. "That's the kind of drama I *don't* need, thankyouverymuch."

"Dad, can you come here a minute?" Sean's voice came from out in the hall.

"As soon as I finish with this onion," I called out in response.

"Could you come now?" Sean's tone sounded more urgent.

"Okay." I handed the onion to Laura and wiped my hands on a dishcloth before I

27

went out to the hallway.

Sean stood there, a puzzled expression on his face, as he stared at a large piece of paper he held gingerly by two corners. As I moved closer to him, he glanced at me.

"I found this on the floor by the front door," Sean said. "Someone must have slipped it through the mail slot. It's offensive." He turned the sheet so I could see it clearly.

The paper was a photograph, a publicity shot of Laura. I had one like it framed on my bedside table.

But my copy of the photo didn't have a red *A* painted on Laura's forehead.

THREE

Sean shifted position so we could examine the photograph together. "You think Lawton is responsible for this?"

"Why would he do such a thing?" My anger was building over this insult to my daughter.

Then a chilling thought struck me. Was it a threat of some kind instead?

Diesel rubbed against my legs and muttered. He always picked up on my emotions, and he didn't like it when I was upset or angry. I rubbed his head to reassure him.

"Other than you and me, who else in Athena knows her? Or even knows she's here?" Sean continued to stare at the photograph.

"Good point, although I can't imagine why he'd do something like this." I locked gazes with Sean. "I don't want her to see this."

"See what?"

I was so intent on the photograph that I failed to hear Laura come up behind Sean and me in the hall. I nudged Sean, hoping he would hide the photograph, but he didn't move.

"I think she should see it," Sean said. "I wanted you to see it first, Dad."

"What are you hiding from me?" Laura stood in front of me, right hand on her hip, head cocked in the same direction. She wrinkled her nose and frowned, sure signs of irritation from her.

"This." Sean turned the photograph toward her.

Laura's eyes widened, and then she laughed. "So Damitra's in town. I didn't figure it would take her long, once she heard I'd be spending several months here."

"Who is Damitra, pray tell? And why do you think she's responsible for this?" I was surprised that Laura appeared to take it so lightly.

"Damitra Vane." Laura rolled her eyes. "She's this nutcase Connor dated before me. Basically harmless, but she's crazy jealous. Calls herself an actress, but she's terrible. The only reason she ever gets cast in anything is her open-leg policy with casting directors." She flashed a wicked grin at me. "Oh, and her giant boobs."

Sean burst out laughing. I could feel my lips twitch, but I wasn't ready to dismiss the incident. The altered photograph set off an unpleasant tingle in my gut, and I feared Laura might be dismissing this too quickly.

"How would she know you're here?" Sean asked.

"We have mutual friends in LA, and one of them probably told her I was coming to Athena." Laura shrugged. "Plus I'm sure she's heard me talk about my father and remembered Dad's name. Then all she had to do was look up the address in the phone book."

"She sounds like a stalker to me," I said.

My daughter put her arm around my waist. "Come on now, Dad, don't start worrying. I promise you Damitra is harmless. To me, anyway. Connor's the one who should be looking over his shoulder. She follows him everywhere."

"Has she ever done anything physically aggressive toward you?" I wasn't ready to drop the matter.

"No, she hasn't. Just stupid little tricks like this." Laura stepped back and crossed her arms over her stomach. Her nose wrinkled. "You don't need to get all protective, either of you." She glared at her brother. "I'm perfectly capable of handling this myself."

Diesel rubbed against Laura, obviously bothered by her heightened emotions. "See, you're upsetting Diesel, and that's not good." She crouched by the cat and cooed softly to him as she scratched his head.

I was still concerned, but I could see there was no point in discussing this further. I'd have a quiet word with Sean later, ask him to nose around and find out whether this Damitra Vane was in Athena. In the meantime I intended to keep an eye on Laura — as much as I could without riling her. "Let's get back to preparing dinner," I said. "You finish the salad, and I'll reheat the risotto. Sean, you set the table."

My children and my cat followed me into the kitchen. Laura applied herself to the salad and, once her back was turned, Sean and I exchanged glances. He gave a quick nod, and I knew he understood what I wanted.

"Will Justin be here for dinner?" Sean asked, his tone nonchalant as he pulled plates from the cabinet.

"No, he's with his dad this weekend," I said. "He'll be back Sunday evening."

Justin Wardlaw, a sophomore at Athena College, was my other boarder besides Stewart. When I inherited this large house from my late aunt Dottie, I kept up her tradition of renting rooms to students attending Athena. Justin boarded with me last year, and now he was almost family.

"How is he doing?" Laura asked. "He seemed like such a sweet kid when I was here for the holidays. I felt bad for him, after all he went through."

"He's doing fine." I popped the dish of risotto into the oven and set the temperature and the timer. "He occasionally has some rough moments, but he's handling everything well, considering." Last fall Justin had been a suspect in a murder case and had suffered some serious personal losses. With his father and me, he had a strong support system, and Diesel, who adored him, was a huge help as well.

"The risotto will need about fifteen minutes to reheat," I said. "In the meantime, shall we start on the salad?"

"Ta-dah." Laura presented the bowl of leafy greens, peppers, and onion in a sweeping gesture and set it on the table.

After we each chose a drink for the meal, we sat down, and Laura dished out the salad. While we ate Laura regaled us with some amusing anecdotes from her recent auditions, and I listened for the buzzer on the oven.

Sean talked about a couple of the cases he'd worked on over the summer as we enjoyed the risotto. While he studied for the Mississippi bar exam, Sean was doing investigative work for Athena's best-known lawyer, Q. C. Pendergrast and his associate, his daughter Alexandra. Sean and I met the legendary Pendergrast and Alexandra a few months ago when I was hired to inventory the rare book collection of one of the lawyer's late clients, James Delacorte. Though Sean and Alexandra didn't hit it off at first, they now worked well together, and I was beginning to suspect that Alexandra could very well be my daughter-in-law one of these days.

When we finished our meal, Sean insisted he would clean the kitchen and sent Laura and me off. We made ourselves comfortable on the couch in the living room. The cat sprawled between us, his head and upper torso in Laura's lap, his back legs and tail against my leg. He was one blissful kitty. His purr rumbled, making the origin of his name obvious.

Laura wanted to hear more about the Delacorte murder case, and I obliged with a summary of the details. Laura loved mysteries as much as I did, and soon the conversation turned to books. Sean joined us then, and we talked for nearly three hours. Diesel remained between Laura and me the entire time, thoroughly content.

Around ten o'clock I yawned and declared that I was ready for bed. "You stay up as long as you like," I said. Both my children were night owls, but I wasn't. "Ready for bed, Diesel?"

The cat lifted his head from Laura's lap and yawned at me. He rolled over and stretched as I stood up from the couch, and he meowed three times at Laura.

"It's okay, sweet boy, you go on up to bed. I'll see you tomorrow." Laura kissed his nose and scratched behind his ears. He jumped to the floor across the coffee table. Thanks to his size, he had little trouble leaping that far.

I bent to kiss Laura's forehead, and she then kissed my cheek. "Good night, love," I said. "See you in the morning." I squeezed Sean's shoulder and wished him good night.

As Diesel and I headed up the stairs, I heard Sean and Laura talking about having some coffee, and I knew they didn't mean decaf. I shuddered. How could they drink regular coffee this late at night and then expect to sleep? *Ah, youth,* I told myself.

Before long Diesel and I were in bed, the cat with his head on his pillow, lying on his side facing me. I rubbed his head and down his side several times, and he rewarded me with chirps of contentment. He was soon asleep, and I drifted off not long after.

At some point during the night a barking dog woke me, and I rolled over. The sounds came from the stairwell. That meant Stewart was home, and so was Dante, his poodle. Dante originally belonged to Sean, but once Stewart moved in and started fussing over him, the dog switched his adoration to my boarder. Sean seemed happy with this because, even though he was fond of the little fellow, he wasn't that keen on having a dog. He had taken Dante to keep him from being sent to a shelter and brought him along when he moved to Athena back in the spring.

Diesel and Dante got along pretty well, though occasionally Dante turned rambunctious and Diesel had to calm him down. Since the cat was about five times the size of the dog, Diesel always had the upper hand — or paw, that is.

The next thing I knew my alarm went off at seven. I sat up, groggy, and reached over to silence it. I saw that Diesel wasn't with me. Most days he didn't get out of bed until I did, but when there was a new guest in the house, he sometimes went visiting in the morning. I expected he was in Laura's room happily curled up next to her.

I breakfasted alone, and it was nearly ten before anyone else appeared downstairs. After that the day sped by. As I expected, Stewart and Laura really hit it off, and Laura kept Stewart entertained with bits of Hollywood gossip. Stewart insisted on cooking lunch for everyone, and Sean and Laura cleaned the kitchen afterward.

After lunch Sean pulled me aside for a brief conversation. Earlier in the day he'd called around town and verified that Damitra Vane was indeed here. She was staying at Farrington House, the best hotel in Athena. He also looked her up on the Internet Movie Database and showed me her picture on his laptop. She was beautiful, in what I thought of as a plastic, Hollywood manner. Her expression was vacant, and she didn't look all that bright.

"Since she's definitely here in town, looks like Laura could be right about the source of the photograph." Sean powered down his laptop and set it aside.

"I guess, but I still don't like the situation. I have a good mind to go over there right now and talk to her."

"Why don't you let me do that?" Sean said. "As Laura's lawyer. Maybe frighten her enough with legal repercussions that she'll back off and leave Laura alone."

"Sounds like a plan. Thanks, son." I paused to think for a moment. "Why don't you wait until Laura and I leave for the cocktail party? That way you won't have to make up some errand."

"Good idea," Sean said. "What time are you leaving?"

"Around five," I said.

The arrangements made, I spent the rest of the afternoon enjoying myself, talking with my daughter and her new best friend, Stewart. The two of them together entertained me, trading gossipy trivia about movie stars past and present.

Laura disappeared upstairs at four to get ready for the party, and I went up shortly afterward to do the same. Diesel stayed downstairs with Sean, Stewart, and Dante. He wouldn't be happy when Laura and I left the house, because I wasn't going to take him with me as I usually did.

Stewart solved that problem by taking Diesel and Dante to the backyard for a play session. When Laura came down the stairs a few minutes before five, I was ready.

She was stunning in a sheath of turquoise silk that fit her figure and set off her tanned skin perfectly. Dangling silver-and-turquoise earrings that once belonged to her mother accentuated the long line of her neck. Her lustrous dark hair was pulled back in a chignon, her curls for once sleekly restrained. She carried a small clutch the color of her dress, and her high-heel shoes were a shade darker. I'd forgotten just how mature and elegant she could look.

"Maybe I should carry a big stick with me." I smiled at her as she reached the bottom of the stairs. "They'll be swarming all over you."

Laura laughed. "You are so good for my ego."

As I backed the car out of the garage, Laura pulled an invitation from her purse. "The address is 1744 Rosemary Street. Do you know where that is?"

"Only a few minutes from here," I said. "It's in a neighborhood like ours on the other side of the town square."

At five-fifteen I turned onto Rosemary Street and soon spotted the house. I had to park half a block away, and as I escorted Laura down the walk we both admired the beautiful houses. This neighborhood, like mine, dated from the latter years of the nineteenth century, when the fashion was for large, multistoried houses. The lots were generous, and there were plenty of trees to help shade the houses. The hot summer sun turned the faded red brick of 1744 to pink, and I felt the heat radiating from it as we headed up the walk.

I was perspiring freely by the time we reached the front door, and I itched to lose my jacket and tie. Laura, on the other hand, appeared unaffected by the heat. I rang the doorbell, and we waited.

And waited. I rang again. Sounds of merriment from inside reached us easily, and I suspected no one could hear the doorbell.

"Let's just go in." Laura reached for the knob and swung the door open. I felt a welcome blast of cold air and followed her inside.

The noise was much louder now, and I decided I should have brought earplugs along with a big stick. I'd have a headache before long, thanks to this din. I pulled out my handkerchief and mopped my face and the back of my head. I stuck the sodden linen in my jacket pocket.

We approached a nearby doorway and paused to observe the scene inside the room. The space was large, perhaps thirty by forty, the furniture and wooden floor worn but clean. I counted sixteen people spread out around the room, and they all seemed to be talking and gesturing at once.

I recognized one of them as the host, Ralph Johnston, or Montana, as he now insisted he be called.

There were a few vaguely familiar faces, but no one who I could put a name to besides Ralph. I hated making cocktail-party chitchat with people I didn't know, but for Laura's sake I'd make the effort.

Even so the next couple of hours could well seem like twenty.

FOUR

Ralph — I had a hard time thinking of him as Montana — glanced our way and frowned, looking puzzled. Then recognition seemed to dawn. He left his companion, a heavyset woman in a pink-and-orange caftan, and approached us.

Ralph's protuberant eyes blinked rapidly. His sallow, egg-shaped head with its or-phaned blond forelock and shiny bald dome never failed to remind me of Tweety, the cartoon bird. He even flapped his hands slightly as he halted in front of Laura and bobbed up and down on the balls of his feet.

"You are Laura Harris," he said in a reedy tenor. He stopped flapping and bobbing long enough to extend a hand, and Laura took it with a friendly smile.

"And you're Professor Johnston," she said. "It's a pleasure to meet you finally. Thank you for hiring me for the semester. It's go-ing to be brilliant."

"Oh, my dear, I'm sure it will." Johnston couldn't take his eyes off my daughter, and I felt the lack of a stick keenly.

I cleared my throat and stuck out my hand. "Evening, Johnston. Good to see you. I hope you don't mind my tagging along as Laura's escort."

The erstwhile playwright wrenched his gaze away from Laura and looked blankly at me. Then his eyes cleared, and he shook my hand. "Right. Harris. The librarian." His glance darted to Laura and back to me. "Hard to believe such a beautiful creature sprang from the loins of an old librarian. Though she does have your coloring. Interesting."

He fell silent and stared at Laura.

Now I remembered why I avoided the man whenever we were in the same room at a college function. He and tact were barely acquainted.

"How about something to drink?" I raised my voice to penetrate our host's apparent fog. "I'm pretty thirsty."

"That would be lovely." Laura smiled, and Johnston came out of his reverie.

"Drink. Uh, yeah." Before he said anything more, a short, frowzy redhead in a worn yellow jumpsuit approached and grabbed his arm. From the fumes coming

43

off her I figured she was already pickled, and her slurred speech confirmed it.

"C'mon, Rowf, wanna ask you 'bout sump'n." She swayed toward him, and Johnston grimaced. "When's Connor gonna get here? Said he would be here. But he's not here."

"How the heck should I know when he's going to turn up, Magda? You know what he's like. Why don't you go upstairs and lie down. I think you could use a rest." He tried to pry her fingers from his arm without success. "All right then." He shrugged. "Drinks are in the kitchen. Down the hall and to the right. Help yourselves." He flapped his free arm as Magda dragged him away, asking once more about Connor.

"Who is she?" Laura asked as we headed for the door.

"I think she's his wife, or maybe his ex-wife," I said. "I heard something about them not long ago through the campus grapevine, but I can't remember precisely what it was." Privately I wondered why she was so interested in Connor, but I dismissed the thought as we wandered down the hall.

We found three people in the kitchen. They were involved in an animated discussion of modern musical theater, from what I could discern.

"Lloyd Webber's a prime example of bubble gum for the masses." The speaker, a gaunt young man who had to be at least six-eight, poked the chest of a shorter, husky, bearded man maybe six inches in front of him. A smiling brunette shook her head as she watched the two men. "How can you stand there and defend him as a gifted composer? I mean, come on, dude, seriously? Lloyd Webber?"

"Come on, Nathan, *seriously,* Elton John?" The other man, about Laura's age, mimicked the tones of his opponent. He was about six feet tall, I estimated. "It's freaking musical theater, you jackass. Who the heck expects Strindberg or Ibsen when they go to a musical?" He turned away and caught sight of Laura. His eyes widened, and he smiled.

Nathan wasn't done, it seemed, because he tapped the other man on the shoulder. "Sir Elton is a genius." His opponent paid no attention and stepped closer to Laura and me.

"Let it go, Nathan. Frank's lost interest," the young woman said in bored tones. "Let's grab something to eat." They moved toward the door into the hall.

"Jade's right. Go away," Frank said, his eyes fixed on Laura. He extended a hand.

"You must be Laura Harris. Glad to meet you. Frank Salisbury. I teach set design." His pleasant baritone had a regional twang, Alabama or perhaps Georgia, I thought.

Laura took his hand and offered an impish smile. "Hi, Frank. Nice to meet you." She gestured toward me with her head. "This is my dad, Charlie Harris."

"How do you do, sir?" Frank offered me his hand now, and I shook it, liking the firm grasp. "I've seen you around campus, haven't I?"

"Yes, I'm the archivist and rare book librarian," I said. "I've seen you around, too."

Frank was polite enough to look at me while I talked, but his eyes shifted back to Laura the moment I fell silent. I suppressed a smile.

"Can I get you something to drink?" Frank said. "There's wine, beer, soft drinks, bottled water."

"I'll have a glass of white wine," Laura said, her eyes sparkling. I recognized the signs. Frank was like most of the young men Laura dated through high school and college: an inch or so taller than she, on the husky side, with dark hair and eyes and a full beard. His teeth gleamed as he grinned at Laura.

"Coming right up," Frank said as he turned away. Then, apparently remembering his manners, he turned back. "How about you, Mr. Harris?"

"Charlie, please. And I'll take a glass of red, thanks."

"Charlie it is, then." Frank went to the counter and pulled a bottle of white wine from a cooler, filled a wineglass, and handed it to Laura with a graceful flourish. Then he found the red wine on the counter and presented me with a goblet of it, sans flourish. He picked up his bottle of beer as we thanked him.

"I hope you like children," he told Laura. "I think we should have three." He sipped at his beer, his eyes twinkling.

Laura's laugh rang out. I was taken aback, but my daughter seemed unfazed by such a direct come-on.

"Oh, no, I want at least seven," Laura said, her expression demure.

"Works for me." Frank laughed. "How about I take you around and introduce you to some of the department members? But just remember, I saw you first."

Laura glanced at me, and I nodded. "Lay on, Macduff." Quoting Shakespeare didn't seem out of place in this gathering. Plus it was an old game with Laura and me. She had fallen in love with Shakespeare in the ninth grade, when her class read *Romeo and Juliet.*

She took Frank's proffered arm and threw me a smile as she and her new beau left the kitchen.

Frank seemed like a nice enough young man, certainly more appealing than Connor Lawton. I hoped Laura meant what she said when she claimed she and the playwright were now friends and nothing more.

I had little inclination to return to the party in the living room. There was a table with four chairs near the back door, and I ambled over and took a seat in the corner. I loosened my tie and had another sip of wine. It was a nice vintage, much better than I expected. At most faculty get-togethers, the wine was generally on the cheap side, but this was good stuff.

My solitude lasted only six or seven minutes. I heard a loud obscenity and looked up to see Connor Lawton, dressed in his usual sleeveless shirt and worn jeans, enter the kitchen. I watched as he, obviously unaware of my presence, rooted in the cooler and pulled out a beer. He popped the top and took a long swig. He set the bottle on the counter and pulled a pack of cigarettes and a lighter from his jeans

48

pocket. He tapped out a cigarette and lit it, expelling smoke into the air with a grunt.

He still hadn't noticed me, and I decided to see how long it took him to realize he wasn't alone. He picked up his bottle again and leaned against the counter, smoking and drinking, turned slightly away from me. He quickly finished his drink, deposited the empty bottle on the counter, and pulled another drink from the cooler.

I could see him glancing idly around the room where he stood, and his body stiffened all of a sudden. He stared at something across the room. I followed his gaze but couldn't tell for sure what had caught his attention. The wall held a few photographs, but most of the space was taken up by cabinets. As I watched, Connor set his bottle down and stepped forward a few paces to kneel before one cabinet. He ran his hands over the surface of the door, then grabbed the handle and opened it.

He rocked back on his heels. "I'll be damned," he said in a low voice. Then he started nodding. "Not so nuts after all."

He closed the door and stood. He went back to the counter, had a last drag of his cigarette, dropped his butt in the sink, and grabbed his beer. He strode out of the kitchen, never noting my presence as far as

I could tell.

I drained the last of my wine and went to the counter to refill my glass. I glanced over at the cabinet Connor Lawton had opened, and curiosity got the better of me. I had to see what was in it. What fascinated him about this particular cabinet?

I knelt in front of it. The door was about three feet high and nearly as wide. I tugged it open. The interior was maybe two feet deep and slightly wider and taller than the door dimensions. I examined the contents. Nothing but cleaning supplies. The mingled smells of pine cleaner and furniture polish wafted out to me.

There was nothing remarkable about the cabinet that I could see. Most kitchens had one like it. I shut the door and stood, wondering what this cabinet meant to Connor Lawton.

Then I shook my head. Who knew what might set off a writer's imagination?

I retrieved my wineglass and decided to join the party. I paused in the doorway and scanned the crowd, looking for Laura and Frank. They sat on a sofa to my right. One young man perched on the arm next to Laura, and another, older man leaned against the back, behind where Frank sat. He watched my daughter with a slight smile.

He looked familiar, but I couldn't place him at the moment. I thought I had probably seen him around campus. A few other young men hovered close.

Connor Lawton held court from another sofa a dozen feet away from where Laura sat. Two women occupied the sofa with him, and five more crowded as close as they could, sitting on the floor and arms of the sofa. As I watched, I saw Connor's eyes shift in Laura's direction and back again several times.

This didn't impede the flow of his words, however. I moved a bit closer and tuned in to what he was saying. ". . . going to change the focus of the play, so I'll have to do some rewriting."

The woman I noticed earlier with our host, the one in a pink-and-orange caftan, ventured a question. "Where did this sudden inspiration come from?" She seemed particularly intent on the playwright. For some reason I flashed on an image of a bird dog on point.

Connor frowned at her. "From the subconscious, the home of all inspiration. Things from the past lodge there — people, places, events — and resurface when you least expect it. An artist learns to trust these messages and dig into them, seeking the root and the truth they reveal."

The room around Connor and his acolytes grew silent as he spoke, and when he finished his statement, the only sounds I heard were people breathing.

Someone spoke in an undertone, and I turned to see Frank Salisbury, his head near Laura's. She laughed, and the buzz of conversation resumed.

Connor Lawton uttered an obscenity in a loud voice and jumped up from the sofa. He glared at Laura and Frank for a moment, but they appeared not to notice him. Connor's face reddened, and he took two steps toward Laura's group.

Connor looked furious. I thought I might have to intervene before the situation got out of hand. Instead, the playwright turned and brushed past me into the hall. Moments later the front door slammed.

Personally, I hoped he didn't come back. I'd had about as much of Connor Lawton as I could take for one night. The party would be much less tense without his brooding presence.

FIVE

The women Connor abandoned drifted away from the sofa, all except the heavyset woman in the caftan. She sat down and gazed about her. Something seemed familiar about her face. She caught my eye and beckoned me with a smile.

She patted the sofa beside her. "Please join me." She waited until I was seated to continue. "I recognize you, but you probably don't remember me." She gazed expectantly into my eyes.

She wore her gray hair in a bob cut an inch below her ears, and her hazel eyes focused intently on me. Her face was bare of makeup, with frown lines etched deep in her forehead and a mole high on her right cheek. From this close vantage point I saw that her caftan was decorated with elaborate designs. Hundreds of beads and sequins winked at me, lit by the glow of a nearby lamp. Long earrings in the shape of a peacock's tail, inlaid with iridescent stones, dangled from her earlobes and brushed her shoulders when she moved her head. I detected the subtle hint of lavender and another fragrance, and the scents triggered an elusive memory.

"Sorry, you seem so familiar, but I'm afraid I can't remember your name. How are you connected with the Theater Department?" Maybe I had seen her around campus.

She laughed. "You're Charlie Harris, and I used to babysit you when you were five or six years old." She cocked her head like an inquisitive parrot. "I heard you'd moved back home."

I wracked my brain as I examined her face. Then a name popped into my head. "Sarabeth. Now I remember. You used to sing to me, didn't you?"

"That's right. I'm Sarabeth Conley. I was Sarabeth Norris back then." She chuckled. "Your two favorite songs were 'My Favorite Things' and 'Bibbidi-Bobbidi-Boo' as I recall."

I blushed. When she babysat me Sarabeth was a pretty young girl, maybe fifteen, and I loved sitting next to her in my dad's old armchair while she sang.

Now Sarabeth was sixtyish, and I'd de-

54

scribe her plump face as more handsome than pretty. The odor of lavender seemed stronger now, and I recalled snuggling close to Sarabeth as she read to me, her perfume a light but pleasant presence in my nose.

"I'm the department administrator," Sarabeth said. "Have been for the past twenty-five years. You work in the library, don't you?"

I nodded. "I'm the archivist and rare book cataloger. Part-time, and I volunteer at the public library several days a month." As I conversed with Sarabeth I darted quick glances at the doorway. I hoped Connor Lawton wouldn't come back.

"I visited the public library all the time when I was a girl." Her tone sounded wistful. "These days I don't ever have time to read like I did back then."

"That's too bad," I said. "I'm lucky, I guess, to have a fair amount of time to read. I love mysteries especially." I paused. "When you have time, what do you like to read?"

A faint tinge of red brightened her cheeks. "Romances, Regencies in particular. Mostly I end up rereading my Georgette Heyer novels." Her fingers moved restlessly in her lap.

"Heyer is wonderful, isn't she?" I chuckled. "I have to confess, I love a good historical romance novel occasionally myself, and there's nobody better than Heyer. I like to reread her, too."

Sarabeth perked up at my response, and I figured she was embarrassed — as some readers are — to admit to reading romance novels. A good book is a good book, I've always thought, whatever the genre. I had no patience for snobbery when it came to fiction reading.

I made a casual sweep of the room and began to breathe easier. Still no sign of Connor Lawton.

Sarabeth and I discussed some mutual favorites for a few minutes — Barbara Metzger, Mary Jo Putney, Meredith Duran, Roberta Gellis, among others — and then the conversation veered away from fiction entirely.

"Your daughter is causing a stir." Sarabeth laughed and gestured toward the other sofa. "Like ducks on a june bug, the men here tonight. And not just the straight ones. She's a knockout."

"Thank you," I said. "She's quite an accomplished actress. I'm proud of her."

"I read her résumé." Sarabeth nodded. "All her theater work is great for our program, and her exposure on television is advantageous, too. We're delighted to have her for the semester."

"I am, too." I laughed. "But it was quite a surprise. I didn't find out about it until yesterday."

"I'm sure you're glad to have her home for a few months." Sarabeth glanced away. "It's hard not being able to see them when you want."

I detected a note of pain in her voice, and when I spoke my tone was gentle. "Do you have children?"

"No, not really." Sarabeth's gaze remained fixed away from me. "A much-younger brother who is more like a son, but that's all." Some private sorrow seemed to engulf her.

I wasn't quite sure how to respond to that, so I picked up on an earlier remark. "Laura living in California is tough," I said. "I'm sure she'll enjoy the semester here, but then she'll be off to Hollywood again." Where Connor Lawton would return eventually, and that thought unsettled me.

Sarabeth faced me again. "How well does she know Connor Lawton?"

I was taken aback by the question. For a moment I thought she'd read my mind. "They're friends," I said in a cautious tone. I wasn't about to discuss my daughter's private life with a relative stranger. "They've worked together in Los Angeles."

Sarabeth cocked an eyebrow. "Judging from his behavior, Connor wants to be more than friends. He acted downright jealous."

I shifted uncomfortably on the couch. I'd thought much the same thing. "He'll have to deal with it. Laura's not interested." I figured that was safe enough as a response to her blatant curiosity.

"He's an intense young man," Sarabeth said. "That comes through in his plays."

With her long tenure in the department, she probably knew far more about modern playwrights — Connor included — than I did. "I'm not familiar with his work."

"He's gifted." Her tone turned sour as she continued. "But he has all the tact and personality of a buzz saw, and that may do him in. At some point he'll meet somebody he can't run over." She glanced at her watch. "You'll have to pardon me, Charlie. It's been nice chatting with you, but I have something I need to take care of." She rose stiffly from the sofa.

I stood and earned a faint smile from Sarabeth for my old-fashioned courtesy. "I look forward to seeing you again." She nodded before she turned and walked away.

I surveyed the room. I spotted a couple of slightly familiar faces in the crowd, but there was no one I had a burning desire to corner for a conversation. Instead I ambled over to check out the food on the dining table.

The spread consisted of the usual cocktail shrimp, cheese and crackers, and fruit and raw vegetables with spinach dip. I picked up one of the small plates and helped myself to a snack. I returned to the sofa to munch and finish my wine.

I emptied my plate within minutes and contemplated heading back for more. I could easily fill up on cheese and crackers — the reincarnated mouse in me — but I figured Stewart would be making dinner, as he often did. Whatever he cooked, I wanted to be sure I had room for it.

I deposited my empty plate and wineglass on a tray near the table. As I turned back Laura was approaching, her new conquest, Frank, in tow.

"Dad, would you mind if I went to dinner with Frank?" She smiled, and I detected a tinge of guilt in her tone.

I was disappointed. I'd hoped to spend more time with her tonight. But I also found it difficult to deny my daughter the chance to have fun with someone her age. I felt heartily thankful Connor Lawton wasn't on her arm. Frank Salisbury looked like a far better prospect to me, even on such limited acquaintance.

"No, honey, y'all go on and have a good time. Did you bring your key with you?" I could always stay up until she came home and let her in myself, but I knew how well that would go over.

"It's in my bag." She leaned forward and kissed my cheek. She whispered in my ear, "Thanks. You're the best. And don't worry."

"Thank you, sir." Frank Salisbury regarded me with a serious expression. "I promise to bring her home safe and sound."

For a moment I felt like we had time-warped into the 1950s. Frank had a gravitas I seldom experienced with Laura's dates, and I respected him for it.

"I appreciate that," I said with a stern smile.

Laura winked before they turned away and headed for the door.

I scanned the room for my host. With Laura gone, I didn't see much point in staying. Ralph had disappeared. Perhaps he was ministering to his wife upstairs.

No sign of him in the kitchen either. I'd done my best to behave like a proper guest, but with no host in sight, what else could I do?

Outside, the humid August evening hit me, and I shrugged off my jacket. I took a few steps down the walk, and then the sight of a man standing on the sidewalk in front of the house next door stopped me.

Why was Connor Lawton still hanging around? He swayed a little, seemingly transfixed by the neighboring house. Did he see something I couldn't?

I decided I wasn't curious enough to accost him for answers. Instead I headed down the walk and turned away from Connor toward my car.

"Hey! Hold on a minute."

I muttered, "Damn," and turned to see Lawton gesturing imperiously to me. "Wanna talk to you a minute," he said.

I was tempted to ignore him, but too many generations of well-bred Southern ancestors wouldn't let me. I ambled toward him and stopped a few paces away.

"Can I help you?" My tone could freeze water.

Lawton appeared impervious. He waved toward the house he'd been peering at and said, "Who lives here?" From his left hand dangled a three-quarters-empty bottle of Jack Daniels.

"I'm afraid I don't know," I said. "But if you go to the library tomorrow one of the staff can help you find out."

"Right." Connor nodded. "Should've

61

thought of that." He gazed at the house again. "Probably further back, too." He swigged some bourbon.

"Yes, or you can go to the county courthouse a few blocks away and check the records." By now I burned with curiosity. Was he interested in buying the house?

I waited a moment, but Lawton's focus on the house didn't waver. "Well, if that's all," I said and turned away.

Lawton came out of his reverie. "No, hang on." His gaze burned into mine. "You're Laura's dad, aren't you?"

"Yes."

Lawton nodded. "Figured. I didn't put it together before, but when I saw her tonight, and now you, the resemblance hit me. Plus the library thing. She told me her dad's a librarian."

"Yes, I am," I said. "If that's all, I'll be on my way."

Lawton grabbed my arm before I could move away. "That's *not* all." He let go when I shook my arm and scowled at him. "Tell Laura I said she can hang around with that freaking fairy set designer all she wants, but she'll end up back with me. Count on it."

I struggled to keep my tone cool. "That's really up to Laura. She told me she's not interested in you anymore, and I'd advise you to take that to heart. Find someone else."

Lawton's face reddened, and I felt the anger radiating from him.

"That's crap." He spit on the ground. "She belongs to me, and I'll beat the hell out of anyone who tries to keep me away from her."

SIX

Good thing I didn't have a blunt weapon in my hands, or Connor Lawton's head would have several dents in it. Ordinarily I'm not a violent man, but the belligerent playwright brought out the worst in me.

I was so angry I couldn't speak. Words tangled together in my brain. I took a couple of deep breaths before responding. "Back off, buster. You leave my daughter alone. Same goes for anyone she chooses to date. You cross the line, and I'll have you in jail so fast you'll think tomorrow is yesterday." I loomed over him, and evidently what he read in my expression made him uneasy enough to step back.

"You don't scare me, old man." He sneered, but I could tell he wasn't as confident as his words made him sound. "You're the one who should back off."

I pulled out my cell phone and punched in a number I knew all too well. When the dispatcher answered, I said, "I'd like to speak to Chief Deputy Berry, please. Tell her it's Charlie Harris."

I twisted the phone away from my mouth. "She's a close personal friend, and she owes me a few favors. Like clapping your sorry behind in jail for a few days."

In my ear the dispatcher said, "I'm sorry, sir, but the chief deputy ain't available right now. Can someone else help you?"

That wasn't in the plan. What should I do now?

Then I saw I didn't have to do anything. Connor Lawton tucked tail and almost ran away from me.

With grim satisfaction I thanked the deputy and ended the call. I watched as Lawton hopped into a car half a block away and peeled out. I stuck my phone back in my pocket and headed to my car.

When I reached home some minutes later and entered the kitchen, I announced in a loud voice that I was home, but no one responded. Usually Diesel was waiting, but not tonight. In the hallway I hung my jacket and tie over the banister, then rolled up my sleeves as I walked to the screened-in back porch.

I detected the aroma of Sean's cigar when I opened the door, and before I took two steps, Diesel greeted me with a loud warble of complaint. I rubbed his head. "Sorry, boy, but I couldn't take you. You'd have had a ball, I'm sure." He enjoyed meeting new people and going places, unlike any other cat I've known.

He kept scolding — it would take a few minutes before I'd be allowed back in his good graces. He stared up at me, and I smiled at him. Above us the whir of the ceiling fan stirred the warm air and made it bearable to be away from air conditioning.

"That cat beats all. I've never heard one talk the way he does." Sean laughed. "How was the party?" He occupied an old armchair near the end of the porch to my right, his favorite spot to relax with a cigar.

I'd rather he didn't smoke, but the aroma reminded me of my grandpa Harris. He'd enjoyed his cigars with a shot or two of bourbon well into his nineties, and I'd loved him dearly. Ever since his death over twenty years ago, the smell of a good stogie — health risks aside — triggered pleasant memories.

"The party was okay, nothing special." I sat on the weather-beaten sofa near him, and Diesel jumped up beside me. He deigned to put one paw on my leg. I scratched his back and his head, and he purred in contentment. "Laura played the belle of the ball, such as it was. She went out to dinner with someone she met from the Theater Department named Frank Salisbury. Seems like a nice young man."

Sean shook his head as he emitted more smoke. We both watched as it whirled toward the ceiling fan over his head. "She sure doesn't waste any time."

"Neither did he."

Sean flashed a grin at my dry tone.

"Connor Lawton reacted like a jerk at seeing Laura with another man." I described the scene in the house. "Then, when I left the party, I found him outside staring at the house next door." Again I wondered about that, but now wasn't the time to indulge in speculation. "He accosted me and threatened violence to anyone who stood between him and Laura."

"What?" Sean sat bolt upright. "Tell me exactly what he said."

I repeated the conversation as best I could remember, and Sean scowled the entire time.

"Somebody should teach that jackass a lesson."

"I agree," I said. "But I don't want you getting into a fight with him. I'll speak to Kanesha Berry about it and see if she'll have

67

a talk with him."

Sean laughed. "If she can't scare the crap out of him, nobody can. She sure as heck intimidates me." He drew on his cigar. "I doubt his verbal threat gives grounds for a restraining order, but the deputy can tell us."

"I hope it doesn't come to that. Maybe Kanesha can calm him down. Laura seems so excited about teaching this semester. I don't want anything to ruin that for her."

"We won't let that happen." Sean tapped ash into the ashtray and took another puff before he continued. "Lawton may have his hands full anyway. Damitra Vane will probably keep him too busy to think about Laura or any other woman.

"You have to meet her, Dad. I thought Laura was exaggerating about her intelligence level. Ol' Diesel there is like a Ph.D. compared to Ms. Vane." He shook his head. "Talking to her exhausted me. She has the attention span of a goldfish. If that."

"How frustrating. Was she responsible for the offensive picture?" I didn't care to meet her. I simply wanted her not to bother Laura.

"Yes. And dumb as she is, she still has a kind of low cunning. Took me a few minutes, but I finally got her to admit to put-

68

ting the photograph through the mail slot." Sean drew on his cigar again.

"What else did you say to her?"

"I told her I was Laura's lawyer and that Laura would sue her if she kept up the harassment. I had to explain what the big word meant, and once I did she looked frightened. Swore up and down she wouldn't bother Laura anymore."

"Did you also tell her Laura has no interest in Connor romantically? That they're just friends, according to Laura?" I wanted every detail of that conversation.

"I'm not fresh out of law school. I knew what to tell her, and I handled it." Sean's tone had an edge to it, and I realized I had offended him.

Diesel meowed, alert as ever to changes in the emotional temperature. I stroked his head, and he settled back down.

"I'm sorry, son, I didn't mean to question your abilities." Even after five months of working on strengthening our relationship, I still managed to annoy my son on occasion. "Put it down to overprotectiveness."

"It's okay, Dad. I overreacted." Sean had the grace to appear abashed.

I smiled to indicate I understood. "Did Ms. Vane make threats against Lawton?"

Sean laughed. "Not exactly. She said she'd

69

be watching to make sure no other woman got her claws into him. He belongs to her, and her alone, and no other woman — except she used a more colorful and vulgar word — stands a chance. She expects Connor to come to his senses eventually and realize she's the only one for him."

"Good luck to her, I guess." I shrugged. "As long as she leaves your sister alone, that's all I care about. The same goes for Lawton."

"Even so," Sean said, his tone more serious, "Laura needs to steer clear of both of them."

"I'll talk with her," I said. "And with Kanesha Berry. Now, change of subject. How about dinner?"

Sean expelled smoke and pulled the cigar from his mouth. "I'm good. I had a couple sandwiches before I came out here." He tapped his cigar on the ashtray. "I figured you'd eat at the party."

"I did." I sighed. "Not a lot, but probably enough. I don't really need anything else." I rose from the sofa. "But I could use something to drink. Can I bring you anything?"

"No, thanks." Sean pointed to a bottle of beer on the table by his chair. "Still got a ways to go with this."

"Then I'll leave you to it. I'll call Kanesha

and then probably head upstairs."

"Good night, Dad."

"Night, son." I headed for the door with Diesel at my side. I used the kitchen phone to call the sheriff's department and left a message for Kanesha. I didn't hear from her that evening. I planned to give her until the following evening to get in touch with me, then I'd start calling until I got through to her.

After a quiet Sunday, on Monday morning I headed to work at the college library at a quarter to nine. Diesel wore his harness, and we strolled the few blocks to campus in the warm, thick morning air. We met several people along the way, and we had to stop to let Diesel greet his admiring public. Even after three years, the sight of a gigantic cat on a leash still attracted attention.

Our stroll was so routine, I was able to think about other things as we walked. Kanesha hadn't returned my call yesterday, and I'd left another message before I left for work. Where the heck was she? I should have asked Azalea about that this morning, but I didn't want to cause irritation between mother and daughter. If Azalea knew Kanesha failed to return my calls, she'd probably chastise her daughter severely for bad manners. I'd try again later.

Inside the antebellum home that housed the library's administrative offices, archives, and rare book room, I removed Diesel's leash. He scampered upstairs on his own. I followed in a more leisurely fashion, and he greeted me with a few chirps when I reached my office door.

Diesel preceded me inside. He waited for me to remove his harness, then walked to the window behind my desk and climbed onto the large cushion I keep there for him. This was his special perch, and he loved it. An ancient oak tree right outside often lured birds, and the morning sun warmed him. He yawned and stretched while I booted my computer.

I managed to read three e-mail messages before Melba Gilley, administrative assistant to the library director, Peter Vanderkeller, popped in for her morning visit. Melba and I had known each other since elementary school, and we'd always been friends. She was a knockout in high school, and at fifty-one she retained her figure and her fashion sense.

"Morning, Diesel honey." Melba adored my cat, and Diesel returned the feeling. He sat up and warbled for her, and she blew him a kiss as she slid into the chair by my desk. "And good morning to you, Charlie. What's this I hear about your daughter working in the Theater Department?"

I suppressed a smile. If the campus grapevine could be likened to a computer network, then Melba could be called the hub. I widened my eyes innocently. "Melba, you let me down on this one. How come you didn't know about this last week?"

Melba scowled at me. "Because my usual source didn't tell me about it until after church yesterday, dang her hide." She picked at an invisible piece of lint on her sleeve. "And before you go asking, I'll tell you. It was Sarabeth Conley." She grinned. "She said she used to babysit you when you were a sprout. Said you were a little dickens, too. The only way she could get you to sit still was to sing."

I reddened, and Melba chuckled.

"You were a little dickens in grade school too, as I recall. Always in trouble for talking in class. Until Mrs. Tenney broke you of the habit."

"And as I recall," I said in a wry tone, "I wasn't the only one who got in trouble for talking in class. I remember a holy terror in pigtails who gave about as good as she got."

We both smiled.

"I know you're thrilled to have Laura here

for a whole semester."

I nodded. "I sure am. I don't get to see her that often. I'm proud of her and her career, but I hate that she's so far away."

Melba leaned forward and patted my arm. "That's the rough thing about being a parent, I guess." A shadow passed over her face. Melba had no children, a situation I knew she regretted.

I decided to change the subject. "What have you heard about the resident genius in the Theater Department, Connor Lawton?"

"That he'll be lucky to make it through the year without getting his rear end whupped." Melba shook her head. "He aggravates people left and right. Being a hotshot will carry him only so far."

"Some people think artists should be allowed to behave badly. It's part of their creative personalities."

Melba snorted. "I don't see why. There's no excuse for anybody being that rude. Besides, he ought to know better, being born in the South."

"Born in the South?" That was news to me.

"Right here in Athena as a matter of fact." I could see Melba enjoyed my surprise. "Lived here till he was about four or five, from what I heard. Then his daddy got a job back east. Connecticut, or maybe Vermont." She frowned. "At least, I think that's what Sarabeth said."

Sounded to me like Sarabeth was another hub in the gossip network. I decided I should advise Laura to be careful what she said and did around the Theater Department's administrator.

Since news spread so quickly around campus, I figured I might as well tell Melba about Connor and Laura. She'd find out anyway, and I'd rather she had the real story from me, and not some lurid tale of unrequited passion from another source. "Laura dated him briefly. She said there's a gentler side to him, though I must say I have yet to see it myself." I didn't tell her about Lawton's threats.

I rarely managed to surprise Melba with such juicy tidbits, and I had to work to keep from laughing at her expression.

"At least he has good taste in women. She's better off without him, though, from what I've heard." Melba stood. "Guess I should get my carcass back downstairs before His Majesty gets into a flap over something." Peter Vanderkeller was a bright man, overall a good library director, but he lacked common sense. Without Melba there to keep him organized, I doubt he'd ever get anything done.

Melba bade me good-bye and blew another kiss to Diesel. He meowed for her as she left.

Thankful for the quiet, I went back to my e-mail.

Once I finished that, I moved on to other tasks, like cataloging more books from the Delacorte Collection. I regretted the manner in which Athena College received the bequest — as the result of violent death — but I had to admit I was thrilled to hold first editions of such classics as *Pride and Prejudice, Middlemarch,* and *Vanity Fair* in my hands as I cataloged them.

I surfaced from deep concentration on my work when I heard a knock at the door. I looked up to see Laura striding into the room. She smiled as she halted in front of my desk. "You sure do get into your work, Dad. I had to knock a couple of times before you heard me."

I laughed as I set aside the book I'd been cataloging. "Guilty as charged. I lose track when I'm working." I glanced at my watch and noted the time with surprise. "It's eleven-thirty."

Laura's cheeks dimpled. "You promised to take me to lunch, remember?"

"That I did." I gazed at her for a moment,

remembering our talk yesterday when I'd told her about Connor Lawton's threats of violence.

In the uncanny way she had, my daughter picked up on my thoughts. "Stop worrying, Dad. I told you, Connor isn't brave, for all his big talk. He won't attack anyone. He's all hat and no cattle, like they say in Texas."

"I hope you're right." I still planned to ask Kanesha to speak with him, no matter what Laura said.

Diesel hopped down from the windowsill and padded around the desk to Laura. He meowed at her, and she obliged by scratching his head. The rumble of his purr told us how much he appreciated such treatment.

"You are such a beautiful boy." Laura gazed at Diesel, and he meowed again, as if to say, *I sure am.* Laura and I both laughed.

With the cat once again in his harness and leash we headed out of the library for the student union and the small café there. Overall the food was passable, but their chicken salad — a favorite of both Laura's and mine — was scrumptious.

The shaded patio sported thirty tables, but today only three were occupied. Laura and Diesel chose one in a corner that offered privacy while I went inside for our food. When I exited the front door ten

77

minutes later, I saw Laura frowning up at a voluptuous, tanned blonde talking too loudly and gesturing at her. Diesel growled, his ears back.

As I hurried across the patio, my hands full, I hoped I could stop my cat from attacking the woman.

SEVEN

I'd never seen Diesel behave this way. He was normally a gentle cat. I called out, "Diesel, it's okay." I repeated that as I drew closer.

Laura heard me and glanced down. She reached forward to reassure the cat with her touch. She spoke in a mild tone to the blonde. "Back off, Damitra. You're upsetting the cat."

With not-quite-steady hands I set the tray of food and drinks on the table. "Yes, please lower your voice. There's no need to cause such a ruckus." I glared at Damitra Vane.

The combination of two humans and one large cat facing her down seemed to shock her into silence. She frowned at the cat, next at me, then her gaze rested on Laura.

"What is all this about?" I directed my question to my daughter.

Laura shot a glance of pure loathing at Damitra Vane. "Diesel and I were sitting here, not bothering anyone, and then Damitra popped up and accosted me." She held up a hand when Damitra started to speak. "You shut up, or I'll let Diesel bite off one of your legs."

"Keep that nasty thing away from me." The woman cast a terrified look at Diesel and backed up at least two feet.

I started to protest that Diesel would never do such a thing, but Damitra Vane bolted.

Diesel crowded close to me and chirped. I bent to wrap my arms around his head and chest. I murmured, telling him he was a good boy and that everything was okay.

"Diesel, sweetie, I'm sorry to malign you like that." Laura laughed. "But I figured that would get rid of Damitra. Diesel freaked her out anyway. I told her he was a rare breed of hunting cat from Tibet, and she bought it."

"If she's silly enough to believe that, it's okay by me. She shouldn't have bothered you." I distributed plates and drinks and set the tray aside. "What was she going on about?"

Laura unfolded her napkin and spread it over her lap. "Apparently *my lawyer* visited her Saturday night to warn her to leave me alone. Did you put *my lawyer* up to it, even after I told you I could handle her?" She had a steely glint in her eye as she dipped her fork into the chicken salad.

"It was a mutual effort." I picked up my own fork. "Sean and I both thought it was a good idea. Neither of us is keen on some nutcase — your word, I remind you — harassing you over a man you say is only a friend now."

Laura put her fork down and glared at me. "I am not twelve years old anymore, and you and Sean need to get that through your thick chauvinist heads. I've coped pretty dang well in Hollywood for four years now."

I raised my hands in a gesture of surrender. "Point well taken. Sean and I shouldn't have acted without talking to you first." Now it was my turn to glare a little. "But remember, young lady, no matter how old you are and how capable, you're always going to be my daughter. I reserve the right to be concerned for your well-being."

Laura regarded me with fond amusement. "You're incorrigible." She ate another bite of chicken salad. "This is crazy good."

"By far the best thing on their menu." I savored a forkful before I had a sip of tea. Laura may have thought she deflected me from her conversation with Damitra Vane, but she ought to know her father better than that.

"About Ms. Vane." My tone was mild. "I'm not trying to run your life, but if she plans to hang around town the whole time you're here, I want to know when she harasses you."

Laura gazed at me for a moment, and from her expression I could see she was exasperated. Diesel chose that moment to warble at her — no doubt hinting that chicken salad would be more than welcome — and the sudden tension eased. She smiled. "You men. What am I going to do with you?"

"Answer my question, maybe? What was she going on about?"

Laura capitulated. "Honestly, Dad, it was just more of the same. Evidently Sean didn't frighten Damitra off, because she was haranguing me about Connor. I tried to tell her Connor and I are through, but she won't listen."

"If she causes any further trouble, I'll go to the sheriff's department. I know someone who could probably get through to her."

"Azalea's daughter, you mean?" Laura patted her mouth with her napkin before she picked up her fork for another bite.

"Exactly." I still hadn't heard from Kanesha, and now I had another reason to talk to her. "Kanesha is scary even when she's not trying to be. I'll bet she can make Ms. Vane back off." I gave Diesel a small bite of chicken salad. It disappeared quickly. Then a large paw tapped my leg. One bite was never enough.

"It won't come to that." Laura glanced over my shoulder, and her sudden change of expression startled me. "Oh, crap. Like I really need this right now." She grimaced. "Don't lose your temper, Dad. Let *me* handle this."

"Handle what?" I started to turn, but as the person approaching from behind me spoke, I stilled in my seat.

"Laura, why aren't you answering my calls? Do you know how pissed off I am with you right now?"

Laura suggested what Connor could do with his cell phone and, while not anatomically impossible, it would be painful. I was aghast at my daughter's crudeness, but part of me couldn't blame her. Lawton affected people that way.

I stood to face him. "I told you last night, leave Laura alone. She's not interested in you. If you continue to annoy her, you'll find yourself in jail."

Diesel hissed again, his ears flattened. He

crouched as if he was about to pounce on the playwright, but he relaxed as Laura stroked his head.

Lawton simply shrugged. Then he pulled out a chair and sat. "Relax, Pops, I'm not going to hit anybody. I'd had a little too much to drink last night when I saw you. Take a chill pill and park it." He waved a hand in my direction, then faced Laura. "What's up, babydoll?"

"I cannot *tell* you how much I despise that *loathsome* nickname. It — and you — have all the charm of a baboon's rear end." Laura picked up her tea, and her gaze flicked back and forth between Lawton and the glass. I wouldn't be surprised if Lawton got a face full of iced tea.

Lawton laughed, to my great surprise. "You're not going to throw that at me, are you? Remember, Daddy's watching."

Laura put her glass down. "Connor, you're such an oaf. No wonder Dad's ready to call the police and have them haul you off to jail."

"Hey, I'm being good." Lawton grinned. "Shouldn't good boys be rewarded?"

"Honestly." Laura folded her arms across her chest and glared at her former boyfriend. "Please go away and let us finish our lunch in peace."

Lawton pulled a crumpled pack and lighter from his shirt pocket and extracted a cigarette. He lit it and exhaled smoke that drifted in my direction.

"I've met pigs with better manners than you, Mr. Lawton. I don't care to have your foul smoke in my face." I waved the air to dispel it.

"Sorry." Lawton raised his hands in mock surrender. He drew on his cigarette again and turned his head away from me to exhale. The smoke still floated toward me. He shrugged and stubbed the butt against the bottom of his worn boot. He pitched the spent cigarette into the grass several feet away. "That better?"

I gave him a grudging nod, deciding that a remark about littering would do no good. Instead I sat and picked up my fork again. I hadn't quite lost my appetite, but all the joy had gone out of this meal with my daughter. For Laura's sake I didn't want to scrap with him. I decided the old saw about holding your friends close and your enemies closer had some merit, at least for the moment.

"Wouldn't hurt you to keep your mouth shut and your ears open for a couple of weeks." Laura stabbed so hard at her food I thought she might go right through the plate into the wood of the table. "You could learn a lot from the people in this town about how normal folk behave."

Diesel meowed as he left me to sit by Laura. She cast the playwright a glance of frustration as she scratched the cat's head to let him know she was okay.

"You know my work." The playwright crossed his arms over his chest and returned Laura's fierce gaze. "I don't write about normal people. Normal is boring. Nobody goes to the theater to see *normal.*"

"No, they don't," I said. "But that doesn't mean they don't expect an artist to behave like a decent human being who treats others with respect outside the theater."

"Mind if I quote you on that?" Lawton sneered at me. He turned back to Laura. "What do you think of the revised first act?"

Laura's nostrils flared. "You just e-mailed it to me this morning. I haven't had time even to open the file. I *do* have other things to do, like prepare for the classes I'll be teaching in less than a week."

Lawton grimaced. "You need to read it soon, because I have to give it to the workshop group in a couple of days." He brightened. "Tell you what, have dinner with me tonight, and we can read it together. I'll even cook."

"You don't cook that well." Laura's deadpan made me want to laugh. "I have other plans for tonight."

"You're not dating that fairy who teaches set design, are you?" Lawton glowered.

"It's none of your business whom I spend my time with, *straight* or not. Besides, how could you have time for me when the love of your life is in town?" Laura treated him to a sweet smile.

Lawton's eyes widened, and his mouth dropped open. "Crap. Don't tell me that loony-tune Damitra is here." He let out a stream of profanity that would have done the proverbial sailor proud.

I didn't see any point in a protest at his vulgarity. The man had the hide of five elephants. No, make that five mammoths.

Laura laughed at him. "You'll be too busy hiding from her to pester me, or anyone else for that matter. You two deserve each other."

Lawton stood suddenly, sending his chair skidding backwards. "Don't jerk me around, Laura. Remember who got you the job here." He stared down at my daughter for a moment. "*And* who has connections in Hollywood that can either help or destroy your career." He stalked away.

Laura was so furious she couldn't speak. I watched her struggle to find the words to respond, but by now Lawton was too far away.

"Don't pay any attention to him, sweetheart. He's an arrogant jackass. It's all big talk."

"Unfortunately, it's not. He's really well connected in LA. One word from him in certain ears, and I might as well leave the business." Laura banged the table with both fists. "I swear, I'd like to push him in front of a big truck."

EIGHT

Two weeks sped by. Laura, increasingly anxious over preparations for her classes, spent most of her time holed up in her room or in her campus office. When I did manage to catch her long enough for a conversation, she alternated between excitement and dread. Not unlike her general state before opening night of all her high school and college performances, I recalled.

She made no mention of either Connor Lawton or Damitra Vane during those brief talks. I wasn't sure whether she was hiding things from me, or whether my plea to Kanesha Berry for semiofficial intimidation paid off.

I'd finally caught up with the elusive chief deputy midweek. She gave no reason for taking so long to return my calls, and I didn't ask. I knew better. Instead I explained the situation and asked her to do what she could to keep the conflict from escalating.

She said she'd talk to Connor and Damitra, and with that I had to be content.

This morning, the second Monday of the semester, Laura, Diesel, and I breakfasted together. The rest of the household — Sean, Stewart, Dante, and Justin — had yet to put in an appearance. My housekeeper, Azalea Berry, stood at the stove, and the odor of hotcakes and bacon perfumed the air.

Diesel sat by my chair, nose aquiver, hoping for tidbits. He was as fond of pancakes and bacon as I was. I tried to keep the human food to a minimum, but that adorable face with its imploring eyes was difficult to resist. Only Azalea remained immune from such appeals.

Laura sipped at her coffee. "Would you like to come and watch us workshopping the play, Dad?"

"I'd love to." I added half-and-half to my cup, along with a couple of packets of artificial sweetener. "I've never seen a play being workshopped before. Are you sure it will be all right?" I didn't want any hassle from the playwright. The less I interacted with him directly, the better.

"It'll be fine." Laura smiled. "Connor won't even notice you're there. He'll be totally focused on the stage and the actors."

"Okay, then." I leaned back as Azalea set

plates in front of Laura and me. "Thank you."

Azalea nodded and stood back to watch as Laura and I tucked into the pancakes.

"Mmmmm." Laura chewed with an ecstatic expression. "Azalea, these pancakes are like heaven in my mouth."

Azalea favored Laura with a smile. She had a tender spot for my daughter. "Thank you, Miss Laura. You eat on up, now. You been working too much, and you losing some weight, no matter how I try to feed you good."

Laura's laugh rang out. "I have to work hard to keep my weight down. Your food has spoiled me for my usual diet of carrot and celery sticks. If I didn't keep on the run, I'd be as big as the side of this house."

"Go on now." Azalea actually laughed — a sound I rarely heard. "Little bitty thing like you, ain't no way you gone get that big, even on my food."

"No, I'm the one who seems to gain the weight." I groaned as I regarded my half-finished stack of pancakes.

Azalea gazed at me with no hint of sympathy in her eyes. "You get up and get a move on like Miss Laura do, ain't gone be no moaning about gaining no weight. Yo' trouble is you sitting around reading books and petting that lazy cat of yours 'stead of getting busy." With that pronouncement she turned back to the stove.

I pretended to be outraged. "I'll have you know I walk up and down the stairs in this house several times a day, plus I walk to work at the college." Diesel meowed, as if in support.

Laura giggled, and I would have sworn I saw Azalea's shoulders tremble ever so slightly. I rewarded Diesel with a bite of pancake.

Stewart swept into the room with Dante the poodle hopping excitedly around him. "Good morning, good morning," he sang to the tune of the famous song from *Singin' in the Rain*. Laura joined in, and they went on for a couple of verses. Diesel decided to help them and started warbling. Dante added a few yips to the mix. I watched with a bemused smile.

Azalea shook her head as she set a plate of pancakes and bacon on the table for Stewart. When the choir of four finished, Stewart bowed. I clapped.

"You set on down there and eat yo' breakfast." Azalea pointed to Stewart's plate. "Nobody believe me, I tell 'em how folks carry on in this house." Her lips twitched.

"As you wish, O Goddess of the Spatula."

Stewart blew Azalea a kiss before he sat. "I'm absolutely famished this morning, and I swear I could eat a dozen of your fabulous pancakes and a pound of that magnificently crunchy bacon." He poured a generous amount of syrup over his plate and set to with knife and fork. After the first bite he said, "O bliss, o joy." Dante whimpered and stood on his hind legs to beg.

Azalea shook her head. "You and yo' mess, ain't never seen nothing like the fooling you do. You got to be the craziest white man I ever saw." She sniffed. "With that no-account rat you call a dog too. Go on ahead and give him a bit of pancake so he'll stop that whining. I know you gone do it anyway soon's I turn my back."

"Ah, but you adore me, and my little dog too, admit it." Stewart's angelic expression amused me.

Azalea snorted and flapped a hand at him. "Lord knows, ain't no use in me even trying."

I saw her lips fight a smile before she turned back to the stove. She pretended to be outraged by Stewart's antics, but I could see that she got a kick out of him. She also tolerated Dante much better than she did Diesel.

Stewart entertained us all, I had to admit.

I had misgivings when he first moved in, but for all his outrageousness — "just being a stereotypical flaming queen," he called it — he was basically a kindhearted, solid, dependable man.

"You have a great voice," Stewart said to Laura. "I can't believe you haven't done musical theater."

"Thanks. I did a bit in college, but not since." Laura crunched bacon for a moment. "I haven't had an opportunity, but I do enjoy singing. Mostly in the shower."

"Lucky shower." Stewart grinned. "So, dish. What's the latest with Mr. Tall, Tattooed, and Temperamental? How many people has he insulted lately?"

"How much time do you have?" Laura rolled her eyes. "The whole Theater Department is ready to wring his neck but we're stuck with him. He is a genius, after all." She snickered.

"Is his play any good?" I started to get up to refill my cup but before I could move, Azalea was there with the coffee pot.

Laura considered a moment before she responded. "I think it will be. I read through the first act a couple times this weekend. There are some rough parts, but workshopping it will help."

"How so?" Stewart asked.

"Writing dialogue is tricky. Hearing it in your head is one thing. Hearing it performed is another." She forked a hunk of pancake. "Connor writes brilliant dialogue, but occasionally he's off the mark. Hearing actors reading it can be illuminating, and Connor's good at spotting the problems."

"Can anyone sit in?" Stewart slipped another bite of food to Dante.

"Not just anyone," Laura said with a smile. "But I think I could sneak you in. Along with Dad."

"And Diesel. Remember he'll be with me," I said. At the sound of his name, Diesel meowed.

Stewart chuckled. "Diesel can give us his review. That cat has discriminating taste. What time is the session?"

"Two," Laura said.

"That's not fair. I'll be teaching my organic chemistry class then, with a lab afterward." Stewart gave a theatrical sigh. "Guess I'll have to forego the pleasure of telling the resident genius what I think of his play. At least for now."

"I'll be sure to let him know." Laura grinned.

I pushed back from the table. Time for Diesel and me to finish getting ready for work. "I'll see you this afternoon, Laura.

Have a good day, Stewart. And Azalea, thank you for yet another delicious breakfast."

My housekeeper nodded her head as Laura and Stewart acknowledged my comments.

"I'll be back after I brush my teeth," I told Diesel. I was so used to talking to my cat, I no longer worried about how odd it might sound to other humans. Stewart and Laura were so busy chattering that they probably didn't hear me. Azalea simply shook her head at me.

Diesel gazed up at me. I was convinced he understood what I said to him. He meowed a couple of times in response, and he moved to sit by Laura as I left the kitchen.

Or maybe it was the bite of pancake dangling from her finger that attracted him.

The morning passed quickly. I ate lunch at my desk. Diesel mostly napped, but on occasion he roused enough to warble at the birds in the tree outside his window. He batted at the glass, his large paw going *thunk* when it struck the pane.

At a quarter of two I closed up shop and fitted Diesel into his harness, and we walked to the auditorium two blocks away. Ancient trees shaded our walk, and I was thankful for relief from the blazing afternoon sun. The college occupied land that had once been dense forest. The pre–Civil War founders made sure the campus retained an abundance of green, and administrators since then had not violated the policy.

The auditorium dated from the late nineteenth century and sported all the elegance of Gilded Age architecture, like a mini-Biltmore. Though more ornate than the nearby antebellum buildings in classic Greek Revival style, the Maria Hogan Butler Center for the Performing Arts harmonized well with its neighbors.

Diesel and I mounted the broad steps, paused at the door for a pair of exiting students, then strolled into the cool dimness of the lobby. Whenever I stepped inside the Butler Center, I always fancied I could hear echoes of long-ago productions. Today I heard the air conditioner's low hum and voices from the auditorium ahead. The right-hand set of double doors was propped open, and Diesel and I headed for them.

A few steps inside the theater I paused, and Diesel stood beside me. I sniffed mingled odors of the greasepaint and dust of ages past — or so I fancied — as I gazed with affection over the ornate fixtures and slightly shabby carpet. The seat covers, once a plush wine velvet, had faded to soft pink. I recalled some of the plays I'd seen here as a student thirty years ago — my first live taste of Shakespeare and others.

Diesel shrank against my leg at a sudden burst of noise from the stage. Memories pushed aside, I stared, appalled, as Connor Lawton staggered around the stage, clutching at his throat. No one on stage with him seemed to be paying much attention — except for Laura, who watched his stumbling progress with a scowl. She didn't seem particularly concerned, only annoyed.

What was going on here? Was it a scene from the play?

Lawton gagged loudly, his arms went limp, and he crumpled to the stage. His body jerked twice, then went still.

Deathly still.

NINE

All conversation ceased as every person on stage turned to stare at the prone body of the playwright. My feet felt frozen to the carpet as I continued to watch in growing concern. Perhaps this was serious after all. Lawton lay immobile. Diesel, sensing my unease, muttered and rubbed against my right leg.

Then, to my great relief, Lawton pushed himself to his feet in one swift move. He regarded the company with contempt.

"Based on the reading I heard, the audience will stagger out of here and die like I did just now. If that's the best you can do" — he turned to glare at Laura — "and the best your *acting coach* can teach you, I might as well cancel the production."

The general look of dismay around him made me want to storm up there and give Lawton a piece of my mind. Even if the reading was as bad as Lawton proclaimed, it surely couldn't have been bad enough to warrant such vitriol.

My daughter apparently agreed with me. Her face flushed red. She stepped forward until she was almost nose to nose with the irate playwright. "You're being a complete jackass, Connor, and you know it. You're pissed at me, and you shouldn't take it out on the students." She expelled a harsh breath. "Besides, if you insist on rewriting the scenes every night and then giving the cast three minutes to look over the new pages, you'll get what you get. Your expectations are ridiculous."

Lawton didn't appeared fazed by Laura's counterattack. "What I expect is for your so-called *actors*" — the word dripped with contempt — "to act, not read as if English were an incomprehensible tongue. Pardon me if that's *ridiculous*."

I started down the sloping aisle toward the stage, a skittish Diesel at my side. Laura might believe Lawton was a physical coward, but I didn't intend to give him the opportunity to prove her wrong. If he laid one finger on her, I'd break his scrawny neck. I halted midway, however, when I heard another voice.

"This has gone far enough." Ralph Johnston, head of the department, emerged from the wings and made a beeline for the embattled couple. "You will stop this embarrassing display *now*, do you hear me?"

Johnston's words would have had more force had they been delivered in a voice with more conviction, instead of in his quivering tenor. His hands flapped like metronomes out of control, and he skidded to a stop so suddenly that I thought he might knock both Lawton and my daughter off their feet. To steady himself, Johnston stuck his right hand on Lawton's shoulder.

The playwright shrugged off the hand and stepped back from Laura. "This is what happens when I work with freakin' amateurs. You know why I'm rewriting those pages, babydoll. You of all people in this hayseed town ought to understand." Neither he nor my daughter appeared to be paying any attention to Johnston, despite his proximity.

Laura groaned, a sound of mingled exasperation and impatience. "You can't write *and* direct anymore. You should let someone else direct the play. Right now you keep erupting like Vesuvius every five minutes and still expect us to make progress."

"Excellent idea." Johnston bobbed up and down on the balls of his feet, his face alight with excitement. "I think it's a mistake for the playwright to direct his own work. I'm going to take over directing the production. You're too emotional, Lawton, to do a proper job."

Lawton cursed, loudly and fluently, and Johnston tensed, like someone bracing for a collision. Laura stepped back, taking herself out of the picture. I resumed progress toward the stage, in case I needed to intervene between the two men. Diesel came with me, though I could feel resistance on the leash. He didn't care for confrontations any more than I did.

"What do you know about directing a play?" Lawton glared at the other man. He was two inches shorter than Johnston but much more muscular than the reedy department head. "You sure as hell don't know anything about writing them. That piece of garbage you submitted to the American Academy of Drama prize committee was a total waste of my time. You're nuts if you think I'm going to let you have anything to do with *my* work."

Johnston's face paled. He sputtered, but no intelligible words emerged from the sounds. I heard a few titters, quickly hushed, from the crowd of students.

I reached the stage, then, and ran up the stairs stage left. Laura saw me coming and met me at the head. I handed Diesel's leash to her, and she took it. "Be careful," she whispered.

Johnston still seemed unable to articulate, but he drew back his right arm and punched at Lawton's head. The playwright's reflexes were too good, however. He ducked, and Johnston's fist sailed past Lawton's face. The momentum caused Johnston to teeter backward and stumble.

Before Lawton could react, I motioned to a tall, muscular youth a few feet from the other side of the combatants. He responded immediately and stepped forward to grab Ralph Johnston and pull him further away. I stepped in front of Lawton and glared at him.

"Enough." My temper flared, and I knew if the playwright attempted to attack me, I'd knock him back so fast he wouldn't know what hit him. He was much younger than I, but I outweighed him by at least fifty pounds and was several inches taller.

Lawton took one look at my face and apparently read my intent. He stepped back, his hands coming up in a gesture of surrender.

"You should be ashamed of yourself." A new, but familiar, voice startled both the playwright and me. I glanced aside to see

Sarabeth Conley, Johnston's administrative assistant, her expression one of grim determination, striding toward us.

Lawton glanced at her and paled. He took two more steps back, almost to the edge of the stage. Sarabeth, tall and heavyset, was a formidable sight, like Boudicca defying the Romans. She stopped a couple of feet away and raked Lawton with a glance of disgust. "You were raised better than this. How long do you think you can get away with treating people like idiots before someone teaches you a lesson you won't recover from?"

With that she turned away and focused her attention on Ralph Johnston. The light caught her caftan, the same one she had worn at the party, and played off the many beads and sequins. The muscular student had released him, and Johnston was breathing deeply to regain his composure. When Sarabeth slid an arm around his shoulders, he spoke. "First I must offer my apologies to you all. My behavior was inexcusable, though I feel justified in saying that I was the subject of extreme provocation." He paused for a deep breath. "I'm going straight to the president of the college to report his incident, Lawton. I'm going to do my best to have your contract terminated immediately."

Lawton made a rude gesture, but before the situation could escalate again, Laura stepped forward, Diesel at her side.

"I'm sure that won't be necessary, Professor," she said in her best placatory tone. "Things have certainly gotten out of hand, but I'm sure once Connor has had time to think things over, he'll apologize to you and to everyone else." She glared at Lawton, as if to intimidate him into submission.

Why on earth was my daughter running interference for this cretin? Did she still harbor feelings for him? Or was she simply trying to help a friend who'd gone too far?

"And here I was, thinking maybe you didn't care after all, babydoll." Connor crowed with laughter.

"Don't flatter yourself." Laura had fire in her eyes, and if Lawton knew what was good for him, he'd back off. Laura was like me, with a fuse slow to ignite, but once it did, she would take no prisoners. "I'm looking out for the students, not you."

"I guess that puts me in my place." Lawton's tone was mocking. "Fine. Sorry, Johnston. Guess I got carried away, heat of the moment and all that. I promise I'll chill out." His voice hardened. "But *I'm* going to direct this play. No one else."

I watched Johnston for his reaction. His

pugnacity seemed to have fled, replaced by exhaustion. Sarabeth still had her arm around him, and he appeared to need the support. Johnston waved a hand in Lawton's direction. "Long as you don't browbeat the students anymore, I guess we can go ahead."

"Right, then." Laura moved forward to center stage. "Let's all take ten, then we'll start again from the top of scene two." She clapped her hands, and everyone on stage began to move.

Sarabeth led Johnston to the wings, and the students quickly disappeared.

"So now you're stage manager as well?" Lawton smiled sourly.

"Take a smoke break," Laura advised him. "Maybe some nicotine in your system will calm you down."

"Yes, ma'am." Lawton sketched a derisory bow, then turned and jumped down from the stage. He headed up the aisle toward the door.

Laura turned to me, and I could see the strain in her expression. Diesel rubbed against her legs and chirped. With a quick smile she squatted and hugged the cat against her. Diesel kept chirping and meowing, and Laura told him, "You're the best tonic in the world, big boy."

I moved closer and extended a hand.

Laura grasped it and stood. "Thanks, Dad. I'm glad you and Diesel are here, but I'm sorry you had to witness that."

"I'm sorry you have to deal with that clown." I frowned. "Johnston was right. He ought to see what he can do about cancelling Lawton's contract. He's surely not worth all this hullabaloo."

Laura sighed. "I know he's difficult. Trust me, I've seen him in action several times. But usually after one good blowup he settles down."

"I hope you're right." I put my arm around her, and she rested her head on my shoulder a moment. Diesel rubbed against both our legs. He was so big he could actually touch all four at once.

Movement in the wings stage right caught my attention. A man stood in the shadows. I couldn't see his face, but he moved into the light for a moment. He appeared to be in his mid-forties, with a stocky build, a shock of salt-and-pepper hair, and stubbled cheeks. His rumpled clothing, similar to what the college custodial staff wore but less well kept, lent him a seedy air. He hesitated, then moved forward. He looked vaguely familiar.

I released Laura, and she straightened as the stranger paused in front of us.

"Excuse me." His voice was deep. "Looking for Sarabeth Conley. They said she was here. You seen her?"

"She was here until a few minutes ago," I said. I gestured toward stage left. "She went out that way, but I'm not sure where she is now."

"Thanks." The man nodded and disappeared moments later into the shadows of stage left.

"Do you know him?" I asked.

"I've noticed him a couple of times, hanging around the theater." Laura frowned.

"I've seen him around campus, I think," I said. "Pretty recently, too."

"Oh, I know," Laura said. "He was also at the party we went to. Someone may have introduced him, but I can't recall his name."

"Now I remember. I don't know who he is either." My mind shifted back to the subject of discussion before the stranger appeared. "Now, about Lawton. Why are you going to bat for him? Surely your life would be simpler if Johnston did manage to get him fired."

"Probably." Laura flashed a quick grin. "He got me this job, though, and I owe him something for that. Besides, I love his work. Whatever else he is, he's an amazing writer." She paused. "When he actually finishes a play, that is."

"Is the writing not going well?" The question sounded fatuous to me, given what had ensued on stage earlier, but Laura forestalled me when I tried to explain what I meant.

"I don't think it is. I haven't been around Connor while he's actually writing a play before." Laura massaged her temples and stared down at Diesel, who sat looking up at her. She smiled at him as she continued. "He keeps bringing in revisions. Maybe he's always worked this way, but the plot seems to be turning into a mystery of some kind. He's never written a mystery before. Plus he's introduced a new set of characters, so I'm not really sure where he's going with it."

The chatter of returning students interrupted us before I could probe further. I looked out over the auditorium and spotted Connor Lawton ambling along behind the students.

Laura sighed and set her shoulders. She had seen him, too. As she moved away I heard her say in an undertone, "Once more unto the breach, dear friends, once more."

TEN

"Come on, boy. We'll be in the way here." I patted Diesel's head and led him across the stage past the proscenium arch to the stairs. As I settled into an end seat a few rows back, with Diesel getting comfortable in the aisle beside me, I tried to identify the source of Laura's quotation. I'd heard or read it before, and after a minute or so, I had it. "*Henry V.* Shakespeare, of course," I muttered. Diesel meowed in response, as if he were acknowledging I was right.

Meanwhile the cast had reassembled center stage. With the area bare of any props, even chairs, the space the cast occupied appeared almost desertlike. I couldn't imagine watching a play without some kind of set. This would be an interesting experience.

Connor Lawton stood downstage. From my vantage point his face was a placid mask, his stance relaxed. I hoped he could maintain this mood.

I heard voices behind me, and I turned to see Sarabeth Conley and Ralph Johnston taking seats halfway down the aisle on the other side of the auditorium.

Laura clapped her hands for silence, and I turned back to watch. When the last snatch of conversation died away, she said, "We're going to try this again. Remember what we discussed in class about sight-reading. We haven't had much time to work on that, but do your best." She turned to Lawton. "Where would you like to start?"

"Beginning of the third scene." Lawton crossed his arms across his chest. Pages rustled as the actors found their places. "We'll start with Ferris."

Dead silence followed. One of the students, an attractive brunette, nudged the tall, pudgy young man standing beside her. "That's you, Toby," she hissed.

"Um, right, old man Ferris, that's me." Toby was clearly rattled, and he stared like a mesmerized goldfish at Lawton.

"Take deep breaths, Toby," Laura said in a firm, but kind, tone. "Center yourself, then start."

I saw Lawton shake his head, but he didn't speak. Toby nodded and I could see the change in his face and body language as he followed Laura's instructions.

When he began to speak, I blinked in surprise. Out of his mouth came the quavery voice of an ill, elderly man.

"I tell you, Henrietta, I'm not shelling out any more of my hard-earned savings on that no-good daughter of yours."

The pretty young woman next to Toby responded, her voice sounding surprisingly mature. "She's your daughter too, Herb. Whether you want to admit it or not."

Toby snorted. "Don't see why as I should own up to begetting that shiftless piece of jailbait." He paused to gasp for breath.

"See what happens when you get your dander up?" "Henrietta" shook her head dolefully. "Gives you spasms, and what's the use of that?"

Toby gulped air again before he spoke. "That girl's enough to give a *healthy* man spasms, much less me. I tell you I'm not giving her — or you — any more money."

Another young woman, a chubby blonde, entered the conversation. "But Papa, we can't put her in jail. All you have to do is pay back what she stole. Surely you don't want to see your child behind bars?" She emitted a muffled sob. "You can't do that to my baby sister."

"Quit your caterwauling, Lisbeth." Toby

spoke sharply. "You're so goldarned concerned about Sadie, *you* pay back the money."

"Lisbeth" sobbed again. "I don't have it. The rent's way overdue, and it looks like Johnny might get laid off. Papa, please."

"Reckon you'll be begging for money next, because that no-good bastard you married can't keep a job." Toby coughed so hard his face turned red.

"Herb, calm down." The note of panic in "Henrietta's" voice sounded real to me.

Based on what I was hearing now, I'd have to say these young people were reading well, although I was not in the least impressed by Lawton's "genius." Was this reading significantly better than what Lawton heard earlier? If that was the case, then perhaps his temper tantrum had energized them somehow. I'd have to ask Laura about that.

What a shame, though, that what they were reading was so banal.

"Herb" told his wife to shut up in a crude manner. "Henrietta" uttered his name in shocked protest.

"I'm fixin' to go lie down for a spell," Toby said. He sounded exhausted, his patience at an end. "I don't want to hear any more about Sadie's problems. I'm done with her." He mimed an old man, shuffling out of the room, leaning on a cane.

"Lisbeth" and "Henrietta" exchanged glances, waiting until the old man left the room. Toby stepped back, and the two young women moved closer together as they continued the scene.

"Mama, what are we gonna do?" Lisbeth practically sobbed the words out. "Sadie can't go to jail, she just can't."

I thought the young woman was overdoing the histrionics, and evidently Connor Lawton agreed. He held up a hand. "Hold on a minute." He pointed at "Lisbeth." "What's your name again, doll?"

The young woman blushed and swallowed. "Um, Elaine, Mr. Lawton."

The playwright walked forward, and when he paused beside her, he stood at an angle that allowed me a clear view of his face. I caught a grimace, but then his expression smoothed out. He placed an arm across Elaine's shoulder. "Elaine, you're giving me too much. Dial it back a few notches, understand? All that weeping and wailing and gnashing of teeth this early on, you've got nothing left later on."

He paused long enough for Elaine to nod twice before he went on. "Lisbeth, now, remember she's thirty-two, married, no kids, and Sadie's like her own child because

Mom and Pop are so much older, right? Lisbeth is emotional and not totally wrapped when it comes to Sadie, but you can't let it all go in this scene. Dial it back a little, like I said. Can you do that for me?"

Frankly I was surprised by Lawton's patient tone and demeanor. It almost seemed like a different man had come back from the break.

Elaine gazed at the playwright like Diesel mesmerized by a bird outside the archive window. After a long moment of silence, she swallowed and said, "Yes, sir."

Lawton patted her shoulder. "That's great, doll." He moved back downstage and faced the actors. "Right. Take it from where old man Ferris leaves. Hey, Tobe, excellent job by the way. You've almost nailed it."

Toby blushed and beamed as "Lisbeth" and "Henrietta" prepared to start the scene again. If Lawton kept up "slobbering sugar" like this — what my aunt Dottie would have called it — they'd all adore him and soon forget the earlier tantrum.

"Lisbeth" repeated her lines in more restrained tones, and Lawton nodded.

"Henrietta" picked up from her fictional daughter's lines. "I don't see much hope. Your father's made up his mind. You know how he is when he talks like that. Remember your wedding?" She sighed heavily. "Wasn't nothing on earth going to make him pay for you a decent wedding once he took against Johnny."

Could this possibly get any worse? I was no expert, but the average soap opera probably had better writing. But I soon discovered it *could* get worse.

"He's a mean old bastard, and I hate him." Elaine's face twisted into an ugly mask. "I wish he'd up and die. Let him join the demons in Hell where he belongs."

"Henrietta" drew back her hand and swung it at her daughter's face. The intended blow became a light tap on the cheek, but Elaine drew back and howled as if she'd been struck hard.

"Girl, don't ever let me hear you talking about your father that way. He's had many a sore trial in his life, and he doesn't deserve disrepect like that."

Before Elaine could respond, Lawton surprised everyone by gesturing wildly with both hands and saying, "Enough, enough."

No one onstage moved. They all gaped at the playwright.

Lawton grabbed his ears and rocked his head from side to side. "God, that's awful. Freakin' bloody rank. Sounds like third-rate dinner theater."

I definitely agreed with that, and I sought Laura's face to see her reaction to this outburst. Was Lawton talking about the reading, or was he referring to the words themselves? The pitying glance Laura directed toward Lawton answered my question.

"It's okay, everyone." Laura spoke in an undertone, but thanks to the acoustics of the theater I had no trouble hearing her. "Connor's not talking about your reading."

The actors relaxed visibly. All the while Laura reassured the cast, Lawton continued to mutter, but I couldn't make out what he was saying.

If this was an example of a playwright's method for creating a play, I decided I was glad I didn't have an artistic temperament.

"Everyone, take ten." Laura made shooing motions with her hands, and the actors moved off the stage in a hurry. A couple cast puzzled glances back at Lawton.

Laura approached the playwright, who was still absorbed in his frenzy of negative self-criticism. She slapped the top of his head.

"Ow. That hurt." Lawton let go of his ears to rub his head and glared at her.

"I meant it to." Laura looked and sounded exasperated. "This is not the time for you to get into one of your self-flagellation sessions. You're freaking out the kids, and frankly I'm pretty sick of it myself."

Well done, Laura, I thought. I'd never seen such an emotional grasshopper.

"Who the bloody hell cares whether they're used to it?" Lawton threw up his hands. "If they can't take it, they're never going to last in the theater. You're not doing them any favors by babying them." He shook his head. "Maybe you're not up to the teaching gig after all."

"Nice try, but this isn't about me, Connor. You wrote the stinking dialogue. And I do mean *stinking.*" I knew Laura in this mood. She wasn't about to back down. Would that make Lawton even angrier? Provoke him to violence?

Diesel was not happy with the loud voices and the tangible tension. He crawled under my legs and tried to hide beneath my seat, but of course he was too big. His tail stuck out between my knees. I scratched his back to reassure him, but right then I was growing more concerned for my daughter. Should I go onstage and interfere before this got any uglier?

"Yeah, thanks to you, babydoll. You're my muse, you know that. How can I write anything decent when you're tearing my heart out?" The fight seemed to have gone out of the playwright.

"Don't give me that pathetic little act. That's all it is, and we both know it. *Bourbon* is your muse. Go drink a bottle or two and rewrite the scene. Leave me out of it."

Lawton's expression turned ugly, and he was clenching and unclenching his hands. I was out of my chair and halfway to the stage by the time Laura finished speaking.

Lawton yelled an obscenity at my daughter, and I was so furious I was ready to teach him some manners — with a baseball bat, if necessary.

He didn't stick around to judge the reactions to his vulgarity. Instead, he rushed across the stage and disappeared into the wings.

ELEVEN

Laura was still trembling with anger, her eyes focused in the direction of Lawton's exit, when I reached her moments later. Diesel followed me onto the stage and meowed loudly as he butted his head against my right leg. I extended a hand to rub him while I examined my daughter with concern.

"I'm okay, Dad." Laura flashed a brief smile, but I could see the strain on her face.

I squeezed her shoulder lightly, then dropped my hand. "That was pretty intense. Are you sure you're all right?"

Laura nodded. Her eyes met mine for a moment then shifted away. "Par for the course with Connor whenever he's working on a new play. I went through part of this process once before with him." She gave a shaky laugh. "I should have been more prepared, I suppose."

"I don't see how anyone can work with him if he's like this on every project." I kept my hand on Diesel because the cat still seemed restless. As I glanced down he butted his head against Laura's thigh and meowed.

Laura squatted and threw her arms around Diesel. She pulled his head next to hers and stroked his back. "You are such a sweetie, you know that?" Diesel warbled as if he were agreeing, and Laura laughed. She stroked him a moment longer, then released him to stand. "It's amazing how much better he can make you feel."

"I know." I smiled fondly at my cat. I checked her face and was relieved to see that her expression had lightened. "Will you go on with the rehearsal now?"

The student actors were clustered stage left, and I indicated them with a tilt of my head. Laura glanced their way and motioned for them to join her onstage. "Might as well."

The students surged forward but halted a few feet away.

"Laura, my dear, I must speak with you." Ralph Johnston approached from stage right, and Laura and I turned to him. He nodded in my direction but addressed my daughter. "After that outburst we just witnessed, I have even graver doubts about this production. Lawton seems completely unstable to me, and I'm afraid he will turn violent. He seems particularly fixated on you."

I agreed with the department head and waited to hear Laura's response. I wasn't keen on her having to deal with Lawton any further, but I knew how stubborn my daughter could be.

Laura sounded weary when she spoke. "I understand how you feel, and I've decided that the best thing is for me to remove myself from direct participation in this production. Connor is volatile, but if I'm not present during rehearsals, perhaps he'll be less keyed up."

There were mutters of protest from the students, and Laura flashed them a grateful smile. "I will continue to teach my students, of course, but away from the theater."

Johnston mulled that over for a moment, then nodded. "Very well. That sounds like a sensible workaround to me. But if Lawton doesn't start behaving in a more mature, professional fashion, I will take drastic steps."

"Yes, sir." Laura nodded. She waved to indicate the cast. "Let's get on with our reading. I doubt Connor will be back this afternoon."

"Good, good." Johnston bobbed his head

back and forth. "Sensible. If you need me, call Sarabeth and she'll know where to find me." He strode off down the steps and up the aisle.

Toby, the student actor reading the part of old Mr. Ferris, moved forward. "Laura, we'd all rather work with you. Why don't *you* direct the play?"

Laura smiled at the earnest young man. Though she was only about five years older than he, her poise and assurance made her seem even more mature. "Thank you, Toby. I appreciate the vote of confidence. But I don't have any experience directing." She paused to smile at the cast. "I'll stick to coaching. You will all do just fine. When Connor gets crazy like he did today, try to stay out of his way and let him carry on till he gets it out of his system. He'll get better as the play progresses, I promise you."

Toby exchanged glances with several other cast members. I could see they weren't completely convinced, despite the assured tone with which Laura spoke. I couldn't blame them.

I spoke in an undertone to Laura. "Are you sure about this?"

"I am." Laura met my gaze and didn't look away. "I appreciate your concern, but I can handle this. I'll stay out of Connor's way. End of problem."

"He seems fairly determined to stay in your way. What about his assertion that you're his muse?" I wasn't convinced by Laura's words and manner.

Laura frowned. "Trust me on this, Dad. I wasn't kidding when I said bourbon is his muse. He'll be so absorbed with the play, he won't have time for me. He'll be busy drinking, writing, and smoking too much instead."

There didn't seem to be any point in further argument right now. I still had reservations, but I would keep them to myself for the time being. "Then I guess Diesel and I will head back to the archive. Will we see you at dinner tonight?"

"Probably." Laura pecked me on the cheek before bending to give Diesel one on his nose. "See you men later." She turned to face her students.

Diesel and I exited the stage and walked up the aisle. When we entered the foyer, I spotted Sarabeth Conley in conversation with the man who'd spoken to Laura and me earlier.

". . . to worry about. He doesn't know anything." Sarabeth saw me and fell silent. The man turned and glanced at Diesel and me.

I waved a greeting. The man nodded before turning back. Sarabeth nodded as well but did not speak. Now that I saw the two of them together I noticed a definite resemblance. Her brother, perhaps? As a child I had known only Sarabeth, and I knew nothing about her family. He looked young enough to be her son, maybe in his mid-forties, but Sarabeth told me at the party she had no children. Then I recalled her remark about a much younger brother.

Next time I ran into her, I'd ask her about him. With that thought, I pushed the door open, and Diesel and I stepped outside into the afternoon heat.

We were both happy to reach the cool, dim interior of the archive building a quarter of an hour later. I filled Diesel's water bowl in my office, and he lapped at it thirstily. Then he hopped onto the windowsill and settled down for a nap.

While I checked e-mail, I revisited the events of the afternoon. I didn't like Lawton, and I worried that his interest in Laura could cause a serious problem before the semester ended. Despite my daughter's repeated assurances that she could handle the playwright, like any father concerned with a child's welfare, I felt I should be able to do something more to ensure her safety and well-being.

But what? Short of working Lawton over with a baseball bat — definitely not my usual style — I felt at a loss. If I played the heavy-handed, interfering father, I risked alienating my daughter. That was the last thing I wanted. After damaging my relationship with my son — though it was thankfully now on the mend — I wanted things with Laura to remain healthy and happy.

I stewed over the issue with little result for two hours before I decided I was accomplishing nothing. My attention to my work was sporadic at best, and my mental gyrations over Laura only exhausted my brain.

"Come on, boy. Let's go." I powered down my computer and reached for the cat's harness and leash.

Diesel chirped as he stretched. Then he hopped to the floor and stood still while I fitted him into the harness.

Soon we headed down the sidewalk toward home. Though it was a few minutes past six, the sun still bore down mercilessly. Trees shaded us much of the way, for which I was thankful. I worried every summer about the hot cement of the sidewalk possibly blistering Diesel's pads, but so far that hadn't happened.

In the kitchen we found Justin Wardlaw, my younger boarder, staring into the refrigerator. When Diesel made a beeline for him and warbled, Justin shut the door and dropped to his knees to hug the cat. "Hey, Mr. Charlie, how's it going?"

"Fine." I removed the cat's leash. "How are your classes?"

Justin glanced up at me as he removed Diesel's harness. After a difficult first semester at Athena College, he had settled down and performed well. The trials he faced that first semester had matured him. He'd undergone physical change as well, working out and putting on some weight, cutting his dark hair and growing a beard. No longer a gangly, awkward boy, he looked and acted like the man he'd become.

"They're all good, thanks." Justin hung the harness on its knob near the back door. Diesel followed him, and Justin scratched behind the cat's ears. With a thank-you chirp Diesel disappeared into the utility room, home to his litter box.

"And the work-study job?" I went to the refrigerator for the pitcher of chilled water.

"Pretty cool so far." Justin worked ten hours a week in the History Department. "Dr. Biles asked me to take her notes for her western civ class and put them on the computer." He laughed. "The pages are all tattered, and the print's fading. They must be twenty-five years old. But at least I'm getting a good refresher while I work. I'm planning to take her upper-level medieval history class in the spring if I get permission."

I poured glasses of water for both myself and Justin when he retrieved another glass from the cupboard. "You've excelled in your history classes. I'm sure they'll decide you're ready to tackle a more advanced course."

"Thanks." Justin smiled shyly. "I'm thinking about graduate school in history."

"Good for you." Before I could continue, my cell phone rang. "Excuse me." I set my glass on the counter, pulled the phone out of my pocket, and glanced at the number. It was Laura.

"Hello, sweetheart. What's up?" I picked up my glass for another sip of water.

"It's Connor, Dad." The near panic in Laura's voice alerted me. "He's dead."

Twelve

I was so startled by Laura's words that I spit the mouthful of water back into the glass. My hand shook as I set the glass on the counter.

"Laura, where are you? Are you all right?" I had to get to her as quickly as possible.

Where did I put my keys?

There they were, on their hook by the door.

Laura was crying now. I had to ask her again where she was.

She managed to get out two words: "Connor's place."

"I'll get there as fast I can, sweetheart. Now try to calm down and give me the address." I jingled the keys in my hand, anxious to get to her.

I heard Laura draw a deep breath, then another. She managed to give me the address, and I recognized the street. She was only about five minutes away. "I'm on the way. Have you called 911 yet?"

"No, but I will now." Laura sounded slightly stronger. She ended the call.

I turned to Justin. "No time to explain, but I need to go. Diesel, you can't come with me."

Diesel meowed, and Justin placed a hand on the cat's head. "Don't worry, Mr. Charlie, you go right ahead. I'll keep Diesel company."

"Thanks." Then I was out the back door and scrambling to get into my car.

The address Laura gave me was for an apartment complex on the northeast side of the campus, about three miles away.

I parked in the first open spot I found. As I sprinted toward the complex, I heard a siren in the distance, coming ever closer. I entered through an open archway to an interior courtyard.

My heart pounded hard in my chest as I tried to focus with the late afternoon sun in my eyes. A few feet from me was a sign with apartment numbers affixed to the building. I followed the arrow in the direction indicated, checking the numbers on the doors as I sped by, frantic to reach my daughter.

Apartment 117 was a corner unit at the back, and as I approached it the door swung open. Cell phone clutched in one hand,

Laura stumbled toward me. I hugged her tight to my chest.

"It's okay, sweetheart. I'm here." I repeated those words several times, and Laura grew calmer.

She drew back, and her tear-stained face wrenched my heart. Suddenly she was twelve again, and I wanted to comfort her. But I had to ask one question I neglected to ask earlier. "Honey, did you check him? To be sure, I mean?"

"I freaked out when the 911 operator asked me to do it." Laura regarded me with guilt-stricken eyes. "I just couldn't touch him."

"I'll check." I moved past her to the open door. "Where is he?"

"Right there in the living room." Laura closed her eyes and began deep-breathing exercises.

I stepped inside, and I gagged at the smell of stale cigarette smoke and a couple of odors that hinted at death. I figured then it was probably too late, but I had to check anyway.

The door opened right into the living room. Connor lay sprawled on a couch a few feet away. His head rested against an arm of the couch, and his mouth stretched wide in an unsettling grimace, as if he died in pain. His bloodshot eyes bulged, and there were splotches of red on his face and neck. *Did some kind of poison cause that?*

Could he have killed himself? Maybe his death was the result of some kind of bizarre accident.

Another thought struck me. Those red splotches — weren't they signs of suffocation?

I stepped close enough to feel for a pulse in his left arm, which dangled off the edge of the couch. His fingers brushed the floor, and I braced myself as I touched the inside of his wrist.

No pulse, skin cool to the touch. I'd seen him on stage at the college only a few hours ago. How long had he been dead?

I stepped back and, as I moved toward the door, I noted certain details about the room.

An empty bourbon bottle sat on the floor by the couch. On the side table nearby an ashtray overflowed with ash and cigarette butts. There was a desk in the corner, its surface littered with pens and scraps of paper. The chair sat with its back against the wall.

At the sound of voices outside I turned and hurried out the door.

Two Athena city police officers stood there

with Laura, and they both frowned when they saw me. The older of the two started to speak, but stopped and stared at me.

I recognized him about the time he realized he knew me. "Hello, Officer Williams." He was one of the policemen who'd responded to the call a few months ago when I'd found another dead body. The younger officer stepped past me and entered the apartment. He looked familiar, too. I thought his name was Grimes.

"Mr. Harris, isn't it?" Williams didn't look pleased to see me. "What are you doing here?"

"This is my daughter, Laura. She found the body and called me, and of course I came." I put an arm around my daughter who was still shivering a little, despite the heat.

"You called your father first, Miss Harris? Not 911?" Williams frowned.

"Yes, sir." Laura cleared her throat before she continued. "I'm sorry, I was so shaken by what I found I just wasn't thinking clearly."

"How long have you been here, Mr. Harris?" Williams focused his laser stare on me.

"Only a few minutes. I got here maybe two minutes ahead of you."

Grimes popped out of the apartment then.

He exchanged a look with Williams, and the two of them stepped to one side to confer in low voices.

I checked my daughter. Her normal color was back, and she was breathing more easily. These were good signs, but I wanted to get her away from here as soon as possible. I knew from experience, however, that we would be here for a while.

As I watched Laura, I saw the tears begin to well in her eyes. I pulled out my handkerchief and handed it to her, and she dabbed at her eyes. I opened my arms, and she leaned into them, resting her head against my shoulder. "Honey, I'm so sorry," I whispered. A muffled sob was her response.

"Mr. Harris, I need to ask your daughter some questions since she was first on the scene." Williams spoke politely, but firmly. I held up a hand to stall him for a moment, and he nodded.

"Laura, do you feel like talking to the officer?" I kept my voice low and gentle. I felt Laura nod against my shoulder. She detached herself from my embrace and scrubbed her face with my handkerchief.

"Sorry, Officer, he was a friend of mine. Finding him like that was a shock." Laura began with a quaver in her voice but finished sounding stronger.

"Can you tell us who he is, Miss Harris?" Williams regarded Laura with a neutral expression.

"Connor Lawton," Laura said. "He's a playwright. He's — he was — here as writer-in-residence for the year at Athena College."

Before he could continue his questioning, the clatter of approaching footsteps across the bricked courtyard alerted us to the presence of newcomers. I met the gaze of one of them, and my stomach started to knot up.

Accompanied by two deputies, Kanesha Berry marched toward us. Her grim expression did not bode well for either me or Laura.

Right behind Kanesha and her men came an ambulance crew. The deputies stepped aside to let the other group by. I kept my eyes mostly on Kanesha, and her gaze never wavered from mine.

I braced myself for the storm about to hit, praying that I could somehow protect my daughter from the worst of it.

Thirteen

Officer Williams pointed the ambulance crew toward the open door, then stepped forward to greet Kanesha Berry and the deputies several feet away. They had a low-voiced conversation while Laura and I stood there under the unsmiling watch of Officer Grimes. I was getting impatient. I wanted to take Laura away, because finding a dead body is a horrible experience. She didn't appear to be in shock, but I could imagine how wretched she felt.

As I stood there, inwardly fretting and watching my daughter closely, Laura said quietly, "I'm okay, Dad. This is horrible, but I'll get through it."

"Okay, honey," I said. "But if you feel like you need to get away from here, tell me."

I'd kept one eye on Kanesha Berry while I spoke to Laura, and now the chief deputy moved forward. She stopped a couple of paces in front of me.

"Mr. Harris, I can't say I'm pleased to find you here." Kanesha's expression was impassive, but her voice was tart. "Would you care to explain just why you're here?" She glanced at Laura. "And this is your daughter, I take it?"

"Yes, this is Laura. She's teaching at the college this semester." I introduced Kanesha to Laura before I continued with my explanation. "I'm here because Laura called me and asked me to come. She was upset over what she found, and naturally I responded."

Kanesha nodded. She glanced around the courtyard. "There's a bench in the shade." She gestured with her right hand. "Why don't y'all wait over there? I'll have more questions for you in a few minutes."

"Sure." I was suddenly conscious of the heat again. Shade was a welcome idea. When Laura and I sat, I wasn't surprised to see that Officer Grimes had followed us. He took up position a few feet away inside the shaded area.

Laura and I remained silent as we watched the apartment door. Kanesha had gone inside with her deputies while Officer Williams remained outside. The EMTs came out and found another shaded spot where they could wait until they could remove the body.

Kanesha's "few minutes" passed, and she was still inside the apartment. Patience has never been one of my virtues, and I was feeling more and more anxious. Laura, on the other hand, was the epitome of calm. She sat beside me, her hands lying relaxed in her lap, her eyes closed, her breathing even. She was meditating, I supposed, something I've never learned but probably should.

I decided that watching the apartment door only served to exacerbate my temper. Instead, I focused my gaze on a border of shrubbery beneath the windows of the apartments down the walk. I ignored the presence of Grimes.

I'm not sure how much time passed, but I felt some of my tension ebb away while I stared at the shrubbery. The tightness in my neck and shoulders returned quickly, though, when I heard Kanesha Berry call my name.

I stood and gently placed a hand on Laura's shoulder. Her eyes fluttered open, and she looked up at me. Her gaze slid past me to focus on the chief deputy. I felt a slight tremor in her shoulders before I removed my hand.

Kanesha walked slightly past us before she stopped, and we were forced to turn to face her. I thought it odd but then I realized she

138

had deliberately pulled our gaze away from Lawton's apartment. They were probably about to remove his body. I appreciated her sensitivity. Laura had seen enough horror for one day.

"Miss Harris, how well did you know Mr. Lawton?" Kanesha's tone was clipped.

"Pretty well." Laura paused. "We were in a relationship for several months earlier this year, but we broke up in May." She paused again, then added in a rush, "We stayed friends, though."

Kanesha nodded. "You're teaching at the college this fall?"

Laura explained the facts of how she was hired for the job and Lawton's connection to the process. I was getting impatient again, because I told Kanesha all this when I spoke to her over a week ago about Damitra Vane. But Kanesha was nothing if not methodical in her investigations. She would go over every point as often as it took to find a solution.

"Why did you come to Mr. Lawton's apartment this afternoon?" Kanesha's question was one I wanted to hear answered myself.

"He called and asked me to come over. He wanted to talk to me about the play he's, um, was writing." Laura frowned.

"When did he call you?" Kanesha asked.

"I think it was around four-thirty," Laura replied. "Wait, I can tell you exactly when he called." She pulled her cell phone out of her skirt pocket and touched the screen several times. "It was four thirty-three." She held the phone out to Kanesha, who examined the screen for a moment, then nodded.

"What time did you arrive here?" Kanesha pulled out a small notebook and jotted something down.

Laura's brow furrowed as she considered the question. "Sometime after six." She shook her head. "I don't remember exactly. I just know it was maybe five minutes before I called Dad." She consulted her cell phone then held it out again for the chief deputy's inspection. "It was six-fourteen when I called Dad, so it was probably about six-ten when I got here."

Kanesha made further notations before she asked another question. "How did you get into the apartment? Was the door locked, or do you have a key?"

"I don't have a key." Laura's denial was swift. She colored slightly. "The door was slightly ajar when I got here, so I just walked in. That's when I found him." She glanced away.

Kanesha waited a moment before she

continued. "Tell me exactly what you did after you entered the apartment."

"I think I called out something like 'Connor, I'm here' after I shut the door." Laura closed her eyes, and I figured she was visualizing the scene. She normally had excellent recall, honed by her acting experience, but I hoped she would soon be able to block this from memory.

"There was no answer, of course." Laura opened her eyes. "So I walked on into the living room and saw him lying there on the couch. At first I thought he had been drinking so much he'd passed out, and I was getting angry. He was a heavy drinker, especially when he was in the middle of a new play." She paused a moment, shut her eyes briefly, then opened them again. "Then I realized something was wrong. He wasn't breathing. Usually when he's drunk and asleep he snores, and he wasn't making a sound. I went a few steps closer until I could bend down and look at his face. It was horrible. That's when I knew he was dead."

I put my arm around her, and she sighed heavily.

Kanesha gave Laura a moment to regain her composure before she asked the next question. "What did you do next?"

Laura's right hand crept up, and she massaged her earlobe with her thumb and forefinger. I frowned. Ever since she was a small child, Laura did that whenever she was about to tell an untruth or a partial truth.

"I just stood there, I'm not sure how long, and then I called my father." Laura looked straight at Kanesha as she spoke, but those fingers kept working her earlobe.

What wasn't she telling Kanesha?

"Excuse me, Deputy Berry." An officer I didn't recognize stepped into view.

Kanesha frowned. "What is it, Townsend?"

"Ma'am, there's something I think you'll want to take a look at right quick." Townsend, a hulk of a man who had to be at least six-seven and a good three hundred pounds, had a deep, rumbling voice that reminded me of Diesel's purr.

Kanesha gave her subordinate a sharp nod. "Be right there." She regarded Laura and me. "Sorry about this, but I won't be long." She strode away, Townsend trailing in her wake like a battleship after a canoe.

Laura and I sat down, and I realized that Officer Grimes was still with us. I had forgotten his presence briefly, and I was glad to be reminded of it before I said something potentially damaging to Laura.

I frowned at my daughter, but she seemed to be studiously avoiding my gaze. That was another indication that she had either lied or omitted something from her last response to Kanesha's questioning. I'd have to wait until we were alone before I tackled her about it. I hoped she wasn't going to cause trouble for herself down the line.

Followed by Townsend, Kanesha returned shortly with a small bag in one hand. Laura and I stood again. The chief deputy didn't speak, and I noticed she was staring intently at Laura's face. Laura remained impassive while Kanesha pored over her features.

"Your ears aren't pierced," Kanesha said finally.

What an odd thing to say, I thought, as I glanced at my daughter. Laura wore her hair in a short style that kept her ears exposed. What did pierced ears have to do with anything?

"No, they're not." Laura frowned. "I hate needles, and I'm not fond of earrings either."

"Have either of you ever seen this before?" Kanesha held out the plastic bag she'd been holding, letting it lay flat on her palm.

Laura and I both leaned forward to examine the contents. Inside the bag was a long, dangly earring made of what looked like gold in a series of interconnected geometric shapes. The hook at the top meant it was for pierced ears.

"I've never seen it before," I said.

Laura didn't speak for a moment, but then shook her head. "It looks kind of familiar, but I'm not sure."

"If you happen to remember where you've seen it, I want to know." Kanesha handed the bag to Townsend, who lumbered off.

A loud, braying voice interrupted our conversation. "What's going on here? Where's Connor?"

Kanesha, Laura, and I turned to see Damitra Vane walking rapidly toward Lawton's apartment where three deputies stood at the door. She halted a few feet from them, her rather large chest heaving. The officers seemed riveted on the sight.

Then Damitra Vane spotted Laura and headed toward us. "What the hell's going on here? Has something happened to Connor?" The last few words came out in a wail.

I scarcely heard her, because my attention was focused on her left ear. Hanging from it was the mate to the earring Kanesha had shown us only moments before. Her right ear was bare.

FOURTEEN

"I'm Chief Deputy Berry of the Athena County Sheriff's Department." Kanesha stared hard at the newcomer. "Who are you?"

"Damitra Vane. Connor's girlfriend." Vane darted a poison-laden glance at Laura. "If something's happened to Connor, you can bet *she's* responsible." She jabbed a finger with a two-inch nail, painted bubblegum pink, in Laura's direction. She swayed slightly on her high-heeled espadrilles, and for a moment I feared she might topple over. She was rather top-heavy — a match for Dolly Parton, at the very least.

"I'm sorry to have to tell you this, but Mr. Lawton is deceased." Kanesha spoke more gently than I'd ever heard her.

Damitra Vane goggled at Kanesha. "*Diseased?* Well, he sure as hell didn't get it from me. I'm clean." She scowled at Laura. "That tramp probably gave it to him."

"You dimwit." Laura shook her head in disgust. "Not diseased. *Deceased,* as in dead."

"Dead?" Damitra practically screamed the word. She launched herself toward Laura, claws extended, but Kanesha stepped in front of my daughter. Damitra recoiled, but not quite fast enough. Her nails raked against Kanesha's uniform, and several of them snapped off.

Townsend stepped forward and clasped Damitra's shoulders in his almost dinner plate–sized hands. "You need to calm down, ma'am." He guided her gently backward a couple of steps.

Damitra shook his hands loose. "You big moose, don't touch me. I'll sue you for police brutality."

"Miss Vane, that's enough." When Kanesha used that tone, even big guys like Townsend quailed.

Damitra swallowed, her gaze focused on Kanesha like a cobra facing a mongoose.

"That's better." Kanesha maintained the laser stare. "Now, Miss Vane, I'd like you to accompany Deputy Townsend here. He's going to take you down to the sheriff's department, where I'll be talking to you soon. I have some questions, and I'd prefer to talk there."

146

Damitra nodded. I expected more attitude from her, but I reckoned she'd finally realized she was no match for the chief deputy. She darted a final hate-filled glare at Laura before she let Townsend lead her away.

Kanesha waited until the voluptuous blonde was well out of earshot before she addressed Laura and me again. "You called your father, you said."

It took a moment for the question to register with me. Then I realized Kanesha had returned to the point in her questioning we had reached before Townsend called her away to show her the earring. And that reminded me: What was the significance of that earring? Did it somehow implicate Damitra Vane in Lawton's death?

She had obviously been in Connor's apartment. Perhaps this afternoon?

Laura cleared her throat. "Yes, I called Dad. I sort of panicked, I guess, and couldn't think what else to do. Dad calmed me down and said he'd come over. Then he told me I should call 911. So I did."

"What did you do while you waited for your father and the emergency response personnel to arrive?" Kanesha had her small notebook out again.

Laura's expression went blank, and her

147

right hand came up to her ear again. "I stayed on the phone for several minutes, but I finally hung up on the 911 woman. She kept badgering me to touch Connor." She shuddered. "I told her I wasn't going to. Then I guess I waited outside, because I was so freaked out by . . . well, you know."

That disconcerted me, and I hoped it didn't show on my face. Laura was definitely lying this time, because when I arrived she was inside the apartment. Why was she lying? My stomach started churning. I couldn't believe my daughter was involved in Connor Lawton's death, but her actions made me terribly uneasy. I had to get her alone to question her.

Kanesha regarded Laura in silence for a moment. I couldn't read the deputy's expression. Had she already picked up on Laura's body language?

She might well have done, because Kanesha was sharp and experienced. I had witnessed her in action enough the past year to know that much.

I began to be more afraid for my daughter. If only I could warn her not to lie to Kanesha or mislead her. Then I realized the irony of that. I hadn't always been precisely truthful with Kanesha myself, though I had tried to avoid outright lies. Like father like daughter, I reflected ruefully.

Kanesha focused her attention on me. "Mr. Harris, what about you? What did you do when you arrived on the scene?"

I needed to choose my words with extreme care. "The first thing I did, of course, was to assure myself that Laura hadn't been harmed. Then I went inside to determine whether Lawton was still alive." I described my actions while I was in the apartment. "Then, when I was about to go outside again, I heard the two policemen talking to Laura."

Kanesha finished jotting in her notebook, closed it, and put it and her pen away. "Thank you, Mr. Harris. Now, Miss Harris, I'd like you to accompany me to the sheriff's department for further questioning."

"I don't think that's a good idea." I spoke before I considered the implications of my words. Then I stumbled over my explanation. "I mean, Laura's had quite a shock. I think she needs to go home."

"I understand your concern," Kanesha said. "But I'm afraid I have to insist."

"It's okay, Dad." Laura moved close and threw her arms around me. Her sudden action threw me slightly off balance, and I turned about thirty degrees to the left, away from Kanesha. I steadied myself and held

149

my daughter in my arms.

To my great surprise I felt Laura's right hand slide inside my left pants pocket. Then she pulled her hand out and pushed away from me.

"I'm ready to go with you." Laura addressed Kanesha with composure intact.

I hoped I wasn't standing there with my mouth hanging open. I had to squelch the urge to reach into my pocket to retrieve what Laura had put there.

Kanesha shot me a glance with narrowed eyes. I thought she suspected there was something odd about that sudden embrace, but she didn't question it. Instead she said, "You can come too, Mr. Harris, but you can't be in the room during my interview with your daughter."

"I understand," I said. "Honey, I'll be there to take you home."

Laura nodded, and then Kanesha led her away. I followed them out of the courtyard onto the street and watched — stomach still churning — while Kanesha put Laura into a sheriff's department car. When the door closed and the vehicle pulled away, I walked to my car, my mind racing with questions.

I waited until I was inside the car, though, with the air conditioner running full blast, before I delved into my pocket to find out what Laura had hidden there. The shape felt familiar. I pulled it out and opened my palm, and there it was, an ordinary computer thumb drive.

I stared at it blankly for a moment. Was this from Connor Lawton's apartment? Was this device the reason Laura lied to Kanesha?

I'd have to wait for Laura to explain herself and tell me why she thought this thumb drive was important enough to indulge in covert action to give it to me. What was on it that she didn't want Kanesha to know about?

After a moment I stuffed the device back in my pocket and pulled out my cell phone. Before I headed to the sheriff's department, I ought to call Sean and tell him what was going on. If Laura should need legal representation, Sean might as well be on the spot.

Sean answered quickly. "Hey, Dad, where are you? Justin said you tore out of here without an explanation."

"Sorry about that," I said. "But I didn't really have time to explain anything. Are you at home now? Because I need to talk to you, and I don't want you driving and talking on your phone."

"I'm home," Sean said. "Fire away."

I leaned back against the headrest and

tried to relax. My entire body felt tight and tense. "Connor Lawton is dead, and Laura found him." Then, before Sean could start firing questions at me, I gave him a precis of the situation. When I finished, Sean didn't respond for a moment.

"Bloody hell." I heard him expel a sharp breath. "I'm on my way, Dad." He ended the call before I could respond.

I tucked my cell phone away and put the car in gear. My hands trembled slightly, and I gripped the wheel more firmly. I tried not to think about Laura being arrested for murder on the drive to the sheriff's department.

When I pulled into a parking space some ten minutes later, I was wrestling with a different question.

Why did I think Connor Lawton was murdered?

Lawton had a volatile, even violent, temperament, but he hadn't appeared to be a manic depressive in my brief acquaintance with him. I didn't see him as the suicidal type. Even if he was wrestling with the play and unhappy with the way it was developing, he wouldn't end his life over it. Lawton was a fighter; I was convinced of that.

His death could have been an accident. I considered that possibility again as I walked from the parking lot toward the front door of the sheriff's department. Alcohol poisoning? There was that bottle of bourbon near his body.

Even as these thoughts entered my mind, I had a nasty feeling that Lawton's death was definitely murder.

Inside the sheriff's department, the fluorescent lighting and chilly air brought me out of my reverie. I spoke to the officer at the front desk and explained why I was there. He nodded and pointed to a small waiting area. He said he'd make sure the chief deputy knew I was there.

I was at the water cooler, gulping down my third paper cup of water when Sean arrived. He strode over, the heels of his cowboy boots thudding against the scuffed linoleum. The officer at the desk glanced up, frowned, and went back to whatever he was doing.

Sean squeezed my shoulder. "How are you doing, Dad?"

"I've had better days." I crumpled the paper cup and dropped it in the wastebasket next to the cooler. "But it's Laura I'm worried about. Let's go sit down and talk."

Sean followed me to the waiting area, and we selected seats in the corner, as far from the front desk as possible.

In an undertone I told Sean the one thing I hadn't shared with him during the phone call — Laura's strange action with the thumb drive.

Sean's expression turned grim when I finished. "If that turns out to be a crime scene, and they find out Laura removed that device, she could face some serious charges."

FIFTEEN

Laura's face was so drawn and pale that I didn't have the heart to question her once we were alone in the car. My concern for her well-being was paramount. I didn't understand her relationship with Connor Lawton. She insisted they were no longer romantically involved and even seemed to dislike him, yet she had gone out of her way this afternoon to help him. My late wife and I had reared our children to be loyal to their friends and family, but I had seen little evidence that Lawton deserved such loyalty.

After Laura moved to Hollywood to pursue her dream, she visited infrequently, particularly after her mother died. When she did come to visit, she seemed different in some small ways, the natural effect of her experiences in California. But I had little doubt that at heart she was still my Laura. A verse from Proverbs ran through my head: "Train up a child in the way he should go:

and when he is old, he will not depart from it." We instilled in both our children a strong sense of responsibility for their actions, and though they might occasionally make a small misstep, I knew they were good people. Laura as a child, however, had an overdeveloped sense of responsibility, sometimes taking on more than she should in an effort to help another person. Perhaps this was the case with Connor Lawton.

If so, I felt Laura had made an error in judgment. She should not have removed that thumb drive from Lawton's apartment — and surely she must have, or why slip it into my pocket so furtively?

She and I were due for a heart-to-heart the moment she seemed up to it. By the time we reached home it was a few minutes past eight. My head ached and my stomach grumbled — I needed some caffeine and food, and Laura needed some sustenance as well. Sean pulled his car into the garage shortly after Laura and I entered the kitchen. When he joined us I was putting a chicken, rice, and mushroom casserole in the oven to warm. Stewart had left it in the fridge for us, bless him. Laura sipped a diet soda and stared vacantly at the surface of the table. Diesel, who had greeted us at the door, kept wrapping himself around my legs and complaining with loud chirps and meows over having been left behind.

After a glance at his sister, Sean asked, "What can I do?"

"There are some green beans in a pot in the fridge. Can you put them on to warm? I need to give Diesel some attention before he knocks me over." As Sean moved to comply with my request, I pulled a chair out from the table and sat. Diesel moved between my legs and placed his front paws in my lap. I held his head in both hands and rubbed under his chin with both thumbs. I murmured to him, telling him I was sorry I had to leave him behind, but that Laura had needed me. His purr rumbled as he gazed into my eyes.

Then, to my surprise, he pulled away and padded over to Laura's chair. She was oblivious to his presence, still focused blankly on the table, but he butted his head against her side to get her attention. Jostled out of her reverie, she set her soda down and turned in her chair. Diesel put his front paws in her lap and stretched his head up toward her face. With a sob, Laura bent and wrapped her arms around his upper body and held him close. Diesel meowed, as if in sympathy.

Sean, stirring the pot of beans at the stove,

let go of the spoon and took a tentative step toward his sister. I motioned for him to stop and shook my head. For the moment I figured Diesel, with his sensitivity to humans in distress, might be able to comfort Laura better than either her father or her brother could. Our turns would come.

Sean and I remained silent for the next several minutes while Laura hung on to Diesel and quietly cried. When the oven timer buzzed, Laura lifted a tearstained face and released Diesel. The cat sat back on his hind legs and watched her as she plucked several tissues from the box Sean held out to her. She wiped her face, blew her nose, and crumpled the tissues into a ball.

I went to her and gathered her into my arms when she stood. She rested her head on my shoulder for a moment before pulling away. "I'm okay, Dad," she said, her voice hoarse.

"Why don't you go wash your face, sweetheart, and then we'll eat."

She started to protest that she wasn't hungry, but I asked her when she had eaten last.

"Lunchtime." Laura smiled briefly. "Yeah, I probably should have something." She kissed my cheek. "Back in a few."

"I'm worried about her, Dad," Sean said

the moment Laura was out of the room, Diesel right on her heels. "I think maybe she was still in love with that jerk, and if his death turns out to be something besides suicide or an accident, she could look like the prime suspect."

"I know, son. That concerns me, too." My head throbbed to remind me that I had yet to drink anything caffeinated. I pulled a can of diet soda from the fridge and popped the top. I gulped some down, and moments later the throbbing began to ease. "Let's give her a little time to recover some equilibrium, and then I plan on having a long talk with her about Lawton and all that's happened."

When Laura and Diesel returned, Sean and I had dished out the casserole and the green beans. Laura sat at her place and picked up her fork. She stared at the plate for a moment, as if willing herself to eat, then ate some of the casserole. Sean and I watched her furtively as we too began to eat. Laura's face had regained some color, and as she ate she looked less worn.

Diesel came to sit by my chair and stare up at me, doing his best to look like a cat that hadn't eaten in several days. I fed him three green beans, then shook my head when he meowed for more. He resumed staring, and I went back to my meal, trying to resist that mute appeal.

We ate in silence for a few minutes, and then Laura put her fork down. She regarded her brother and me, a hint of defiance in her eyes. "I know you both probably think I'm crazy, but I don't want to talk about it tonight." She paused. "I promise I'll talk about it tomorrow, but for tonight I just want to be left alone. Please?"

Sean frowned and appeared about to speak, but I forestalled him. "It's okay, sweetheart. I know you're worn out. It's been a horrible day for you, and you need some time to rest. But we have to talk. There are some serious issues to discuss, and we can't duck them for long."

"Yes, sir." Laura smiled briefly before she resumed eating.

I looked across the table at my grown-up daughter, but suddenly all I could see was a little girl, vulnerable and confused. I wanted to pick her up and hold her, tell her that I would make everything better. But then I saw the adult Laura again and knew instinctively that she wouldn't welcome my assurances, at least not tonight.

We finished the meal without further conversation. Laura had a faraway look as she picked at her food, and I could only imagine her thoughts. When Sean and I were done, Sean stood and took our plates to the sink. Laura set her fork down and gazed at me.

"I'm going up to bed. I'm really tired." She came around the table to me and held out her hand. "May I have the thumb drive back for now, Dad?"

I hesitated before I stood to pull it out of my pocket. I clasped it in my hand and regarded my daughter. I didn't want to hurt her feelings and make her think I didn't trust her, but I was concerned about the contents of the device and what Laura planned to do with it.

She knew me only too well. "I promise you I'm not going to do anything to the contents. I won't delete or change anything. We'll look at it together tomorrow and then decide what to do with it." She gazed into my eyes without wavering.

I had to trust my daughter, I decided, and her reasons for having taken the drive from Lawton's apartment. We would catch hell from Kanesha Berry, I knew, but we would face that when the time came.

I dropped the drive into Laura's hand. Her fingers closed around it, and she gave me a sweet smile and a swift peck on the cheek. "Good night." With that she turned and left the kitchen.

Diesel chirped, and I looked down at him. "Go ahead," I told him, and he trotted off after Laura.

Sean had cleared the table already and was putting the dishes into the dishwasher. I thanked him.

He looked troubled. "I have this feeling that something nasty is going to happen because Laura took that drive, Dad. For the life of me I can't figure out why she'd do such a thing. Surely she knows better."

"I think we simply have to trust her, son. I'm not happy about the situation either, but she must have a compelling reason to have done it."

"I guess so." Sean shook his head. "The whole thing's one unpleasant mess, that's for sure. I wonder what the Theater Department is going to do without their star playwright?"

"They might try to find a replacement," I said. Then I had an uneasy thought. "I wonder if anyone has informed Ralph Johnston about this."

"Would the sheriff's department know to?"

"They might," I said as I thought about it. "Surely in her questioning of Laura, Kanesha would have asked her what she knew about Lawton's next of kin. Johnston was his employer, so to speak."

"I wouldn't worry about it then." Sean squeezed my shoulder. "You've got enough to think about without dealing with that."

I definitely didn't feel like I had the energy tonight to talk to Ralph Johnston. He would probably go into hysterics, and I didn't have the patience to cope with that. Kanesha would have notified the college. She was very thorough.

"I think I'll head upstairs then."

"I'm going to relax for a while on the back porch," Sean said. That meant he was going out to smoke a cigar — his way of relaxing.

I bade him good night, then trudged upstairs to my room. After changing into my pajamas, I read for a while, keeping an eye out for Diesel. By the time I turned out the light he hadn't come, but I left the door ajar in case he returned during the night.

Restless thoughts kept me awake for a good hour or more but eventually I drifted off to sleep. At some point I was dimly aware that Diesel was on the bed with me, and then I drifted off again. I awoke the next morning feeling logy, but I couldn't loll in bed. There was much to do today.

Laura hadn't appeared for breakfast by the time I was ready to leave for work. I was eager to talk to her, but I didn't want to disturb her. She needed rest, and my questions could wait a while longer. Perhaps by lunchtime she would be ready to talk.

Diesel and I arrived at the archive a few minutes early, and we had a quiet morning. Melba didn't appear for her usual visit, but I remembered that she was taking the day off. Just as well, because I didn't feel up to answering questions about the events of yesterday.

At nine my cell phone rang. Sean's number came up on the screen. I barely had time to say, "Hello," before he launched into frantic speech. "Laura's gone, Dad, and she must have left the house before you and I had breakfast. I just tried her cell phone, but she didn't answer."

My heart thudded in my chest. Where was my daughter?

And, more important, was she safe?

Sixteen

I suddenly felt cold all over. I forced myself to take a couple of deep breaths. "Maybe she's here on campus in her office." That thought comforted me. "She's probably so focused on whatever she's doing that she's ignoring the cell phone."

"Maybe." Sean didn't sound convinced.

"I'm going over there right now, and I'll call you as soon as I know something." I paused for a breath. "You keep calling her cell."

"Will do."

I stuffed my phone in my pocket and reached for Diesel's harness and leash. "Come on, boy. We've got to check on Laura."

Diesel, perhaps attuned to my urgent tone, leapt down from his perch in the window and stood patiently while I buckled on his harness in record time. Once I attached the leash, he darted around the desk, and I had to hurry to keep up with him.

I paused only long enough to lock the office door. Then we scooted down the stairs and out the back door of the building. I jogged as quickly as I could, and Diesel kept pace with me. The walk to the building that housed the Theater Department normally took under ten minutes. This morning I probably made it in four.

I tried to keep my thoughts focused on the positive, but doubt kept niggling at me. Laura had to be all right. She had to.

We pounded up the walk to the fine arts building. Like many on our campus it dated from the mid- to late nineteenth century, its once-red brick weathered to a rosy pink, offset by white windows and doors. I jerked one of the double doors open. I was thankful no one was in my way, because I probably would have barreled over anyone who impeded my progress.

Too impatient for the elevator, I ran to the stairs, and Diesel scampered up ahead of me. My heart thudded in my chest, and the sweat dripped down my face, but I pressed on. I prayed I wouldn't collapse before I found my daughter safe and sound.

Laura's office lay at the end of the hall, away from the stairs. I ran down the empty hall. Diesel was still slightly ahead of me.

How he knew where we were going, I had no clue, but he was straining at the leash, trying to pull free.

I let him go, and he beat me to Laura's door by a full five seconds.

When I reached the door, I had to pause to catch my breath. I couldn't speak because I was gulping in air. Diesel meowed loudly and scratched at the door, which was slightly ajar. His weight forced it open, and my heart almost failed me when I caught my first glimpse of the interior. Books and papers lay scattered about.

I stepped into the doorway and, still struggling to breathe freely, croaked out my daughter's name. A phone began to ring, and I recognized the ringtone as Laura's. I took another step inside. To my right, perhaps two feet away, was a wall covered with overloaded bookshelves. To my left was a desk, and my heart almost stopped when I saw a woman kneeling over a body on the floor between the desk and another wall of bookshelves behind it.

Diesel disappeared around the edge of the desk, but I heard him chirping and meowing in distress. The sight of my daughter's body on the floor terrified me so that I couldn't speak. Then I could see Diesel, licking Laura's face. The woman started and sat back on her heels.

"What are you doing?" I finally found my voice, and my legs worked again. I strode around the side of the desk and grasped the strange woman's shoulder. She turned her head to look up at me, her expression mirroring the fear of my own.

"I'm trying to help her," she said. She struggled to loosen my hand from her shoulder. "Who the hell are you?"

"Her father," I said, pushing her none too gently out of the way. I dropped to my knees on the worn carpet beside Laura. Her eyes were closed, but her breathing was regular. She looked like she was sleeping. I grasped her hands in mine. They were cold. I started rubbing them, trying to warm them.

"Laura, honey, can you hear me?" While I spoke to her, Diesel kept licking her face. I didn't try to stop him, because I thought any kind of sensory stimulation was good.

Laura's phone started ringing again, and I could sense the woman hovering behind me. "We need to call 911."

"I'm doing it now." I glanced back, and the woman had the office phone in her hand and was punching in numbers.

For the moment I ignored Laura's still-ringing phone, though I knew Sean was probably even more worried by now. I'd call him as soon as I could.

Laura moaned, a low sound that tore at my heart. She blinked several times, then her eyes opened and tried to focus on me. Diesel stopped licking her face but kept talking to her, as I called it.

"My head," Laura whispered. Her face contorted in a grimace of pain. "Hurts. What happened?"

"I don't know, honey," I said. "We've called 911, and they're on the way. You lie still."

Laura frowned. "Where am I?"

"In your office." I stroked her hands, still trying to warm them up. Diesel moved to stand beside me, his eyes intent on Laura's face.

She blinked, then a tremulous smile flashed briefly. "Sweet kitty," she whispered.

"They're on the way," the woman announced behind me.

I turned to nod at her, and with a small shock I realized I knew her. Magda Johnston, Ralph's wife. She looked far different today from the woman I'd seen at the party a week or so ago. For one thing, she appeared to be stone-cold sober, and she was dressed more conservatively, in a gray skirt, purple blouse, and black jacket. Nothing like the garish, blowsy woman from the party.

Laura whispered, "Water. Please. Bottle in desk."

I gazed down at her and nodded. "Don't move," I told her again. I shifted position so I could open the desk drawers. I found the water on the first try. I turned back to Laura and frowned. I didn't think she should move her head until the paramedics arrived and examined her. So how was I going to give her water without choking her?

Laura moved, and I knew she was going to try to sit up. "No," I said. "Stay still. I'm going to dribble some water in your mouth from the side, okay?" That should work, as long as I could hold my hand steady.

"Okay," she said. She opened her mouth as I twisted the cap off the bottle. I knelt over her and held the bottle to the side of her mouth. I tilted it until a tiny trickle of water flowed. Laura swallowed, and I stopped the flow.

We went through this procedure four more times, until Laura said, "That's good."

I capped the bottle and sat back on my heels, regarding my daughter with concern. Where were the EMTs? Surely they would arrive soon.

"They're coming down the hall." Magda Johnston spoke from the doorway. She appeared to be waving at them.

"Thank goodness," I said. I glanced at the desk. The EMTs would need more room to work, so I stood and pushed the desk toward the opposite wall. Magda saw what I was doing and stepped forward to help. Between us we managed to get the desk as far out of the way as possible. I was gently moving Diesel away from Laura as the first member of the team entered the office.

I pulled Diesel to the corner and watched as the other emergency personnel came in. They went to work quickly and efficiently, and one of them asked Laura several questions, such as "What day is it? Who is the president?" Her responses were evidently satisfactory.

Diesel, made nervous by all the strangers in the small office, crawled underneath the desk and watched everything from there. I called Sean to apprise him of the situation but kept the conversation brief. I asked him to come in his car to pick me and Diesel up. He would need to take me to the hospital and then take Diesel home. The emergency room was no place for a feline, even one as well mannered as mine.

One of the EMTs, a woman not much older than Laura, knelt by my daughter and with gloved hands probed her head. I missed what happened next because members of the team kept shifting positions. I heard Laura moan, then the EMT said, "Got a little blood here and a small wound."

"Did you fall and hit your head?" An older member of the team, a man in his late thirties or early forties, posed the question.

"I'm not sure." Laura paused, her tone uncertain. "I don't really remember much. I remember coming into my office early this morning and working, but after that, nothing."

The man turned to me. "Who are you, sir? Any relation?"

"Yes, I'm her father." I introduced myself. "I work here at the college. I became concerned earlier when my daughter didn't answer her cell phone. When I arrived, I found Mrs. Johnston with her."

Magda Johnston hovered in the doorway, and hearing her name, stepped forward. "I stopped by to see Laura, and her door was slightly open. When I stepped inside, I saw her on the floor. I was just checking her out when Mr. Harris arrived."

A campus police officer showed up then, and he took charge of the questioning. Magda Johnston and I repeated our stories. The EMTs placed Laura on a gurney for transport to the hospital, and as they rolled her out of the office I called out that I would be right behind her.

I turned to the campus officer and said, "Someone struck my daughter on the head and knocked her out. I don't know why, but I suspect it has something to do with the death yesterday of her colleague, Connor Lawton. You might want to notify the sheriff's department about this, in case there is a connection."

When I mentioned the dead playwright's name, I heard Magda Johnston whimper. I shot her a quick glance, but her face was averted. Was she upset over what happened to Laura, or was it Lawton's name that elicited a response?

She had been very interested in the playwright at the party, I recalled. At the time I had put it down to her inebriated state, but what if there was more to it?

An even uglier thought came to me then. Was Magda Johnston Laura's assailant?

SEVENTEEN

By the time Sean dropped me off at the hospital, a nurse and an ER physician were examining Laura. The nurse appeared to be cleaning the wound while the doctor watched. The doc, an attractive woman in her forties, asked who I was, and before I could reply, Laura said, "My father." I spotted the doc's name embroidered on her lab coat: LEANN FINCH.

The nurse, a chunky, short man of about thirty, didn't stop what he was doing, but the doc nodded in acknowledgment before she resumed watching the nurse work.

When the nurse finished, the doc bent over Laura. Her gloved fingers probed the back of Laura's head. Laura, on her side facing me, winced.

I stood at the side of the small room and observed the rest of the examination.

After some minutes the doc said, "Your hair is very thick and seems to have cushioned the blow. You don't even need stitches." She nodded at the nurse who took over and finished treating the wound while the doc continued to talk.

"Her reflexes are good, although she's complained of a little dizziness and nausea. She lost consciousness, she told me. Any idea how long she was out?"

"No." I glanced over at Laura, who now appeared to be asleep. I explained what I knew of the situation.

Dr. Finch nodded. "She doesn't have any memory of what happened in the moments leading up to the blow on the head. Not unusual in the circumstances. I want a CT scan to see whether there's any kind of internal trauma." She laid a hand on my arm, evidently having noticed my alarmed expression. "I don't think there will be any. As I said, her hair is very thick, but the blow did break the skin enough for her to bleed. Just a mild concussion probably. The CT scan is a necessary precaution."

"Whatever you think best," I said. I prayed the doc was right and there was no internal injury.

"Once I've had a chance to examine the results of the scan, I'll probably send her home. I'll discuss with you later the kind of aftercare she needs." Dr. Finch smiled warmly. "Any questions?"

"Does she need to stay awake? I've read that you need to keep someone with a concussion awake for a while."

"No, that's not really necessary," Dr. Finch said. "Natural sleep is okay, but if she loses consciousness you'd need to bring her back in." She paused, apparently waiting for further questions, but when I nodded, she smiled and moved to a nearby laptop computer and began typing.

"You can sit here if you like." The nurse's deep voice startled me, because I hadn't seen him approach. He indicated a chair near Laura's bed. "It's going to be a little while before they come to get her for the CT scan."

I thanked him and sat down. My head was about two feet from my daughter's, and as I gazed at her, I could feel my heart rate increase. Seeing her like this brought back sad memories of her mother's times in the hospital.

Then I chided myself for such morbid thoughts. Laura was going to be fine. This was nothing like her mother's case, when pancreatic cancer ravaged her. Laura was young and healthy and would make a rapid recovery, I assured myself.

As I watched, Laura's eyes fluttered open

and she yawned. "Guess I dozed off," she said, her voice weak and low. "When can I go home?"

"They want to do a CT scan first," I said. "The doc wants to make sure there are no internal injuries."

Laura frowned. "Okay."

I checked to see whether Dr. Finch and the nurse were out of the room. They were, and one of them had pulled the door almost shut. I turned back to my daughter.

"Time for a few questions," I said. I hated doing this now, but Laura was in grave danger. "You've been through a lot in less than twenty-four hours, and I need some answers. I want to know what's going on in that pretty, stubborn head of yours."

"Yes, sir." Laura offered a brief smile.

"First, tell me what you remember of this morning," I said.

"I woke up early, around six, I guess." She paused. "I was hungry, so I went downstairs and had some toast and a cup of hot tea. No one else was up, and, I don't know, I guess I had this urge to get out of the house. So I had a quick shower, dressed, and walked over to campus. By then it was seven, probably."

"Why didn't you leave a note?" I tried to keep my tone even, though my aggravation level was rising. "Considering what happened yesterday, didn't you think we might be concerned when you didn't turn up for breakfast?"

"I wasn't thinking about that." Laura looked guilty at this confession of thoughtlessness. "I'm sorry. The last thing I wanted was to worry you, Dad."

"I know, sweetheart." I clasped her right hand and gave it a gentle squeeze. "After you reached campus, what did you do?"

"The weather was so nice, I decided to walk around a bit. I must have wandered for at least an hour, and I ended up in front of the fine arts building. I went up to my office and sat there and stared at the wall for lord knows how long."

"What were you thinking about?" I could have prompted her with a more specific question, but I decided to leave it to her to tell it how she wanted.

Laura was silent for a moment. A shadow passed over her face when she finally spoke. "Mostly just thinking about Connor, I guess. Everything happened so quickly, or at least that's the way it seems now, and I was trying to process it all. It's such a waste."

Tears threatened, and I squeezed her hand

again. "I know, sweetheart. He was too young."

"Yes, he was," Laura said sadly.

I decided to bring the conversation back to her activities this morning. "You were in your office, thinking about all this. What happened next?"

Laura frowned again. "That's where it starts to get hazy. I think I went to bathroom down the hall and then into the faculty lounge. I was going to make some coffee. Yes, that's it. I wanted some coffee, and while I was waiting for the coffeemaker to finish, I sat in the lounge and glanced through one of the scrapbooks Sarabeth Conley has kept over the years. I stayed there while I had my cup of coffee, and then I think I went back to my office." She paused, looking pleased for a moment. Then doubt returned. "And that's it."

I tried to fill in from there, to see if it jogged her memory at all. "So you went back to your office. I presume you'd left the door open?"

Laura nodded. "I don't usually lock it while I'm there, just going in and out."

"The person who struck you must have been in your office, and you surprised him or her, you got knocked on the head, and then the assailant either left or kept ransacking your office." As I described the potential scene, I could feel chills dancing up my spine and settling in the back of my neck. Laura could so easily have been killed.

"Dad, are you okay?" Laura sounded alarmed. "You're really, really pale."

"I'm okay, sweetheart." I tried to give her a reassuring smile, but I wasn't certain how successful I was. At least Laura looked less disturbed. "Thinking about someone hurting you is upsetting."

"I wish I could remember what actually happened when I went back to the office." Laura rubbed her forehead, as if she could call up the memory, like a djinni from a magic lamp. "The next thing I remember is seeing you and Magda Johnston there with me."

"Are you particularly friendly with her?" I hadn't heard Laura talk about the woman that I could recall, so Magda's presence on the scene made me suspicious.

"Not particularly, no." Laura started to shake her head, winced, and stopped. "She'd sort of pop up two or three times a week, asking me questions about Hollywood. She claimed to be a huge fan of that sitcom I guested on a few times. Wanted to know all about stars. But somehow the conversation always ended up with Connor.

I think she really had the hots for him." Her expression indicated her distaste at the thought.

Given what I'd observed at that party, I wasn't terribly surprised by Laura's revelation. "Then I guess her presence in your office wasn't suspicious."

"I guess." Laura thought for a moment. "But I almost didn't recognize her this morning. That's the first time I've ever seen her dressed that plainly, and with almost no makeup. Strange."

"Yes, it was. I've never seen her like that either." That bore some further thought. Was the woman in mourning for Connor Lawton? I wondered what her husband might think about that.

"You don't think she's the person who hit me, do you?"

"I don't know," I said. "It's certainly possible. I could have walked in not long after she struck you, but she wasn't holding anything. Would she have had time to dispose of whatever weapon she used?" Surely the campus police, or even someone from the sheriff's department, was working on that. "If we can answer another question first, however, it might help us to figure out who it was."

"That question being, what was he looking for?" Laura gazed right into my eyes, her expression bland.

"Exactly. And I can think of one answer to that." I waited to hear what she would say.

"Connor's thumb drive." She sighed. "The one I took from his apartment."

"Did you have it with you this morning?"

"No, I left it at home." Her eyes widened in alarm. "You don't think he'll break into the house, do you?"

This was a possibility that hadn't yet occurred to me, and now I felt the first stirring of greater alarm. Then I forced myself to remain calm. "We don't know for sure that's what your attacker was after. First we'd have to know what's on that drive in order to figure out why it might be important." I paused as I regarded my daughter, whose expression had resumed its blandness. "Why did you take it in the first place? Do you know what's on it?"

"I took it because Connor's laptop was missing. The killer must have taken it."

EIGHTEEN

Laura asked for water before I could follow up with a question about the missing laptop. I found a cooler with paper cups just down the short hall from her room in the ER. After she finished, she expressed her thanks.

"Would you like more?" I asked.

"No, that's enough for now."

I set the empty cup on a table nearby, then resumed my seat. "About the laptop. You're sure it's missing? You were in a very upsetting situation and you might have overlooked it."

Laura shuddered and closed her eyes. "It was horrible. You just don't expect to find a person like that. Not somebody young, like Connor." Her eyes opened, and she continued as I clasped her hand. "I stood there for I don't know how long once I realized he wasn't simply drunk and sleeping it off."

"I'm so sorry you had to be the one to find him," I said.

Laura squeezed my hand. "Me, too. But I guess it was meant to be." She paused for a moment. "Anyway, I found him. Then I got myself together enough to call you.

"Before I called 911, I started to take in other details. I glanced over to where he kept his laptop, and it was gone. That was strange, because it should have been there. I checked the other rooms very quickly, but there was no sign of it."

"How long did that take?"

"Probably not much more than a minute. It's a small one-bedroom apartment." Laura shuddered. "I felt strange doing it, but I wanted to find the laptop if I could. Then I remembered what you told me about calling 911, and I did."

"What about the thumb drive?"

"While I was talking to 911, it popped into my head. Connor was really compulsive about backing up his work. He also hid his thumb drive so no one would swipe it."

That sounded more than a little paranoid to me but, for all I knew, most writers might be just as paranoid. "Where did he hide it? And how did you know?"

A faint smile touched Laura's face and then was gone. "I suppose he thought I'd never try to steal it, because I was the one person — or so he said — that he trusted not to reveal his hiding place." She sighed. "He had this urn he took with him wherever he went that's supposed to have his parents' ashes in it. It has a false bottom, and he hid his thumb drive in there."

I couldn't question her further, because the nurse returned, along with the staff who had come to fetch her for her CT scan. I wondered what that thumb drive contained that was so important that my daughter swiped it and didn't tell the sheriff's department or the police about it.

As they wheeled Laura out, the nurse said, "You can wait in here if you like, sir. Or you can go out to the waiting room, and someone will let you know when she's back here."

"Thank you." I smiled. "I think I'll go out to the waiting room so I can use my cell phone."

The nurse nodded, and I followed him out of the room. He pointed the way to the waiting area, and I walked on through a set of double doors into the corridor and down a short hall.

Sean walked into the waiting area as I was about to sit down and call him. He came over and took the seat beside mine.

"I was about to call you."

"How is she?" His expression betrayed his intense concern.

185

I recounted what Dr. Finch had said, concluding with "They just now took her to have the CT scan. If that's clear, they'll release her, and we can take her home."

Sean relaxed. "I hope that scan comes out clear. I don't want to think about any other possibility. Oh, before I forget, I called the library and talked to your friend Melba and explained that you probably wouldn't be back today."

"Thank you," I said. "That totally slipped my mind."

"And no wonder, given what's been happening." Sean shook his head. "Has she been able to tell you what the heck she was doing, going off like that this morning?"

I recounted to Sean what his sister told me about her morning. I had reached the point where Laura regained consciousness when I glanced toward the door and saw Kanesha Berry bearing down on us.

"Good afternoon, Deputy Berry." I stood and extended a hand, and Sean did the same when he caught sight of her.

"Gentlemen." Kanesha shook our hands in turn, her expression as cool and remote as usual. "How is your daughter?"

Once again I shared what Dr. Finch told me. "They're doing the CT scan right now. I'm hoping to be able to take her home before long."

"I hope they don't find any internal injury." Kanesha motioned to the seats Sean and I were occupying when she arrived. "Please sit. I'd like to talk to you." She pulled a stand-alone chair over and placed it so that she faced us directly.

"What can we do for you, Deputy?" Sean sounded wary to me, and I wondered whether he was about to go into lawyer mode. I devoutly hoped Laura wasn't going to need a lawyer before this was over.

Kanesha pulled a small notebook out of a pocket and flipped through it until she found the page she wanted. "I have the report from the campus police, and I have personally been to the scene. I'm taking this very seriously, I just want to assure you. I'd like you to tell me, Mr. Harris, what you did and observed."

How many times now had I gone through this? I repressed a sigh and gave the deputy the information she requested.

Kanesha jotted a few things down as I talked. When I finished, she thanked me. "I also need to talk to your daughter as soon as possible."

"If they release her, can it wait until I get her home?" I didn't want Laura to have to be here longer than was necessary. None of us was keen on spending time in a hospital after what my late wife went through.

"Sure." Kanesha tapped the notebook with her pen while she regarded me. "You have any idea why someone'd attack your daughter like that? There haven't been any incidents like that on campus for about ten years, according to the campus police."

I frowned. I had to be careful what I said to her, because I didn't want to cause trouble for Laura. I had to talk to my daughter about that blasted thumb drive and urge her to turn it over to Kanesha.

Kanesha continued to stare at me, and I realized I had let the silence extend a bit too long. "Surely it must have something to do with the death of Connor Lawton."

"Why would you say that?" Kanesha didn't let up with that laserlike fix on my face.

"The circumstances of his death are definitely odd," Sean replied, his tone cool. He was slipping into lawyer mode. "He and my sister were good friends, and she may have been targeted because of that. Do you know where Damitra Vane was this morning? She has expressed considerable hostility to Laura."

"The police are checking on Ms. Vane's whereabouts this morning." Kanesha focused that gimlet eye on Sean. "Why would Ms. Vane attack your sister? Because she thought Ms. Harris had something to do with Lawton's death?"

Sean's face darkened at that last question, and I wasn't pleased with it myself.

"My daughter had nothing to do with that man's death." I tried to keep my voice level, but I could feel myself becoming heated as I spoke. "She had the unpleasant experience of finding him, that's all."

Kanesha shifted back to me. "I hope for her sake that's all it turns out to be."

I suddenly felt like a hypocrite, because I knew my daughter was holding back potential evidence from the investigation. Evidently I masked my consternation well, because Kanesha didn't push me further. Instead, she said, "I'll need both you and Ms. Harris to come to the sheriff's department to make your statements and sign them." She stood. "Also, please call and let me know if Ms. Harris will be going home today. I'd really like to talk to her this afternoon."

"Certainly," I said. I decided to venture a question of my own, even though Kanesha might bite my head off for asking it. "Is it definite yet that Connor Lawton was murdered?"

A quick glance at her face let me know she was peeved with me. She regarded me coolly for a moment. "Why do *you* think he was murdered? Are you some kind of expert now that you've been involved in three homicides?"

"No, I don't think any such thing." I was trying to hold on to my temper. She probably thought I was baiting her, but that was not my intention. "My daughter found a corpse one day and was attacked the next. I'm concerned for her welfare, and if this turns out to be a murder investigation, I'll be even more worried."

My words hit home — I could see it by a subtle change in Kanesha's expression.

"We're treating Connor Lawton's death as suspicious," she said. "That's really all I can tell you at the moment. Now, if you'll excuse me, gentlemen, I need to move on." With that she turned and walked away.

Sean muttered an uncomplimentary word at the chief deputy's retreating back, and I frowned at him. Kanesha could be deliberately unpleasant, but I didn't like him displaying such poor manners.

He had the grace to appear abashed when he caught my frown. "Sorry, Dad. But she really irks me."

"Of course she does," I said. "She seems

to love playing *bad cop* most of the time." I glanced at my watch. "I wish they'd hurry up and tell us about that scan."

"She's going to be fine, Dad." Sean spoke with assurance, and I prayed he was right.

I decided to ask him something that had been preying on my mind for a while now. Doing it would put him in an awkward position, but my concern for Laura propelled me forward. "Son, did Laura ever talk to you much about Connor Lawton? She never mentioned him to me."

Sean regarded me with a bland expression. "Yeah, we talked about him a few times, I guess."

"Did she ever get really serious about him? He seemed like such a jerk to me, yet she seemed to go out of her way to defend him. Even when he was driving her crazy, too. I'm just trying to figure out why she kept putting up with him."

He looked away for a moment, and I sensed he was trying to come to a decision. When he met my gaze again, he nodded. "Yeah, she did get pretty serious. She'll probably wring my neck when she finds out I told you this, but he asked her to marry him back in May, and she said yes."

NINETEEN

My own daughter engaged, and I didn't even know about it? My first reaction was hurt. Why hadn't Laura told me about this? Did she no longer feel comfortable confiding in me?

Sean must have read my expression because he put a hand on my shoulder and gave it a squeeze. "Chill, Dad, it's not what you think. Laura would have told you, but the engagement lasted maybe two weeks. She broke it off."

That mollified me somewhat, but there was still the fact that Laura had never mentioned to me — in our several-times-weekly phone conversations — that she'd met anyone who was serious marriage material. I kept that observation to myself, though.

"I'm sure glad she changed her mind." I managed to keep my tone light, despite the fact that I was still smarting. "I can't imagine how I would have dealt with him as a son-in-law."

"No chance of that now."

"You're right, of course." I shook my head.

"Remember how she was always bringing home those odd kids in her class, the ones who never quite fit in?" Sean smiled.

"I'd forgotten that. She seemed to have an affinity for any lame duck that came along." Connor Lawton would have qualified as a lame duck, I supposed, just on a bigger scale.

"I used to think she ought to be a counselor or a teacher because she was so determined to help those kids fit in." He laughed. "But then the acting bug bit her in high school, and it was pretty clear what she wanted to do."

I felt a little better about Laura's insistent defense of Lawton now. I'd been worried she was still in love with him and would be even more deeply hurt by his death as a consequence.

"Mr. Harris." I glanced up to see the person at the ER admissions desk waving at me. I got up and walked over to her.

"Your daughter's back in her room if you want to go see her again." She smiled, and I thanked her.

I motioned for Sean to join me. "This is

her brother. Is it okay for him to go with me?"

"Of course." She peeled a visitor badge off a sheet on her desk and handed it to Sean, who stuck it on his shirt.

Laura was sitting up when Sean and I walked into her room. Her face brightened at the sight of us, and Sean went straight to her. He leaned down and gave her a quick hug. "You always have to find a way to be the center of attention. I thought you might have outgrown that." He grinned.

Laura balled up her fist and punched him lightly in the stomach. "Toad." She grinned back at him.

"How was the test?" I asked as I moved closer.

"Not too bad." Laura shrugged. "I hope they let me go home soon. I'm getting really hungry."

"That's a good sign." Sean winked at me. "If the monster is hungry, she can't be hurt all that much."

Laura punched him again, and he doubled over and groaned. "Now *I* need an X-ray," he said, sounding pitiful.

"I'm not the only actor in the family." She paused for a beat. "But I am the only good one." Laura's dry tone made me laugh, and Sean straightened up, grinning.

"You must be feeling better, sweetheart," I said.

"I think the pain medication has kicked in." Laura smiled. "Whatever it was made the headache go away, mostly. I feel a little floaty."

"Hold on to that," Sean said. "Kanesha Berry was here. She wants to question you about what happened."

"Right now?" Laura frowned.

"No, later, after you're home," I said. "That is, if the doctor releases you today."

"I wish they'd come tell us the results of that scan." Sean motioned for me to take the chair, then went to stand to one side of the bed, by a large cabinet. "How long does it take?"

"I have no idea," I said. "Not long, I hope." I patted Laura's hand. "I'm thinking positively. You'll be going home with Sean and me soon."

"That she will." Dr. Finch walked into the room. She stopped near the bed, and Laura quickly introduced her brother. The doc nodded, then addressed her patient. "I'm pleased to tell you that there was no sign of any internal injuries."

I gave a silent but utterly thankful prayer for those results.

"The nurse will be here in a few minutes

with some aftercare instructions, and he'll go over them with you. Main thing, be sure to follow up with your own doctor. Problems can pop up after the fact, and if you feel that anything is wrong, go to the doctor right away, or come back to the ER." The doc turned to leave.

"Thank you, Doctor," I said, and Laura echoed me.

With a last, quick smile, Dr. Finch departed.

Within five minutes the stocky nurse returned. There were the usual papers to be signed, and he went over the doc's instructions with us.

He went to find a wheelchair, and soon Sean was wheeling Laura out of the ER toward the entrance. I stayed with Laura while Sean went to retrieve his car.

"Are you going to feel up to talking to Kanesha?" I asked.

"I suppose," Laura said. "Will you be with me?"

"If Kanesha will let me," I said. "I'm thinking she probably won't."

Laura sighed. "Figures."

"Before you talk to Kanesha, you and I need to discuss a few things." I spotted Sean approaching. "The sooner the better, I think."

"Yes, sir," she said. "I'm really sorry about all this, Dad."

"No need to apologize. We just need to get this sorted out, so you can get on with your job."

Laura's laugh sounded bitter. "If I have one. With no Connor and no new play, I'm not sure what we'll do."

"Ralph Johnston will come up with something." I helped her out of the wheelchair and into the car. I took the wheelchair back into the ER and left it inside the door, out of the way. The nurse at the admissions desk nodded to acknowledge it.

I climbed into the backseat with Laura. Sean put the car into gear and drove slowly out of the hospital parking lot. He kept up a sedate pace all the way home.

"About that thumb drive," I said in a tone I hope brooked no argument. "What is so all-fired important about it?"

Laura stared out the window. "For one thing, it has the play on it — at least whatever amount of the play that Connor managed to write."

That much I figured. "What else?"

"Correspondence, of course, and notes." Laura shrugged as she turned back to gaze at me. "He also kept notes about all sorts of things. At least that's what he told me. He never let me see what he had on it, or even what he had on his laptop. He was really secretive about it all."

"If it turns out he was murdered," Sean said as he glanced into the rearview mirror, "you think there could be clues of some kind on that drive?"

"I sure hope so," Laura said.

"Why did you feel like you had to take it?" I was still puzzled by Laura's actions. "Why didn't you simply give it to Kanesha? As it stands now, it could be deemed inadmissible evidence. What do you think, Sean?"

"You could be right," Sean replied. "Criminal law isn't my forte, but a competent defense attorney could probably get it disallowed."

"I didn't think about any of that." Laura rubbed her forehead. "I guess I just thought it was important to see whatever is on it. If I turned it over to the deputy right away, I'd probably never get to see it all."

"Do you think there's going to be something really personal — something about you — on the drive?" That made me nervous. Connor had acted more than a bit obsessed with Laura, and who knew what he could have written about her.

"There could be." Laura glanced at me,

then away. "I guess I should tell you, Dad, Connor asked me to marry him several months ago, and I said yes." She cut a sideways glance to see my reaction.

I frowned. "Why didn't you tell me that before?"

"I wasn't sure you'd approve." Laura sounded defensive. "But we didn't stay engaged very long, only a couple of weeks. By then I figured there was no point in telling you about it."

"It's okay," I said, glad she had finally told me herself. I caught Sean's glance in the mirror and nodded slightly. I waited a moment, then continued. "You should never be afraid to tell me anything, sweetheart. I'll always be on your side, no matter what."

Laura leaned against me. "I know, and I'm sorry. I should have talked to you about it."

"When we get home," Sean said, "I think we should see what's on that thumb drive. Then you need to turn it over right away to Deputy Berry."

"I agree." I patted Laura's hand. "Kanesha's bright and capable. We can trust her."

"Good," Laura said. "But I still want to know what's on that drive." She hesitated. "I just have this feeling that it's important. Mostly because of what Connor said."

"Said? When?" Sean asked.

"That last phone conversation we had." Laura sounded sad. "He was half-bombed when he called me, and when he was like that, he'd mutter a lot. Right before he hung up, he said, 'The play's the thing.' Those were the last words I heard him speak."

TWENTY

"We're home," Sean announced as he turned the car into the driveway. "That phrase — 'The play's the thing' — sounds familiar. Where have I heard it before?"

"Hamlet," Laura and I said in unison. I smiled and deferred to the actor in the family. Laura supplied the whole quotation. "I'll have grounds / More relative than this — the play's the thing / Wherein I'll catch the conscience of the King."

"That was Hamlet talking about his uncle, right?" Sean pulled into the garage and shut the motor off.

"Yes," Laura said. "Hamlet wanted a way to test his uncle Claudius to see if he was guilty of killing his father, who was also Claudius's brother."

When Laura paused, I added to her comment. "He wrote a play and put in some lines about regicide to see if Claudius reacted."

Sean opened Laura's door and offered her his arm. She accepted the gesture with a smile, and I followed them into the house.

Diesel met us a few feet inside the kitchen door, and he warbled up a storm at all of us. He went straight to Laura, though, and rubbed himself against her legs. She cooed at him, telling him what a wonderful kitty he was and how much she adored him. He kept talking to her, ignoring Sean and me.

Sean led his sister to the table and pulled out a chair for her. When Laura sat, Diesel moved in front of her and put both his front paws on her legs. He gazed up into her face and meowed. She scratched his head. "I'm doing okay, sweet kitty."

I glanced at the clock and was amazed to note that the time was only seven minutes past noon. The morning seemed a day long because so much had happened.

"I'll fix lunch." Something fast and easy, I decided. "How about tomato soup and grilled cheese sandwiches?" Strictly comfort food. Sean and Laura had both, as children and as adolescents, asked for the combination whenever they were sick, and comfort seemed a good idea now.

"Yes, please," Laura said with a big smile, and Sean nodded. Diesel finally stopped talking and settled down by Laura's chair.

He still hadn't acknowledged my presence.

"Sean, why don't you make Laura some hot tea while I get started?" I went to work preparing our lunch.

As I worked and Laura sipped at her tea, we resumed our conversation about Connor Lawton's quoting from *Hamlet*.

Sean stirred his tea as he spoke. "The question is, I guess, was Lawton writing about a real murder in his play?"

"And if he was, was he trying to 'catch the conscience' of someone he thought was a killer?" I added some heavy cream to the soup before I started on the grilled cheese sandwiches.

"Good questions," Laura said. She sipped at her tea. "That's why I wanted to keep the thumb drive, at least for a short time. With the laptop missing, the only complete copy of what Connor had written is on that drive. I'm sure of that. We have some pages we've been using for the workshopping, but we don't have that many."

"If it turns out that he was murdered," Sean said, "then there could be a strong connection between the play and the killer."

"That sounds reasonable to me." I buttered bread while I waited for the skillet to heat. "And it would mean the killer is someone who saw the workshopping or somehow managed to read as much of the play as Lawton had written."

"The problem for me is that, based on the bits of the play we workshopped, I can't remember anything in it that had anything to do with a murder. Though there were elements that made it seem like a mystery novel." Laura scowled before she drank more of her tea. "It just doesn't make sense."

"Then maybe the incriminating bit is in some part of the play you didn't workshop," Sean said. "We'll just have to read it and see what we can find."

My cell phone rang, forestalling conversation for the moment. I set down the knife and the piece of bread I was buttering and pulled out my phone. I recognized the number that came up on the screen. "Hello," I said, and Kanesha Berry responded with a quick greeting.

"What can I do for you, Deputy Berry?" I asked.

"I'd like to ask your daughter some questions, as I told you earlier." Kanesha's tone was brisk. "I can be there in about fifteen minutes. Will that work?"

"We're getting ready to eat lunch. Let me check with Laura and see how she feels." I muted the phone and explained what Kanesha wanted.

Laura looked alarmed for a moment, then she shrugged. "Might as well get it over with."

I relayed her assent to Kanesha and added, "We might still be eating lunch when you get here."

"No problem. I'll be there in fifteen." Kanesha ended the call.

I tucked my phone away and went back to the grilled cheese. "She'll be here in fifteen minutes."

"Then I'd better go copy the files off that thumb drive right now." Laura made a move to stand, but winced and subsided into her chair. "Maybe Sean could do it."

"Make me an accessory, eh?" Sean grinned as he stood. "I expect you to come up with all the bail money. Where is it? I'll just copy it onto my laptop for now."

"On the dresser next to my makeup bag," Laura replied.

Sean headed out of the kitchen.

"I'll feel better when we've turned it over to Kanesha." I flipped the grilled cheeses over, one after the other. Then I began to ladle up the soup.

As I set a bowl down in front of Laura, she looked at me, her expression serious. "Do you think she'll charge me with anything, Dad? What do they call it, obstruction?"

"Something like that," I said. I patted her shoulder in what I hoped was a reassuring manner. "She's going to be really ticked off about it, probably. At least, based on my own past experience with her, that's what I'd predict." I sighed and patted her again. "But I think she won't go as far as charging you with obstruction or whatever it is." I hoped fervently that I was right about that.

Laura echoed my thoughts. "I sure hope you're right. The thought of maybe going to jail makes me sick to my stomach."

"It won't come to that." I went back to the stove and removed two sandwiches from the skillet, added some butter, and put another sandwich in. I plated one and gave it to my daughter. "Eat."

Laura flashed a grateful smile. She dipped up some soup and tasted it. She sighed after she swallowed. "Totally yum. It's that cream you add. Love it." She spooned more into her mouth.

I placed bowls of soup on the table for Sean and me. Then I finished the third sandwich and plated it. I sat down across from Laura and tasted the soup myself.

We ate in silence, and I kept expecting Sean to return. When several minutes passed and he didn't appear, I was curious. "What's taking Sean so long, I wonder? How much could that thumb drive possibly hold?"

Laura shrugged. "I'm not sure, but it could be eight gigabytes for all I know. Connor backed up all his stuff on it, so there could be a ton of files to copy."

I didn't know they made thumb drives with that kind of capacity, but I wasn't the most tech-savvy person in the world to begin with.

Laura and I finished our meal, and still Sean hadn't appeared. "Maybe he's having technical problems," I said. "Could it require a password?"

"I doubt it," Laura said. "Maybe I should go check."

"No, you stay where you are. I'll go. Would you like more soup first?"

"About half a bowl, if there's enough left," Laura said.

I gave her what she requested, and when I glanced down at Diesel he looked up at me and meowed. I bent to rub his head. "Guess I'm forgiven finally, eh, boy?" He meowed again.

I headed for the stairs, and when I was about halfway up, Sean appeared at the head of the stairs. He stopped and scowled when he saw me.

"What's wrong?" I asked, stopping where I was.

"I can't find the blasted thumb drive," he said, and I could hear the frustration in his voice. "It isn't where Laura said it was, and I've practically torn her room apart looking for it. It's not there."

"Where the heck could it be?" As I spoke the words, I had an appalling thought.

While we were at the hospital, had someone broken into the house and taken the thumb drive?

The doorbell rang, and both Sean and I tensed.

That could only be Kanesha. Confessing to taking the thumb drive was bad enough. Now we'd have to explain that it was missing.

Kanesha would go ballistic.

Twenty-One

Sean grimaced at me. "What are you going to tell her?" He moved down the stairs closer to me.

"I guess we'll have to tell her everything." I turned to face the front door. My legs suddenly felt leaden. I didn't want to open that door and have to deal with Kanesha. But I had little choice.

"That sucks." Sean passed me, and I persuaded my legs into motion. While I headed for the door, Sean turned toward the kitchen. "I'll break the good news to Laura."

The bell rang again. "Coming," I muttered. When I reached the door, I grabbed the knob and pulled it open. "Afternoon, Dep. . . ."

My voice trailed off because I realized Kanesha Berry wasn't standing on my front doorstep.

Instead, Frank Salisbury, his expression

one of deep concern, stood there. "Afternoon, sir. I just heard about Laura and wanted to stop by and make sure she's okay."

My first thought was, where was Kanesha? She'd told me she was coming right over and should have been here by now. But I wasn't going to ignore a small blessing. Maybe she'd been delayed. That would give me more time to think.

In the meantime, I welcomed Frank into the house. "Laura's doing fine," I assured the young man as I showed him the way to the kitchen. His grim expression didn't lighten, however, until he saw Laura for himself.

Sean and Laura broke off their conversation when Frank and I walked through the door. Sean looked relieved, while Laura looked like a child receiving a much-desired present.

Sean prudently moved out of the way because I didn't think Frank even realized he was there, he was so intent on Laura. He went straight to her and knelt by her chair. "Darling, how are you? When I get my hands on whoever harmed you, I'm going to rip his arms off."

He had it bad, and from what I could see, so did my daughter. She flung her arms around her suitor — that was how I would think of him from now on — and simply said, "Oh Frank." He slid his arms around her, and they stayed locked together for what seemed like several minutes.

Sean glanced at me and rolled his eyes. I suppressed a smile. I wanted to know a lot more about Frank before I would feel truly comfortable with him as serious son-in-law material, though my early impressions of him were favorable. For now I gave him good marks for the way he made my daughter smile and perk up by his mere presence.

When Laura and Frank detached themselves, Frank pulled a chair close to hers and sat. Diesel came around from Laura's other side and warbled at Frank, who laughed and patted the cat's head. "Hey, buddy, have you been taking care of my girl for me?"

Diesel meowed several times, as if giving Frank a report on Laura's well-being, and we all laughed. Diesel glanced back and forth between Laura and Frank, and I would have sworn that, for a moment at least, he smiled. Then he rose and trotted over to me. He head-butted my right leg, and I figured I'd finally been forgiven for leaving him at home earlier.

I beckoned for Sean to join me, and we

moved into the hall to give Frank and Laura some privacy — not that they seemed to realize we were still in the room. Diesel came with us.

Sean glanced at his watch. "Wonder what's keeping the deputy? Thought she'd've been here by now."

I checked the time also. It had been almost half an hour since I'd talked to Kanesha. "Something else popped up to claim her attention, I'm sure."

As if on cue, the phone rang, and I walked back into the kitchen to answer it. I figured it was Kanesha, and I was right.

"My apologies for not calling sooner but something came up that demanded my immediate attention." Kanesha's tone was brisk as ever. "I'm probably going to be detained an hour or so. I'd still like to come by."

"That's fine." I wondered whether she could hear the relief in my voice. "See you then."

After I hung up the phone, I saw that Laura, Frank, and Sean were watching me. I shared the contents of the call, and Laura visibly relaxed as Sean and I exchanged glances.

Frank frowned as he gazed at Laura. "Are you sure you're up to talking to the cops, darling? You should get some rest." He turned back to me. "Don't you agree, sir?"

Laura regarded Frank fondly. "I'm okay, sweetie. I'm going to have to talk to her sooner or later, and it might as well be sooner. I want to get it over with."

"If you're sure you're up to it." Frank didn't look happy.

"If you'll excuse us, Sean and I have something to take care of." I smiled at the doting couple. "Give a shout if you need anything."

Sean followed me out of the kitchen along with Diesel. We paused in the hall near the foot of the stairs.

"What do you want me to do?" Sean asked.

"Before Kanesha arrives, I want to determine whether someone broke into the house while we were at the hospital. Check all the windows and doors on the ground floor and even on the second floor, I guess."

Sean's eyes narrowed. "It infuriates me to think that someone might have been in this house."

"Me too, son." I grimaced. "Maybe it's time I thought about an alarm system."

"Might not be a bad idea."

"I'll look into it," I said. "Meanwhile, let's get on with the inspection. You take the second floor, and Diesel and I will check down here."

Diesel meowed when he heard his name. He was sitting in what I call his sentinel position, like one of those ancient Egyptian cat statues.

Sean grinned at the cat before he headed upstairs.

"Come on, boy, might as well start in the living room." Diesel padded along behind me as I began to check the windows.

Since most of the windows in this room faced the street, I didn't think it likely an intruder would choose one of them for a point of entry. I checked anyway. The side windows were more likely entry points because there were high shrubs and trees on that side of the house that could screen a person bent on mischief from view from the street.

From the living room I moved on to the rest of the rooms on the ground floor. I found not a sign of forced entry anywhere. The door to the porch was secure, and its lock hadn't been tampered with.

I realized I hadn't checked the front door, so my assistant and I walked back to it. I opened it and squatted to examine the lock. Diesel stuck his head up beside mine, as if he too were checking the lock, and warbled.

"That's right, boy," I said with a smile. "No signs here either." I stood and stepped out the door, pulling it shut behind the cat and me. "Let's check the windows from the outside."

Diesel rarely went out into the front yard without his halter and leash, but I trusted him not to bolt. He was, like many of his breed, timid about some things and preferred to stick close to me outside. He stayed with me as we made the circuit around the perimeter of the house.

I was sweating profusely by the time we reached the front door again. I pulled out my key to unlock the door, and when Diesel and I stepped inside, Sean was coming down the stairs.

"Did you find anything?" I pulled out my handkerchief to blot the sweat on my forehead.

"Not a blessed thing. What about you?"

"No sign of any kind of break-in." I shook my head. "The only thing I can think of is that someone with a key let the person into the house."

"Do you really think either Stewart or Justin would do that?" Sean leaned against the banister. "I don't. Azalea wasn't here today either, and I'm sure she wouldn't let a stranger roam through the house unattended."

"You're right," I said. "Azalea's definitely out, but I want to check with Stewart and Justin, just in case."

"I'll call them." Sean pulled his cell phone out. "I don't think either one of them was in the house when I dropped Diesel off here. But I suppose one of them could have come back to the house after I headed to the hospital."

"While you check, I'm going to get some water." Diesel preceded me into the kitchen and disappeared in the direction of the utility room, where I kept his food and water bowls and his litter box.

Frank and Laura were deep in conversation when I walked in and at first didn't appear to have noticed me. I greeted them, and they both started. I smiled as I filled a glass with tap water and drank it down thirstily.

"Laura's brought me up to date on everything, sir." Frank stood and walked over to near where I stood by the sink. "I'm really concerned for her safety, and I want you to know I'll do whatever I can to help keep her safe."

"My knight in shining armor." Laura's tone was teasingly affectionate.

Frank flashed her a grin. "Sir Frank at

your service, milady." Then he sobered. "Seriously, I can arrange to be with her a lot of the time she's on campus, and when I can't, I think I can arrange for a couple of students to help."

"That's kind of you, Frank." I was touched by his offer. "I appreciate your concern for Laura." Then I had a flash of fear — what if Frank was the one who had attacked Laura? What if his devotion to her was simply a screen for some darker motive?

I tried to keep my expression bland, and Frank didn't seem to have noticed anything. Then another terrifying thought hit me: What if Frank killed Connor Lawton to make sure he couldn't woo Laura back?

TWENTY-TWO

For a moment I couldn't breathe. Diesel must have sensed my distress, because he rubbed against my legs and warbled loudly.

Frank smiled as he looked down at the cat. "He sure is affectionate. I've never been that fond of cats, but this guy could make me change my mind." He bent slightly to rub Diesel's head, and Diesel meowed at him. When Frank stopped rubbing, the cat butted his head against the man's leg.

As Frank laughed at Diesel and petted him again, I relaxed. Diesel liked Frank, and I took that as a strong endorsement that Frank was okay. In the time since I first rescued a hungry kitten from the public library parking lot three years ago, I had learned that Diesel had an uncanny ability to judge character.

If Frank noticed any oddness in my manner, he gave no sign. Sean walked into the kitchen then, and I welcomed the diversion.

He brandished his cell phone. "Neither one was here to let anyone into the house." He slipped the phone into his pocket.

"What does that mean?" Laura asked.

I hastened to explain about the missing thumb drive. "Sean called both Stewart and Justin to ask whether they'd been home this morning while we were all at the hospital. And whether they'd let anyone into the house."

"Dad and I couldn't find any signs of forced entry." Sean threw up his hands. "So if nobody broke in or was let in by someone who lives here, then what the heck happened to that dang thumb drive?"

"You're sure you left it on the dresser?" I asked. "You didn't perhaps squirrel it away somewhere?"

"I left it on the dresser. I didn't even consider hiding it." Laura shrugged. "It must be here somewhere."

Diesel meowed and rubbed against my legs.

Four pairs of human eyes slowly focused on one large kitty. Then the humans exchanged glances.

"I never thought of Diesel taking it." Laura shook her head. "Does he take things?"

"Every once in a while," I said. "He's like

most kids. He likes toys and shiny things. Did you leave your bedroom door open this morning when you left?"

"I did." Laura stretched a hand toward Diesel. "Here, sweet kitty, come here." Diesel chirped and walked over to Laura, who took his large head in both hands and bent to kiss his nose. "Did you take my toy, Diesel?"

Diesel meowed, and we all had to laugh. I felt some of the tension slowly drain away. "The trick now is going to be finding it," I said. "He likes to hide his toys and then pull them out when he wants to play with them."

"Why don't you just ask him where it is?" Sean laughed. "You're always talking to him, and he sure seems to understand a lot of what you say."

I caught Frank exchanging a skeptical glance with Laura. Neither of them had of course spent as much time around Diesel as Sean, so I couldn't really expect them to believe it could happen.

"Might as well try." I shrugged. "Come here, Diesel." I squatted to put my head on a level with his. For the moment, however, Diesel didn't appear too interested in doing what I wanted. He remained with Laura.

"Go on, Diesel, go to Daddy." Laura gave the cat a gentle nudge on the backside to propel him toward me.

Diesel twitched his tail a couple of times, but he did what Laura told him. When he was close to me, I stroked his head. "Diesel, where's your toy? Go find your toy."

The cat cocked his head sideways and gazed into my eyes for a moment. I repeated the instruction to find his toy. He chirped and pulled away from me. We all watched as he trotted out of the kitchen. Sean made a move to follow him, but I called him back.

"Let him go on his own," I said as I straightened.

"Might as well sit, then." Sean suited actions to words. I took my usual spot at the table, and Frank sat down by Laura.

Diesel reappeared then, carrying something in his mouth. As he moved closer to me I could see that it was one of the catnip mice I buy him every so often. He stopped right in front of me, dropped the mouse at my feet, and sat back on his haunches. He warbled.

"You're a very good boy," I told him and scratched his head. "Thanks for bringing your toy. But I need another toy. Will you go get it?"

Diesel gazed up at me for a moment, and I could almost have sworn that he sighed before he turned and ambled away again.

"How many of those things does he have?" Frank asked.

"Over a dozen, at least," I said. I hoped he wasn't going to end up bringing in every single catnip toy before this was over.

That, fortunately, didn't happen. I did, however, have a small pile of mice at my feet — with Sean and Frank ready to start ripping the house apart — before Diesel finally returned with a shining thumb drive protruding from his mouth.

I gave Diesel even more praise as I accepted this final gift. I quickly handed it over to Sean, who scurried upstairs with it. A glance at my watch showed me that Kanesha's promised hour was almost up. I hoped Sean could copy the files on the drive before she arrived.

Next I went to one of the cabinets and found the box of special treats Diesel loved. I thought he deserved several, and he watched with great interest as I shook some out in my hand. He reared up on his hind legs in his eagerness to get one of the semi-crunchy bits, and I bent to let him take them from my hand.

After he ate the last crunchy treat, he licked my hand and meowed. I told him again what a good boy he was, and Laura and Frank echoed me.

The doorbell rang, and this time I knew it had to be Kanesha.

Laura looked straight at me and smiled. " 'But screw your courage to the sticking-place, and we'll not fail.' "

Frank frowned. "*Macbeth*? Isn't that what Lady Macbeth says about murdering Duncan?"

"You're right," Laura said, wrinkling her nose. "I'd forgotten the context. That's what I get for quoting Shakespeare without stopping to think."

I headed for the door, and Diesel came with me. I realized belatedly that I still held the box of treats. He, ever the optimist, hoped more would be forthcoming.

"Sorry, boy, it's got to be all business now."

Diesel meowed as I stopped in front of the door. I opened it, ready to greet Kanesha. Instead, to my surprise, Ralph and Magda Johnston occupied the doorstep.

"Good afternoon." Ralph smiled briefly. "Magda and I were in the neighborhood, and we wanted to find out how Laura is doing. Magda was quite upset this morning."

Magda nodded, a bit uncertainly, I thought. "Finding poor Laura unconscious like that was, well, upsetting."

"Yes, it was." I stood back and motioned

for them to enter with the hand that still held the box of cat treats. "Please come in, and you can say hello to Laura."

Magda, with Ralph close on her heels, walked into the house. Upon catching sight of Diesel, hovering behind me, Magda stopped so suddenly that Ralph stumbled into her.

"What on earth is that?" Magda paled and held a hand in front of her, as if to ward off an imminent attack.

"It's just a big pussycat, for heaven's sake. He's not going to attack you."

Magda flushed at Ralph's derisive tone. "How would I know that? I've never seen a house cat that large, now, have I?"

The bickering didn't sit well with Diesel. He moved restlessly behind me, muttering. He didn't seem to care for either Ralph or Magda, and I took note of that.

"Diesel is gentle and friendly," I said in a neutral tone. "Don't let his size intimidate you." I smiled. "Laura's in the kitchen with Frank Salisbury. If you'll follow me, I'll take you to her."

Magda nodded, not looking at all convinced by my reassurances about Diesel. The cat ignored the two guests and scampered ahead of me into the kitchen.

"Laura, you have visitors," I announced

as we entered the kitchen. "Mr. and Mrs. Johnston dropped by to see how you're doing."

Diesel planted himself in front of Laura, as if to protect her from our guests, and I had to suppress a smile. He rarely took an active dislike to people, so his response to the Johnstons was all the more marked.

"Laura, my dear girl, how are you? Afternoon." Ralph nodded in Frank's direction. "I just can't imagine who on earth would attack you like that." He stepped as close to Laura as he could, but Diesel kept him a good two feet away.

Magda hovered behind her husband and peered around him at Laura. "You look much better than you did this morning."

Laura offered them a wan smile. "Thank you for coming to check on me. I've got a bit of a headache, but otherwise I'm doing okay."

"Excellent news, excellent." Ralph beamed at her as Magda contributed, "So glad you're okay."

"I simply can't imagine who on earth would attack you like that." Ralph was nothing if not repetitive. "Do you have any clue, any clue at all, who it might have been?"

Was he merely concerned, as a caring department head should be? Or did he have a more sinister reason for asking that question? I recalled my earlier thought that Magda could have been the one to strike Laura, with me happening upon the scene not long after.

As Laura responded in the negative to the question about clues, I heard the doorbell ring. As I slipped away to answer it, I wondered whether Kanesha had finally arrived. I glanced at my watch and noted that nearly an hour and a half had passed since I last spoke to her.

My stomach knotted in anticipation of the difficult interview that would shortly take place. Kanesha was going to be so angry with Laura and, of course, with me.

When I opened the door, I was almost relieved to see Damitra Vane there instead.

TWENTY-THREE

Before I could say anything, Damitra Vane brushed past me into the entranceway. Her perfume was so overwhelming I felt like gagging. Had she bathed in it?

"Where *is* she? Where *is* the bitch?" The woman's voice came out almost as a shriek. She was clearly agitated, her expression wild, her arms jerking, but that was no excuse for her ill-bred language.

My temper flared red-hot. "If you *ever* refer to my daughter in that tasteless, vulgar manner in my hearing again, Miss Vane, I will slap you six ways from Sunday. Are we clear on that?" I loomed over her, despite the ridiculously high heels she wore, and glared right down into her eyes.

I had never slapped a woman in my life, and I didn't plan to start, but Damitra Vane didn't have to know that. Her manner toward Laura infuriated me, and I was not going to tolerate it.

I wasn't done. "Furthermore, unless you want to be kicked out of this house immediately, you *will* apologize."

Damitra Vane stared at me and shrank back a couple of steps as I continued to radiate fury over her complete breach of manners. When she spoke, her voice came out as little more than a whisper.

"I'm sorry, I'm just very upset. I'm not thinking very good right now." She paused to lick her lips. "Uh, who are *you?*"

I doubted her ability to think well under any circumstances. I'd never seen such a vacuous expression on a person in all my life. She looked like she had to concentrate just to get her mouth to open, and after that effort, she had little mental energy left to control what came out of it. I couldn't help but agree with Sean's evaluation of her. My cat was far smarter than this poor woman.

"I am Laura's father, remember?" Her retention was obviously poor, since I had mentioned my daughter moments before.

"Oh, yeah." Ms. Vane nodded. "Mr., um, Harvey?"

"Harris." I was rapidly losing patience with this woman. "I think you'd best be on your way, Ms. Vane. My daughter has nothing to say to you."

"Oh, yes I do." I turned to see Laura bearing down on us like the proverbial avenging angel. "You've got some nerve showing up here. I thought you'd be out of the country by now."

Damitra frowned. "Why would I go anywhere? I went to Mexico a month ago."

Laura rolled her eyes. "How do you get dressed by yourself? Good grief, Damitra, I'm talking about Connor. Aren't you afraid you're going to be arrested for his murder? If I were you I'd light out back to Mexico."

This was a side of Laura I'd not seen before, and I couldn't really blame her for being so acidulous. Damitra Vane was a huge irritant, and I couldn't take much more of her myself.

"I didn't kill Connor." Damitra's face had an obstinate set to it now. "If anybody killed him, *you* did. He was coming back to me, and *you* couldn't stand it."

Frank appeared behind Laura, and Diesel trotted around Frank to stand in front of her. If a cat could glare balefully, Diesel was doing it. He made a rumbling noise low in his throat, and I recognized that sound. He didn't like Damitra Vane.

Laura, quick to seize again on the woman's vacuity and fear of my large cat, said, "Attack, Diesel. Rip her leg off."

Frank made a muffled sound I assumed

229

was laughter, and I was hard put not to guffaw myself. Our behavior violated all rules of Southern hospitality, but with a "guest" like Damitra Vane, the rules flew out the door.

Like Damitra Vane, as it turned out. She gaped at Diesel for a couple of seconds, heard him growl and saw him take a step forward. Before I could open the door for her, she jerked it open and sprinted out of it and down the walk, narrowly missing Kanesha Berry, who moved out of the way with maybe a second to spare.

How the woman ran in those high heels I hadn't a clue, but as long as she was out of my house and out of my sight, I didn't care — for the moment, at least. I considered her a strong suspect in Connor Lawton's death. Should it turn out to be murder, I added to myself.

Kanesha proceeded up the walk, an intense frown on her face. I waited in the doorway with Diesel, who started chirping when he spotted the deputy. Despite the thorny relationship between Kanesha and me, Diesel liked her. She was still a bit uneasy around him, but she had at least learned to appreciate him.

"What's going on with Ms. Vane?" Kanesha stopped a couple of feet away from me on the walk. She smiled down at Diesel. "What did you do, sic the cat on her?"

I couldn't help but laugh, and Kanesha's startled gaze met my eyes. "Actually, yes, Laura threatened her with Diesel, and she apparently believes that my cat is some kind of exotic hunting feline that preys on humans. So off she went."

Kanesha shook her head, while a smile tugged at the corners of her mouth. "If she goes to the police and wants to bring assault charges, I'll volunteer to be a character witness for the cat." Then her expression sobered. "She's not in much of a position to bother you and your family. There are a number of questions for her to answer."

"Please, come in," I said, stepping back into the house and motioning with my right hand. Diesel scooted behind me. Frank and Laura had disappeared. "Questions like what her earring was doing in Lawton's apartment? Was it under his body on the sofa?" I'd thought a lot about that earring since yesterday and concluded it must have been beneath the corpse.

Kanesha grimaced as she walked past me and Diesel. "No comment."

I took that as a *yes*.

Ralph and Magda Johnston popped out of the kitchen, but they stopped short at the sight of Kanesha. They exchanged uneasy glances before they advanced toward us.

"Morning, Miz Berry." Ralph's nervous smile made me suspicious. Did he feel guilty about something?

Magda had a sickly yellow cast to her skin now, and she bobbed her head at Kanesha and muttered a few words I didn't hear clearly.

"Morning, Mr. Johnston, Miz Johnston." Kanesha nodded at the couple who were now inching themselves toward the front door, their eyes locked on the deputy.

"So glad Laura is okay," Ralph Johnston said to me as he and Magda reached the door. Magda nodded. "We must be going, though."

"Thanks for stopping by," I said as I opened the door for them. Diesel warbled, but I didn't think either one of them noticed. They couldn't get out the door and down the walk fast enough.

I shut the door behind them and turned to Kanesha. "Strange behavior, wouldn't you say? They acted like they were terrified of you."

Kanesha stared at me for a moment, her expression deadpan. "I have that effect on some people."

The woman did have a sense of humor

after all. I sputtered with laughter, and Diesel meowed a couple of times. Kanesha maintained her demeanor, though I would have sworn I saw one corner of her mouth twitch slightly.

"Come on in the kitchen," I said when I stopped laughing. "Laura's in here with a visitor." I motioned for her to precede me.

When we walked into the kitchen, Diesel ahead of us, Laura and Frank sat at the table, involved in an animated discussion. I worried that Laura was overdoing it, because to my eye she was beginning to look a bit flushed — a sure sign that she was tired and needed rest.

Sean was there as well. He nodded and gave me a thumbs-up to indicate he'd been successful in copying the files on the thumb drive.

The conversation broke off as Laura and Frank caught sight of Kanesha. Sean and Frank stood, as properly reared Southern men should do when a woman enters a room. It might be interpreted negatively in other parts of the country, but here in Mississippi it was just plain good manners, not chauvinism.

Kanesha nodded in response to Sean's greeting. "Afternoon, Mr. Harris, Miss Harris." She regarded Frank with her customary enigmatic expression.

"Frank Salisbury, ma'am." Frank stepped forward and extended a hand. "Friend of Laura's."

Kanesha gave his hand a quick shake. "Chief Deputy Kanesha Berry." Then her attention focused on Laura. "I have some questions for you, Ms. Harris. I realize you're probably tired and not feeling all that good after what you went through the past couple of days. But I need answers."

"I understand, Deputy." Laura smiled, but I could see the strain in her face. She had overtired herself, and I should have been more zealous about keeping people away from her so she could rest.

"Good. Is there somewhere we can talk privately?" Kanesha shot pointed looks at Sean and Frank.

"Here's fine with me," Laura said.

Sean said, "I'll get out of the way, then."

Frank, however, frowned and stood beside Laura. "Are you sure you're up to this, darling?" He regarded her with evident concern.

Laura patted his hand and said, "I'll be fine. You go on, and I'll call you later." Frank didn't appear convinced, but he didn't argue. He gave her a quick kiss before he nodded and followed Sean out of the kitchen.

"Can I offer you anything to drink, Deputy?" I moved toward the sink. "Laura, honey, what about you?" I intended to stay in the room unless Kanesha threw me out.

"Wouldn't mind some water," Kanesha replied.

"Nothing for me, Dad," Laura said.

While I filled a glass with cold water from a pitcher in the fridge, Kanesha walked over to the table and sat down in the chair recently vacated by Frank.

Diesel, I noticed, took up position between Laura and Kanesha. He looked back and forth between them.

Kanesha thanked me when I handed her the glass of water. I sat down at the other end of the table from Laura, and all I got from Kanesha was a raised eyebrow. Then she turned back to Laura.

"The incident this morning." Kanesha had a sip of water, then set the glass on the table. "Tell me everything you remember, from the moment you arrived on campus."

Laura nodded and took a couple of deep, calming breaths before she answered. "I walked to campus from here. Must have been about seven when I left the house, and I rambled around campus for a while. I glanced at my watch when I reached the building, and it was a couple minutes past eight."

Kanesha pulled a notebook from her uniform pocket, along with a pen, and jotted the times down. "Did you see anyone in the building when you arrived?"

Laura frowned. "No, I didn't. But I heard someone, in the stairwell. I always take the stairs, helps me keep fit. When I was about halfway up the first flight — there are two short ones per floor — I heard footsteps above me, but I didn't think anything about them until now."

"You didn't catch a glimpse of this person?"

"No." Laura shook her head. "When I reached the second floor, I exited into the hallway and walked down to my office. Oh, I stopped by the staff lounge on the way to see if anyone was there, but there wasn't. So I went on to my office and pulled out my notes on the play to work on."

Kanesha made more notes. There was silence for a few moments while she wrote. She looked up at Laura. "Clear and concise, like your father." The ghost of a grin hovered around her lips, then disappeared.

Diesel chose that moment to meow rather loudly, and Laura and I both smiled. Kanesha glanced down at the cat, her expression bland.

"You were working on your notes," Kanesha said, prompting Laura.

"I meant to, but I couldn't seem to focus." Laura frowned. "I just stared at the wall for a long time. Eventually I needed to go to the bathroom. I remember going down the hall to the ladies' room near the stairs. And I obviously made it back to my office, but I'm afraid that's where my memories of the morning end. Until I woke up, that is."

"How long would you say you sat in your office before you went to the bathroom? Kanesha drained her water glass as she waited for an answer.

Laura thought about it for a moment. "Probably thirty minutes, at least. I seem to remember checking my watch at one point, and it was about eight forty-five. I think."

"Good." Kanesha nodded. She turned to me. "What time did you arrive on the scene?"

I had been thinking about that and trying to remember. The morning's events seemed oddly distant now, but I forced myself to concentrate. "Sean called me about nine to say he couldn't get Laura to answer her cell phone, so I decided to see if she was in her office. I ran, along with Diesel, from my office to Laura's, and it took only four or five minutes, maybe. So I'd say I found Laura in her office, with Magda Johnston kneeling over her, between nine-ten and nine-fifteen."

Kanesha made more notes as she resumed questioning Laura. "What you've told me so far is from your visual memory." She waited for Laura to nod in the affirmative before she continued. "But there are other kinds of memories, auditory memories, or scent ones. Think about it for a moment. Did you hear anything or smell anything in the moments before you were struck?"

Laura stared at the deputy for a long moment. "That's really strange," she said finally. "There *was* an odd smell. But what was it?" She had a look of deep concentration.

Neither Kanesha nor I said anything. Diesel, however, chose that moment to warble. "No comments from the peanut gallery," Kanesha said in a low voice.

Laura didn't appear to have heard either the cat or the deputy. Suddenly she smiled. "Motor oil. That was what I smelled. Motor oil."

TWENTY-FOUR

Motor oil, I thought. *How very strange. Was Laura's attacker a mechanic?* This certainly bore more thought. Who among the people associated with Connor might be around motor oil?

"That's an unusual scent," Kanesha commented. "Does it bring anyone you might know to mind?"

Laura shook her head slowly. "Not that I can think of. That really is weird, isn't it? Motor oil."

"At some point, you might remember something else." Kanesha tapped her notebook with the pen. "Can you think of any reason why someone would attack you?"

Laura glanced at me, her expression one of mute appeal. "Damitra Vane has accosted Laura at least twice that I know of," I said. "I wouldn't put it past her to attack my daughter physically."

Kanesha faced me. "Miss Vane was at the

sheriff's department when the attack took place." She turned back to Laura. "Who else?"

Once again Laura's eyes sought mine. I took a seat at the table, and Kanesha's eyes narrowed as they focused on me. "The attacker might have been after something in Laura's possession." My stomach knotted as I spoke. This wasn't going to be pleasant.

"Like what?" Kanesha frowned at me.

"This." Laura had the thumb drive in her hand, extended in Kanesha's direction. Her hand trembled slightly.

"Place it on the table." Kanesha stared hard at Laura as she did as the deputy asked. "What is it?"

"It was Connor's," Laura said. She paused for a deep breath. "He backed up all the files on his laptop on it. Have you found his laptop?"

"No, we haven't. How long have you had this?" Kanesha's tone was harsh.

"Since yesterday. Connor asked me to keep it for him." Laura focused on the table as she lied to the deputy. "He was kind of paranoid about anything happening to it."

I frowned at my daughter. What did she think she was doing? Taking the thumb drive from the scene was bad enough. Now she was compounding the act by lying about it.

"Could I have a paper towel to wrap this in?" Kanesha directed her request to me, and I hastened to comply. She took the paper towel and wrapped the thumb drive in it, then tucked it into one of her pockets.

"Thank you," she said to Laura. "I wish I'd had it sooner, but I reckon you weren't in too good a condition to think about it before now."

Laura smiled faintly. "No, I wasn't." She still wouldn't look at me.

What should I do? I wondered. Rat out my daughter and tell Kanesha the truth? How would Laura react if I did such a thing? I was annoyed with her for putting me in this position, but I decided that, for the moment, I'd have to go along with her.

"Have you looked at the files on this thing?" Kanesha patted her pocket.

"No, I haven't." Laura placed subtle emphasis on the pronoun, and I wasn't certain whether Kanesha picked up on it. "Was Connor murdered?"

Her blunt question startled me, but Kanesha didn't appear bothered by it. "We have reason to believe he didn't die naturally, and I'm currently treating this as a murder inquiry."

I waited to hear further details, but I should have known better. Kanesha

241

wouldn't tell us one jot more of information than she wanted us to have. I had thought all along that Lawton had been murdered, and now I was even more worried for my daughter's safety than before. I started to ask Kanesha about protection for Laura, but she forestalled me with another question.

"Did Mr. Lawton have any enemies that you're aware of?"

Laura appeared to be tiring rapidly. She rubbed her forehead and closed her eyes as she answered. "Not enemies *per se*, but he definitely had people angry with him."

"Like who?" Kanesha had her pen and notebook poised to write.

I decided to answer for Laura. The sooner this ended, the better. She needed rest. "Ralph Johnston for one. He was upset with Lawton yesterday over the way Lawton was behaving during the workshopping session. He even threatened to go to the president of the college to try to have Lawton's contract cancelled."

Kanesha frowned at me, whether in irritation over my answering instead of Laura I didn't know. "What happened during this workshopping session? And what is it?"

Laura answered before I could continue. "The actors read their parts so the director

— Connor, in this case, and he was also the playwright — can hear how it sounds on-stage." She shrugged. "Connor was up to his usual behavior — histrionics, yelling at the student actors, at me, you name it. He wasn't happy with anyone, least of all himself." She finally looked at me. "Dad, could I have some more tea?"

"Of course, sweetheart." I jumped up to make the tea for her.

"I'll need a list of everyone who was at this session yesterday," Kanesha said.

"I'll have to look at my class roll for all the names," Laura said. "I haven't learned everyone's surnames yet." She paused. "I don't seriously think any of the students are involved. They barely knew him."

"Maybe," Kanesha said. "But they'll all need to be interviewed. Who else disliked him?"

"Damitra Vane." Laura grimaced. "She probably didn't dislike him. She'd go on and on about how much she loved him and he loved her. But Connor didn't, and didn't want to be involved with her. But she wouldn't leave him alone."

I set Laura's mug of tea in front of her, and she slipped her hands around it with a faint smile of thanks for me. After a moment she lifted it and had a few sips of the tea. Her face regained a bit of color.

"What about you?" Kanesha slipped the question in so smoothly that at first I wasn't sure I'd heard it.

"Me?" Laura paled slightly. "I didn't dislike him. He annoyed the heck out of me, sure, but I was used to him. I didn't let him bother me."

"You were engaged to him at one time, I believe."

I wondered where she got that information. After brief reflection I decided Damitra Vane must have told her.

"Yes, I was. But I ended it a few months ago." Laura drank more tea.

"He got you the job here, didn't he?" Kanesha leaned forward in her chair, her gaze intent on my daughter.

Laura shrugged. "Yes, he did. He knew I was between gigs, plus he knew my dad lived here. He could be kind, you know." She blinked away sudden tears.

"Were you still in love with him?" Kanesha's tone had gained an edge.

Laura's reply was sharp and short. "No."

"So you had no motive to harm him?" Kanesha sounded harsh.

"No, I didn't." Laura's eyes flashed as she responded. "He drove me nuts sometimes, but I'd never harm him permanently." She stood. "I'm not feeling very well. I want to go lie down."

"Thank you, Miss Harris." Kanesha set her notebook on the table. "That's all for now. I will probably have more questions for you later."

Through all of this Diesel had remained silent — so silent, in fact, that I'd forgotten he was there. Now, however, he made his presence known. He meowed loudly as Laura bade the deputy good-bye and followed her out of the room. Her pace was slow, but steady. She appeared tired but able to make her way upstairs on her own. Diesel stayed with her.

Kanesha reclaimed my attention. "Now I have a few questions for you, Mr. Harris."

"Sure, go ahead." I braced myself. What should I do if she asked me about that dang thumb drive? I was going to have quite a talk with my daughter, and soon.

"Tell me about this morning," Kanesha said. "How you came to find your daughter and what you saw."

I drew my lightly scrambled wits together and focused on what the deputy wanted. I spent the next several minutes taking her through the events of the morning from my perspective.

When I finished, her first question focused

on Laura's olfactory memory. "Did you smell motor oil?"

"Not that I recall. I think if I'd smelled anything like that on Magda Johnston, though, I'd remember it."

Kanesha stood. "I think that's it for now."

As I escorted her out of the kitchen, I brought up the subject I'd been concerned about ever since I found Laura unconscious this morning. "I'm worried that whoever attacked Laura will try again." We stopped at the front door.

"You have every right to be." Kanesha looked grim. "We don't know yet what the attacker was after. It could have been random, but I don't think it was. Until we know for sure why your daughter was assaulted, you do need to be concerned for her safety. I'll talk to the police department to see if there's anything they can do to keep an eye on her. In the meantime, keep her home as much as possible, and if she has to go out, make sure she doesn't go alone."

"Thank you, Deputy," I said as I opened the door. "Anything you can do to keep her safe, I'd appreciate it."

"That's my job." Kanesha stopped on the doorstep and fixed me with her laser stare. "Just one more thing, Mr. Harris. I know your daughter's lying to me about something. And I don't like that, not one little bit."

She turned and headed down the sidewalk toward her vehicle.

TWENTY-FIVE

I felt an icy prickle on the back of my neck at Kanesha's words. Should I have told her the truth?

I almost called out to her, but another thought struck me. Laura would be very hurt if I went behind her back and talked to the deputy, and I didn't want that.

Laura's reasons for lying to Kanesha eluded me at the moment, unless she did it in a misguided attempt to protect me. She didn't realize, however, that her failure to tell the truth would simply make things far worse when Kanesha figured it out. And she would; I was sure of that.

I closed the door, then headed upstairs to check on Laura. Her door was ajar, and I paused at the threshold and called her name softly. When there was no response, I stuck my head inside far enough to see the bed.

Laura appeared to be asleep, lying on her side, her breathing even, one arm curled around Diesel. The cat spooned with her, his head under her chin. I watched for a moment. Diesel blinked at me a couple of times, as if to tell me he had everything under control and to go away. I smiled and withdrew, pulling the door almost shut.

Back downstairs, the house quiet around me, I began to feel restless. Yielding to impulse, I grabbed my keys and headed for the garage. I hadn't talked to Helen Louise Brady for several days, and I had a sudden hankering to see her. We hadn't been able to reschedule the dinner we'd planned the night of Laura's cocktail party. I also thought it would be nice to have something from her bakery for dessert tonight. An image of her *gâteau au chocolat* flashed in my mind, and I was practically licking my lips as I backed the car out of the garage and pointed it toward the town square.

I found a spot on the square across from the bakery and parked. The afternoon sun blazed, and I shaded my eyes as I waited to cross the street. When I stepped under the bakery's awning, I paused to peer in through the window. At mid-afternoon there were only three tables occupied, and I didn't see Helen Louise anywhere.

As I entered, I hoped she was in the kitchen and not out for a while. I had to

249

admit to myself that I came here more to see her than to buy a cake. I inhaled the delicious scents of freshly baked pastries and butter and various flavors all mingled together as I wandered over to the display cases. I could probably gain a couple of pounds from sniffing in here. I bent to have a closer look at a plate of éclairs.

"Charlie, my dear, what a pleasant surprise."

I turned to my left to see Helen Louise beaming at me from behind the counter. I moved closer and smiled.

"But where's Diesel?" Helen Louise, rake-thin and nearly six feet tall, frowned as she peered over the counter around me. "Isn't he with you? I hope he's not ill."

"He's fine," I said. "I left him at home with Laura, napping."

"Well, I suppose it's okay this one time, but you know the only reason I allow you in here is because you usually bring that gorgeous kitty with you." Helen Louise chuckled.

I sighed heavily, going along with the joke. "Yes, I know, and here I thought you were beginning to like me for myself and not *mon chat très beau.*"

Helen Louise laughed at my sally. She had spent several years in Paris, studying her art, and ever since she came back to Athena she tended to sprinkle her conversations with the occasional word or phrase of French. My accent was not that good, but I think the effort amused her.

"Do you have time for a chat? How about some coffee and an éclair?"

"You read my mind." I smiled. "My mouth will overrule my waistline and say yes to the éclair."

"Have a seat, and I'll be with you in a moment." Helen Louise gestured toward our usual table, in the corner near the cash register.

Sitting at the table without Diesel at my feet was odd. I was so used to having him with me almost all the time that I felt like part of me was missing. Helen Louise returned then, bearing a tray with two cups of coffee and two éclairs. She deftly served them before sitting next to me.

She clasped my hand for a moment and gave it a squeeze. "I heard about the death of Laura's friend at the college. How awful for her."

"Yes, it was terrible. She was the one who found him." I added two small scoops of sugar to my coffee.

Helen Louise grimaced. "I hadn't heard

that. Poor Laura. Is there anything I can do?"

"Not at the moment," I said. "She's doing okay, all things considered. But unfortunately, there's more."

Helen Louise sipped at her coffee and nibbled her éclair as I related the events of the day. Had the attack on Laura happened only this morning?

"What was the person after?" Helen Louise's eyes blazed. "I'd love to get a hold of whoever did it."

"You'll have to get in line." I smiled briefly. "We think the person was after a thumb drive that belonged to Connor." I told her the rest of it, the real version, not Laura's made-up one. I trusted Helen Louise implicitly, and I valued her perspective on things. She had been a lawyer before chucking it over in order to follow her dream of opening her own French-style bakery.

"Kanesha may string you both up before she's done with you." Helen Louise frowned. "I wish Laura hadn't been so impulsive and taken that blasted thing to begin with. This isn't going to look good when Kanesha finds out the truth."

"I know." I sighed. "Laura is usually so levelheaded, but I suppose the shock of finding Lawton like that knocked her so off balance that she didn't think clearly about the implications."

"No, she probably didn't. Did she have strong feelings for him?"

"They were engaged briefly," I said. "A fact I didn't know until recently. Laura swore up and down she wasn't in love with him any longer. In fact, she seems to be infatuated with a young man in the Theater Department, Frank Salisbury. Do you know him?"

Helen Louise nodded. Of course she knew him — she knew practically everyone in Athena. "He's a fine young man. His mother, a widow, goes to my church, and Frank often attends with her."

"I'm glad to hear that, because Laura seems serious about him, even though they've only known each other a couple of weeks." I shook my head. "And he seems just as besotted with her. I don't know what will happen when the time comes for Laura to go back to Los Angeles." I had two more bites of my éclair and wanted to sigh from sheer pleasure.

"They'll work it out, never fear." Helen Louise chuckled. "Who knows? Laura might decide to chuck Hollywood and settle down here with Frank."

"I wouldn't mind that, I have to admit." I sipped my coffee. "I worry about her out there. You hear so many stories of bad things happening to young actors."

"You and Jackie reared her well." Helen Louise patted my hand. "She has a strong foundation, unlike a lot of those kids."

"Thank you." I liked to think that my late wife and I had done our best with our two children. "I have to confess, though, I'm really floored over this situation with her lying to Kanesha. And Kanesha knows Laura is lying about something. She told me that."

"Laura has a valid reason, at least in her mind, for doing what she did." Helen Louise regarded me with a thoughtful expression. "I'm sure she'll eventually tell you what that reason is."

"I'm sure she will, but in the meantime, what must Kanesha be thinking?" I tore the remainder of my éclair into several pieces. "She hasn't said so, of course, but Laura is probably her chief suspect."

"She has to consider Laura." Helen Louise's tone was matter-of-fact. "She wouldn't be doing her job properly otherwise. You know that."

"Yes, you're right," I said. "But that doesn't make it any easier. I know my daughter did not kill that man."

"Are you sure someone killed him? That it wasn't an accident? He was a heavy drinker, by all accounts, and couldn't his death have been alcohol poisoning of some kind?"

"Kanesha told us she is treating it as a homicide, more or less. He was an unpleasant man, and I've no doubt several people might have wanted him dead. Laura wasn't one of them."

"He was not the sort to endear himself to anyone." Helen Louise shook her head. "He came in here frequently, and with several different women. His behavior toward them was not gentlemanly, to say the least."

"Was one of them Damitra Vane?" I described her to Helen Louise.

"My lord, yes, she was with him a couple of times. She's about as dim as a three-watt bulb, and he treated her like dirt."

"She claims she was in love with him, and he with her. In fact, she'd been threatening Laura to stay away from him." I drained my coffee and set the cup down.

"She'd have had to threaten several other women as well." Helen Louise snorted in disgust. "I couldn't see the attraction myself, but evidently that type of man appeals to some women. Even women old enough to know better. Married women, in fact."

"Like who?" I scented possible leads. The

more suspects Kanesha had, the more likely she was to back off from Laura. Or so I hoped.

Helen Louise leaned closer. "Magda Johnston, for one. They came in here together four or five times, and the way they were carrying on it was all too obvious they were having an affair. And Ralph Johnston is the jealous type."

TWENTY-SIX

Ralph Johnston detested Connor Lawton
— I had seen evidence of that myself yesterday morning. At the time I had thought it
based on Lawton's behavior in his professional role. But if he and Magda Johnston
were having an affair, and Ralph knew
about it — that added another dimension
to the situation.

"Do you think Ralph knew?"

Helen Louise grimaced. "I imagine he did,
because it's not the first time Magda's
strayed. Nor the second or the third."

"It always amazes me how you know so
much of what's going on in this town." I
shook my head. "I guess running a business
like this, you tend to see all kinds of things."

"That's true." Helen Louise laughed.
"Throw in the beauty parlor and church,
and that pretty much covers everything.
Magda goes to the same beauty parlor I do,
and what those beauticians and their cus-

tomers don't know about what's going on in Athena isn't worth knowing. Same with the altar and flower guilds and the senior women's Bible study class."

I had never really thought about the sources of Helen Louise's information. I'd simply come to rely on her knowing who was who and what was what in Athena. "I'll take your word for it." A stray memory surfaced. "I thought I heard somewhere that Ralph and Magda were divorced, or were getting divorced."

Helen Louise rolled her eyes. "They're always on the brink of divorce. They've actually been divorced twice. They're on their third marriage."

"That's nuts." My mind boggled at the idea.

"Tell me about it. They have their lawyers on speed dial, I'm sure."

I had to laugh at that. The situation sounded truly bizarre. Then I sobered. "If they're that crazy, then do you think one of them might be willing to kill? If they thought someone else posed a serious threat to their warped relationship?"

Helen Louise shrugged. "Anything is possible. Ralph does have a temper. He tried to beat up one of Magda's boyfriends once. Didn't work out too well for him, though, because the guy was a jock and hurt Ralph enough to put him in the hospital."

"If they have a history like that, then I reckon Kanesha must know all about it." That thought cheered me. With two loons like that to consider, the deputy ought to look at Laura as a much less serious suspect.

"They're well known to both the police and the sheriff's departments," Helen Louise said. "Not to mention their neighbors. I'd sure hate to live next door to them."

"Why do people involve themselves with such obviously toxic relationships?" I was still puzzling over that. I just couldn't understand it.

"Beats me." Helen Louise massaged the sides of her neck with both hands. "Sorry, neck and shoulders are a bit tired."

"No wonder, with all the baking you do." She worked very hard, six days a week, plus long hours that started at five A.M. and didn't end until seven in the evening when the bakery closed. "You need more help."

"I know." She sighed. "I keep meaning to advertise for someone, but there never seems to be enough time to get to it."

"Plus finding someone who can meet your exacting standards." I smiled at her.

"Some people do." She smiled, a distinct twinkle in her eyes.

"The added benefit of having more help here and more time off means you could spend more time with friends, you know."

Helen Louise nodded. "I do know. That's certainly a powerful inducement." She paused for a moment. "It sure would be nice to have something remotely resembling a personal life for the first time in years."

I leaned forward and grasped her right hand. The strong, capable fingers rested lightly in my palm. "I couldn't agree more."

A faint flush appeared in Helen Louise's cheeks, and she squeezed my hand. She started to speak, but the voice of her part-time helper interrupted. "Miz Brady, there's something wrong with the cappuccino machine."

I glanced to my left to see Debbie, an adenoidal high school senior, staring avidly at her boss's hand, still in mine.

Helen Louise flashed me a wry grin and pulled her hand away as she stood. "All right, Debbie, I'll come take a look at it."

I stood also. "I'd better pick out dessert for tonight and head back home. They'll all be wondering where I am."

"Debbie, help Mr. Harris."

The girl nodded at Helen Louise's command. "Yes, ma'am. What would you like?" She headed behind the counter to the display case.

I walked over and stared at the contents for a moment, then pointed out one of the two remaining chocolate cakes. "I'll take that one."

While Debbie extracted the cake and prepared it for me to carry home, I watched Helen Louise fiddle with her cappuccino maker. "I'll see you soon, I hope," I said.

She turned to smile at me. "Definitely. And before I go to bed tonight, I'm going to have an ad ready to run in the paper."

"Good." We grinned at each other until Debbie called out to me that my cake was ready to go. I went to the cash register to pay and was soon on my way out the door, with one last glance back at Helen Louise. She was once again absorbed in her task while Debbie lounged at the cash register and stared into space.

On the brief drive home, I thought mostly about Helen Louise. We had known each other since childhood, and through high school and college she had been a good friend to both my late wife, Jackie, and me. We gradually lost touch when Helen Louise moved east to attend law school and Jackie and I married and moved to Texas for me to enter library school. The letters and cards dwindled to a trickle over the years, and on the increasingly infrequent occasions when I brought my family home to visit we never seemed to have the time to connect with many of our classmates. Helen Louise spent some of those years in Paris, and, with few family members of her own still in Athena, she'd rarely visited either.

She came back permanently and opened her bakery about three years before Jackie and my aunt Dottie died and I decided to move back myself. Getting to know her again after so many years helped ease some of the pains of transition into my new life, but I never expected our friendship to develop into something more. Sean and Laura appeared to be happy that I was seeing Helen Louise, and somehow I thought Jackie would be happy for me, too.

I woke from my happy daze as the car turned into my driveway. I blinked. I had driven home on autopilot, I supposed. My stomach did a little flip at the thought of what I might have done in my distracted state, but fortunately the traffic in Athena was never heavy in the late afternoon. I resolved to be more careful as I parked in the garage.

In the kitchen I stowed the cake in the fridge, and when I shut the door I felt pressure against my legs. I glanced down to see

Diesel looking up at me. He chirped a couple of times, and I scratched his head. "Hello, boy. Are you glad to see me? I sure am glad to see you." He chirped again, his way of saying yes, I supposed.

"How is Laura doing? Did you take good care of her?" I realized how foolish it was to ask the cat questions like that, but that never stopped me. Besides, he almost always responded when I did ask him something. Like now, when he meowed several times, almost as if he were giving me a report.

"You and that cat." Sean chuckled.

Startled, I whirled around to see him in the doorway. My response was a little tart. "You should be used to it by now."

"Oh, I am, I am." He grinned at me and arched one eyebrow as he continued. "I'm keeping the butterfly net handy, just in case."

I had to laugh at that. Then I noticed a sheaf of papers in his hand. "What have you got there?"

"Stuff from Lawton's thumb drive." Sean stepped forward into the room and pulled out a chair at the table. "Laura's still resting, far as I know. So I decided to go ahead and have a look at the contents. I picked a few things to print."

I took a seat to Sean's left, and Diesel

came to sit by me. "What kinds of things?"

"Mostly letters and e-mails." Sean fanned the pages out on the table between us. "There's more upstairs in my room, including the play he was working on. But I thought starting with his more recent correspondence might be a good plan."

"Have you found anything of interest yet?" I glanced down at the pages in front of me. Ralph Johnston's name leapt out at me from the page on top.

"Read that one." Sean indicated the page I had noticed. His smug tone as he continued piqued my interest. "Wait till you see what's in that letter."

I scanned it quickly, and my eyes widened as the contents of the letter sank in. "If Ralph knew about this . . ." My voice trailed off.

Sean nodded. "He'd want to kill Lawton for sure."

TWENTY-SEVEN

I read the letter again, this time more slowly, to absorb every detail. Addressed to the director of the American Academy of Drama, it offered Connor Lawton's review of a play submitted in consideration for the Laurette Taylor Fellowship in Dramaturgy. Lawton was apparently a member of the judging panel for the fellowship.

The author of the play in question was Montana (aka Ralph) Johnston. Lawton's comments savaged the man and his work. Phrases like *tediously derivative* and *staggeringly boring* made me wince on Ralph's behalf. Lawton closed the letter with the complaint that he couldn't understand why he was expected to waste his time on work that was so *manifestly substandard.*

I set the letter down and looked at Sean. "Connor made it plain he didn't like Ralph's play. But if he knew Lawton had written *that,* he would certainly be furious. I know I would."

"A simple *no* would have been enough, I'd think." Sean shook his head. "Looks to me like Lawton went out of his way to be a jerk about it. Even if the play was as bad as he says, he didn't have to say it like that."

"No, he didn't, but in my experience some critics can't resist the temptation to be as nasty as possible. I suppose it feeds their egos somehow to tear other people down so viciously."

"Lawton had a colossal ego, from everything I've observed and things Laura told me." Sean tapped the letter with his forefinger. "Deputy Berry will look into this, I'm sure, whenever she gets around to reading the letter. You think maybe you should talk to her, make sure she gets to it right away?"

"I doubt she'd thank me if I did." I rubbed my forehead to ease the tension that was threatening to bring on a headache. "No, it's better to let her assess this on her own. She already has enough on Ralph and Magda Johnston to consider them prime suspects."

"Like what?" Sean leaned back in his chair and stretched his long legs farther under the table.

Diesel chose that moment to let me know

he needed attention. I felt a large paw on my thigh and heard a couple of insistent meows. He stood on his hind legs, now with both front paws braced on my thigh, and his head was about level with mine. I put my hand on the back of his head and drew it nose to nose with mine.

"You are incorrigible and shameless, and you know it," I told him. His response was to lick my chin, and I laughed and pulled away. I kept my hand on his head as he sat on his haunches and stared up at me. A few good rubs between his ears, and he was content to let me resume my conversation with my smirking son.

"Now I know what I have to do to get your attention." Sean chuckled.

I chose to ignore that little sally. "Back to your question. I had an interesting chat with Helen Louise when I went to pick up some dessert for tonight." I gave Sean a rundown of what I'd learned about Magda and Ralph, their marriage, and her propensity for having affairs.

Sean rolled his eyes three times while I talked, but he waited to comment until I finished. "Some advertisement for marriage, those two. They're totally whacked."

"Agreed," I said. "If they're that unstable, I can easily see one of them deciding to kill

Lawton and take him out of the picture."

"You think Magda Johnston attacked Laura?"

I pondered that for a moment. "It's certainly possible, especially if she considered Laura a rival. But that would have made more sense before Lawton was killed. I can't see her doing it after he was dead. Plus, there was the odd smell."

"What are you talking about?" Sean looked puzzled. "What smell?"

"Sorry, I forgot you weren't in the room when Laura told Kanesha about that." I explained briefly. "I didn't notice any smell like that with Magda in the room, so it must have been some other person. And before Magda found Laura. I think that probably clears her."

"Maybe so." Sean didn't look convinced. "But she's obviously a nutcase. I wouldn't count her out just yet."

"I'm not. She and Ralph are at the top of my list." I glanced down at the papers on the table. "But I can't stare at the forest and not look at the individual trees, so to speak. What more is there? Anything that might point a finger at someone else?"

Sean straightened in his chair and leaned forward, elbows on the table. "Heck, yeah. Damitra Vane. There are some e-mails that will make you blush." He chuckled. "I know I did when I read them."

I frowned. "What do you mean?"

"Exchanges between Lawton and different Hollywood guys, all about what Damitra Vane will do to get a part, and how good she is at certain activities." He waggled his eyebrows.

"Sexual activities?"

Sean nodded. "Pretty disgusting, too. If she knows he talked about her like this — basically saying she's nothing more than a prostitute and too dumb to realize it — I don't think she'd be too happy with him."

My head began to ache in earnest. Connor Lawton defiled everything he touched, or so I was beginning to feel. It made me sick to my stomach to think of my daughter involved with such a man. What was she thinking? Did she not know what he was really like?

If I found out she was aware of all this and still associated with Lawton despite it, I'd be hugely disappointed in her. She had been reared better than this.

Sean must have read at least some of my thoughts in my expression, because he looked increasingly disturbed.

"No, Dad, I know what you're thinking. I'm sure Laura didn't know about any of this. She'd never condone crap like this."

"What are you talking about?" Laura's sharp tone surprised both of us. "What wouldn't I condone?"

I turned to see her standing in the kitchen doorway. She scowled at Sean and me as she advanced toward us. Diesel went to her, chirping a welcome. She paused several feet from me to pat Diesel's head.

"Come sit down, sweetheart. How are you feeling?" I stood and pulled out a chair for her.

"I'm feeling better, thanks." Laura sat and folded her arms across her chest. Her expression turned mulish. "What are you two talking about? Something to do with me, I know."

I resumed my seat, and Sean and I exchanged glances. He shrugged, and I knew it was up to me to answer Laura.

"Sean printed some of the files from the thumb drive." I indicated the papers on the table with a slight jerk of my head. "We've examined them, and they reveal some nasty aspects to Lawton's personality." I paused for a moment. "Aspects that I can't believe you knew about, frankly, or you wouldn't have remained a friend."

Laura stared hard at me and then at her brother. Slowly, as if reluctant, she reached for the papers and pulled them toward her. She drew a deep breath and began to read the one on top — Lawton's savage letter about Ralph Johnston's play.

"How about some tea? Or something to eat?" I asked.

"Hot tea would be nice." Laura's gaze didn't waver from the letter as she spoke.

With a motion of his hand that indicated I should remain seated, Sean got up to make the tea for her. I nodded, then watched with mounting concern and unease as Laura read through the short stack of papers.

She was still reading when Sean set the cup of tea in front of her. She picked it up and took a few sips as she continued to read. Her face reddened and then paled a few times before she put the last paper down.

"That pig. 'Experience, manhood, honour, ne'er before did violate so itself.' " She shook her head.

"Shakespeare, right?" Sean glanced at me.

"I think so," I said when Laura failed to respond. "But I'm not sure of the play."

"*Antony and Cleopatra*," Laura said. "And here's another one: 'Slave, souless villain, dog! O rarely base!' " She rubbed her eyes, and I could see she was crying. "I could think of a lot more, if I weren't so angry with him."

Before I could move, Sean got up and knelt by her, putting his arm around her. She leaned her head against his shoulder, and he held her until she calmed. Then he kissed her forehead before resuming his seat.

Laura looked at me, lovely even after crying, and my heart melted. "Sweetheart, I'm so sorry that you have to know about such vulgar things. You had no idea about any of this, did you?"

"No, Daddy, I didn't." She shrugged, her expression a mixture of puzzlement and sadness. "He could be an ass sometimes, but never anything like this with me. He could be really cutting with things he said, but it was only here in Athena that I saw him turn really nasty."

"You probably brought out the best in him. Around you, at least for a while, he tried to be a better person. I'd like to think that anyway." I leaned forward and grasped one of her hands. Her fingers curled around mine and held tight for a moment.

"Poor Damitra." Laura sighed. "I can't be too irritated with her now, even though she's a giant pain most of the time. I had no idea she was being treated like that. Men are such pigs, sometimes." She smiled briefly at Sean and me in turn. "With certain exceptions, thankfully." She drained her cup and rose from the table. "I think I'll have more tea. When are we going to eat? I'm starving."

By now it was almost six o'clock, and I discovered that I too was hungry. "Let me see what our options are." I went to the fridge and checked inside. Azalea generally kept us supplied with casseroles and other ready-made meals, and I found a large dish labeled CKN SPCH that I translated as a chicken and spinach dish.

I announced my find, and both Laura and Sean agreed that sounded fine. Into the oven it went to heat while I prepared a salad. Sean started a fresh pitcher of iced tea — one of the best kitchen gadgets I ever bought was an iced tea maker — and we sat down to a hearty meal twenty minutes later.

While we ate I kept a covert watch on Laura. She was quieter than usual, and I knew the revelations about Connor Lawton's true character had bothered her. She caught me a couple of times and offered what I considered a brave smile each time. If she wanted to talk, I would be ready, but I figured she would need some time to herself to process everything.

Stewart and Dante appeared as we were finishing, and Diesel greeted his playmate with a plaintive warble. Dante bounced up and down around the much larger cat, whimpering and emitting the occasional short bark. As the humans watched with bemused smiles, Diesel placed one of his paws on the dog's back and pushed him down. Dante knew who the alpha was and submitted meekly.

Laura excused herself, pleading tiredness, and after Sean and I both gave her quick hugs, she departed upstairs. Diesel came to me and warbled a couple of times before he turned and followed Laura. I knew he was telling me he would take good care of my daughter.

Sean and I sat with Stewart as he consumed the remains of the casserole and the salad. I pretended not to notice when he slipped tidbits of chicken to Dante. The dog would have turned into a complete butterball by now, the way Stewart fed him from the table, if it weren't for the vigorous exercise he got playing with Diesel in the backyard at least twice a day.

We filled Stewart in on the latest developments, and he was properly horrified over the attack on Laura. "When you find out who was responsible, let me know," he said, his face darkened by anger. "I'll help beat the crap out of the jerk."

Sean grinned and said, "It's a deal."

Not long after that I decided I was ready to go upstairs and try to relax. I probably should have read more of the files from Lawton's thumb drive, but I was too tired. This had been a long and difficult day, and my headache had come back with a vengeance.

Upstairs I took some aspirin and got ready for bed. I tried to read for a few minutes, but I found it difficult to concentrate. I put the book aside and turned out the light.

Sometimes when I'm really tired, my mind fixes itself into a seemingly endless loop, and I have trouble going to sleep. I figured tonight might be that way because of all the stress of the day. But I soon drifted off.

I awoke sometime later to the sound of an alarm and the smell of smoke.

TWENTY-EIGHT

Three nerve-wracking, exhausting hours later, I sat in the kitchen with my family, both two- and four-legged, to take stock of our situation.

"I'll never complain about your filthy habit, ever again." Laura cast a tired but fond glance at her brother.

"Same here, I think." I suppressed a yawn. "We're incredibly lucky you happened to be on the back porch. The damage could have been so much worse." Diesel meowed and rubbed against my thigh. I scratched his head to reassure him. The noise and excitement tonight had frightened him badly.

"I just wish I'd caught the bastard." Sean, fatigue obvious in his expression and posture, frowned.

"At least you scared him off before he could set more fires." Stewart shivered and clutched Dante closer to his chest. The dog whimpered and tried to lick Stewart's chin.

Sean had gone out to the back porch around ten to have a cigar and unwind. When he finished an hour or so later, he decided to stay there a while longer. He liked to sit there in the darkness. The glow from the street lights at the front of the house barely penetrated, and he found the atmosphere conducive to thought.

As often happened, however, he drifted off in his chair, he told us. He awoke sometime later to sounds of an intruder in the backyard. Before he could even get out of the chair to investigate, he heard the noise of the fire as it took hold at the corner of the porch. He yelled as he scrambled through the door into the yard. He barely made out a dark shape as it fled around the corner of the house.

Sean continued to yell for help as he ran for the water hose to douse the flames. Both Laura and Justin, whose bedrooms overlook the back of the house, heard him. Laura called 911 while Justin ran downstairs, clad only in his underwear and a ratty T-shirt, to help Sean. Stewart soon followed after, handing his dog over to Laura, who also had Diesel with her. I woke up during this and was almost mindless with worry until I knew everyone was safely out of the house.

By the time the fire department and the

police arrived, the fire was almost out. I met them on the front walk along with Laura, Diesel, and Dante. The firemen went into immediate action, and Sean, Stewart, and Justin joined us in the front a little later.

Time blurred after that. Between the questions from the police and the fire chief, I felt my head spinning. Neighbors had come from several nearby houses and stood on the sidewalk near the street, held back by two policemen. Diesel cowered against me, overcome by the number of strange people and the noisy activity going on around us. I did my best to reassure him, but before long I felt about as bewildered as he did.

Finally the fire department was satisfied the fire was out, without a lot of damage, I was happy to hear. Everyone submitted to thorough questioning, and by three-thirty we were all together in the kitchen trying to make sense of what happened.

"What I don't get is, why would someone want to burn down this house?" Justin shook his head. "It makes no sense."

"It's my fault." Laura, her expression grim, glanced at each of us in turn. "Whoever killed Connor must think I know something. Either that or someone hates me so much he doesn't care whom he harms. I'm sorry to be the cause of this."

"Nonsense," I said, my voice a little heated. "You don't have anything to apologize for."

"Thanks, Dad." Laura smiled briefly.

"The police are going to watch the house," Sean reminded us.

"The rest of the night, at least." Stewart frowned. "But what about tomorrow and after?"

"I'll help keep watch. My earliest class is at ten, so I can stay up late and sleep in a little." Justin gazed at Laura like a puppy watching its owner and hoping for a treat.

"Thank you, Justin," I said, trying not to smile. "That won't be necessary. The police will keep watching the house, and I'm sure once Kanesha Berry has heard about this, the sheriff's department will probably get involved. If all else fails, I'll hire a security firm to protect the house until whoever did it is caught."

"I *hate* this. All because of that jackass Connor." Laura's savage tone shocked us all, I think. "I wish I'd never met him."

I wish you hadn't either, I thought. I would never say that to her, however. She was exhausted, as indeed we all were, not to mention the high level of stress she was under.

"It's time everyone went back to bed." Sean stood. "Come on, there's nothing more we can do now. We'll be safe with the police keeping an eye on the house."

Stewart, with Dante still in his arms, stood also. "Good idea. I don't know about the rest of you, but I can use all the beauty sleep I can get." He fluttered his eyelashes at Sean. "I have to look my best for my hunky housemate, or he won't pay any attention to me."

Sean guffawed. "Face it, Princess Not-So-Charming, you need more than sleep to get *my* attention."

Stewart placed his free hand over his heart and pretended to swoon. Dante barked. "So cruel, so heartless." He paused. "And so full of it. I'm more man than you could ever handle anyway." He swept past Sean and strutted his way out of the kitchen and up the stairs.

Justin looked slightly shocked at this interplay between Stewart and Sean, but he should have been used to it by now. Laura and I laughed, and Sean pretended to be wounded. His wide grin spoiled the effect, however.

"Off to bed, all of you," I said. "Come on, Diesel. We need our beauty sleep, too." I made shooing motions with my hands and started turning out lights.

The three preceded Diesel and me upstairs. As I headed for my bed I silently blessed Stewart. He always knew how — and when — to break the tension. We all needed to recover our balance, and by getting us to laugh, Stewart had us off to a good start.

The next morning, after a sound sleep, I woke to the phone ringing. I groaned. A short sleep, because the clock informed me that it was two minutes past seven. I fumbled for the receiver, wanting to answer it before anyone else was wakened by it.

"Hello." I wanted to say, *Who the heck is calling here this early?,* but good manners forbade me. I noticed Diesel was not beside me on the bed. He was probably with Laura.

"Mr. Harris? Kanesha Berry here." Her clipped tones indicated she was in business-as-usual mode. I expected her to call about the fire, but not so early. Did the woman never sleep?

"Good morning, Deputy. What can I do for you?"

"I hear you had some excitement last night at your house. Mind filling me in on what happened?"

I gave her a quick summary, and when I

finished, she didn't respond right away. I waited a few moments, then was about to ask her if she was still on the line, when she spoke.

"Why do you think someone tried to burn your house down, Mr. Harris?"

Her matter-of-fact tone chilled me. The reality of what happened finally started to sink in. I had been too dazed last night to take it in completely, but now I realized someone intended to kill us all.

"Mr. Harris?"

"Sorry, Deputy, but reality is setting in." I paused for a steadying breath. "Obviously the person who did it is afraid one of us knows something that will implicate him — or possibly *her* — in Connor Lawton's death."

"And what would that be?" Kanesha's clinical tone did nothing to abate the chill. "You must have some idea, surely."

"Lawton's thumb drive, I suppose. There must be something on it that's dangerous for the arsonist." A new thought struck me. "Although I'm not really certain why that person would think it's still in the house."

"I agree that there's potentially important evidence on the drive. I'm not convinced, however, that the arsonist thought it was still in your house and not in police custody," Kanesha said. "Are you sure there's not something else, something your daughter's holding back, for example?"

The only information Laura was holding back — that I was aware of, anyway — was that she took the drive from Lawton's apartment after his death. How she came by it suddenly didn't seem that significant to me. The importance of the drive was in its contents, not its provenance.

"You'll have to ask Laura that yourself, Deputy." The strain in my voice was evident to me, and probably to Kanesha as well. How she would interpret that, I had no idea.

"I'm not happy that Miss Harris didn't turn that drive over to me right away."

"I can understand that," I said. I wasn't happy about it either, but Laura had her reasons, misguided though they were.

"I have a computer consultant examining it." Kanesha's tone could have frozen water. "If she discovers that anything on that drive was changed or deleted after Mr. Lawton's death, your daughter is going to be in serious trouble, Mr. Harris."

TWENTY-NINE

Kanesha's statement — no, it was a threat — robbed me of speech. The danger of Laura's situation hit me hard.

I realized Kanesha was waiting for a response. In my frostiest tone I replied, "You won't find any evidence of tampering, Deputy." Time to go on the offensive. "What are you doing about protecting my family from another attempt at murder? I thought your department was going to keep an eye on my daughter in case of another attack."

I would like to have seen Kanesha's face just then because I did not receive an immediate reply.

When she did speak, her tone was grudging. "I'm real sorry about that, Mr. Harris. Frankly, I didn't see any need to keep a watch on her at night. I didn't expect anything like what happened."

"My whole family could have died or been critically injured." I wasn't ready to accept her apology. She had screwed up, and she knew it. Maybe it was petty of me, but I thought she needed to squirm a bit longer.

"You've made your point already." The tartness returned. "It won't happen again. You've got my word on that."

"Thank you. Now, if you don't have any more questions for me, I have things to do."

"That's it for now," Kanesha said. "When I need to talk to you or your daughter again, I'll let you know."

The dial tone buzzed in my ear, and I hung up the phone. I sat there for a moment, feeling another headache coming on. I decided I needed water, because my throat felt parched. I headed into the bathroom.

Ten minutes later I was downstairs making coffee. The house was quiet around me, and were it not for the smell of smoke that lingered, the events of last night might have been only a bad dream. I decided to wait until I'd had at least one cup of coffee before I went out back to assess the damage. I needed caffeine in my system before I could deal with that level of reality.

While I waited for the coffee to finish, I thought about our predicament. Laura wouldn't be safe until Lawton's killer was in custody. I didn't doubt Kanesha's ability to catch the guy, at least in the long run. I

285

didn't, however, see any reason not to help the investigation along in any way I could. Kanesha would consider it interference, as she had before, but I wasn't going to let that stop me. I knew I could count on Sean as well.

I grinned. If I fancied myself as Holmes, Sean certainly made a more than capable Watson. More like Nero and Archie, I thought a bit ruefully, as I patted my stomach. I wasn't anywhere near a seventh of a ton like Nero, but that was only because of concerted effort on my part. Azalea's cooking, though distinctly different from that of Fritz Brenner, was every bit as calorie-laden and mouthwatering.

The coffeemaker beeped to let me know it had finished. As I poured myself a cup, I glanced at the clock. Nearly eight now. And speaking of Azalea, here she was coming through the back door.

"Morning, Mr. Charlie." She set her capacious bag down on the counter and rummaged inside it for her apron.

"Morning, Azalea. How are you?" I was glad I'd remembered to put on my robe this morning. Considering how sleep-deprived I felt, I could easily have been caught in my pj's, and Azalea would have been highly affronted by that.

"Doing right fine." Azalea paused in tying the apron behind her back and sniffed. "Why's there smoke in the air?" She frowned. "You ain't been using the fireplace, surely, this time of year." She finished with her apron and stood glaring at me.

"No, not the fireplace." I explained what happened, and her eyes grew round with outrage.

"Thank the Lord y'all wasn't hurt." She closed her eyes, and I could tell she was offering a silent prayer. Then her eyes opened again, and I could almost feel the sparks jumping out of them. "What Miss Dottie would think, well, I thank the Lord she be resting safe in His arms. She sure loved this house."

For a brief moment I felt guilty — as if it were my fault the house had been damaged. I doubted that was Azalea's intent, but I knew how close she and my late aunt had been. Azalea took the care of this house seriously, considering it her duty to Aunt Dottie. Sometimes I felt I was here only on sufferance and that if Azalea thought I should go, I'd have to.

"What you need is a good breakfast." With that announcement Azalea headed to the refrigerator. "I'm gone whip up some pancakes. You want bacon or sausage with 'em?"

"Bacon, please." I could never resist Azalea's bacon, fried to crisp perfection every time.

Plaintive meows sounded nearby, and I turned to see Diesel trot into the kitchen. He came to me and put his front paws on my leg, then butted his head against my side as if determined to make me notice him.

"Good morning, boy," I said as I scratched between his ears. "Did you take good care of Laura last night?"

As Diesel chirped in response, I heard a snort from Azalea's direction. I grinned. "Diesel, you tell Azalea you understand every word I say and that you're a good watch-cat."

Diesel chirped a few times more, and I watched Azalea's back as she stood at the counter, mixing pancake batter. Her head shook back and forth three times, and I could imagine her expression. I thought she secretly found Diesel entertaining, but she would never admit it.

"I think I'll go get the paper." I stood as I made my announcement. Diesel, instead of following me to the front door, ambled toward the utility room and his litter box.

The sun was bright, and the day already hot when I opened the front door. The paper lay a few feet down the walk, and as I headed for it I saw the police car parked on the street in front of my house. After I retrieved the paper, I stood for a moment and watched the car. The officer inside saw me and inclined his head. I nodded back, then turned and headed inside again.

Reassured by the police presence outside, I felt a little lighter of heart as I returned to the kitchen. I informed Azalea that our police guard was on duty, and she nodded to acknowledge that she heard me.

I opened the paper — the *Commercial Appeal* from Memphis — and began reading. Diesel returned and made himself comfortable by my chair. He knew pancakes were in the offing and hoped to score a few bites. I really had become lax about letting him have human food, although I consoled myself with the knowledge that, with his size and appetite, he ate far more of his own food than he did treats from the table. He had regular checkups with his vet, and Dr. Romano was always pleased with his general state of health. She did remind me, though, to keep the treats to a minimum.

By the time Diesel and I finished our pancakes and Azalea started on the laundry in the utility room, none of the other occupants of the house had yet appeared. I went upstairs to dress and brush my teeth, then grabbed my cell phone before Diesel and I went out back to inspect the damage to the house.

Diesel hunted in the flowerbeds while I stood in the hot morning sun and began to sweat. I shaded my eyes with my hand and started my examination.

The porch ran the whole length of the back of the house, and the fire had started to the left of it on the west side. The white paint had blackened and bubbled in a mostly circular patch about four feet wide. Thanks to Sean's quick response, the fire hadn't had time to gain hold. From what I could see, it hadn't managed to burn through the wood into the interior.

Feeling vastly relieved, I stepped back and for the first time noticed the state of the flowerbeds. The firemen had trampled several azaleas, and the plants would have to be replaced. Thankful the loss wasn't much worse, I retreated to the shade of the porch to cool off and call my insurance agent and then the college library to let them know I wouldn't be in today. I was lucky with the latter call, because my friend Melba, assistant to the library director, was out of the office, and I reached her voice mail instead. I simply told her I wasn't feeling very well and was staying home. She'd hear the truth soon enough. Right now I didn't want to spend an hour on the phone with her while she pumped me for every little detail.

By lunchtime the insurance agent had come and gone, plus one of my high school classmates, a contractor, responded to my call and came to give an estimate on the time and cost for the repairs. My contractor friend said he could have the work done within two weeks, and that sounded fine.

I lunched alone, except for Diesel. Laura had a class to teach this morning, and Sean went along as her bodyguard. Stewart and Justin both had classes as well, and Dante went with Stewart. He was now accustomed to accompanying Stewart on campus, and Stewart claimed the dog was much better behaved than any of his students.

While I enjoyed Azalea's chicken salad, an alternate recipe that included sliced grapes and walnuts, Diesel sat by me and meowed occasionally for a bit of chicken. With the mundane matters of insurance and repair fairly well settled, I was able to concentrate on the ongoing threat to Laura.

I was tempted to go to the sheriff's department and insist on seeing Kanesha. I was impatient to discover whether she had read Lawton's vicious letter about Ralph

Johnston's play. There was also the matter of Lawton's affair with Magda Johnston. Kanesha had to know about that by now.

And what about Damitra Vane? Those e-mails shed a revolting light on Lawton's relationship with her. From what I had seen so far, she had a temper on her, as my late mother would have said. I could see her killing Lawton in a rage over his obscene insults. If she truly believed he was in love with her, his true opinion of her might have pushed her too far.

The more I thought about it, the more I was convinced that I needed to seek Kanesha out right away.

I cleared the table and washed my hands. "Come on, boy," I said to Diesel. "We're going to visit the sheriff's department."

Diesel headed straight for the back door and stopped under the rack on the wall from which his harness and leash hung. He knew what *going* meant. I smiled as I bent to fit him into the harness.

I had my hand on the back door when I heard the front doorbell ring. I hesitated a moment. Azalea would answer it, and I could sneak out and be on my way to the sheriff's department.

Then common sense asserted itself, and I headed for the front door. Diesel padded along with me, and I realized I still held the leash.

I peered out the peephole, and there stood Kanesha, scowling as she rang the bell again. I opened the door and stood aside.

"Afternoon, Deputy. I was just about to come to see you."

Kanesha stepped inside, and I closed the door.

"Come on in the kitchen. Would you like something to drink?" I turned and took a couple of steps, expecting her to follow me.

"Mr. Harris, this isn't a social call."

There was a note in her voice that gave me a bad feeling. I turned back to face her. "What's happened?"

"Damitra Vane is dead."

THIRTY

"Dead?" I repeated the word as I tried to make sense of it. Beside me, Diesel warbled. The sudden tension made him uneasy, and I patted his head. "Murdered?"

Kanesha nodded. "No doubt this time."

I stared at her for a moment. Then I wheeled toward the kitchen. "I need to sit down." Diesel trotted with me. I didn't look back to see whether Kanesha followed.

As I sat I realized my legs were shaky. Diesel hunched up close against my legs, and I stroked his back and murmured to him. All the while my brain was trying to digest the murder of that poor woman.

"What's going on here?" Azalea's voice intruded on my self-absorption. "What you done said to Mr. Charlie?"

Another time I might have been amused at seeing Azalea glaring at her daughter and Kanesha looking guilty and irritated at the same time.

"I'm here on official business, Mama." Kanesha met her mother's accusing gaze head-on now. "This is between Mr. Harris and me."

Azalea snorted in derisory fashion. "Still don't mean you come in here and upset a man. Look how pale he be." Her tone turned solicitous. "You need something to buck you up, Mr. Charlie? You still got some of that brandy from Christmas."

I smiled, hoping to ease the situation. "Thank you, Azalea, I'm okay. Kanesha's — I mean, Deputy Berry's — news startled me, that's all." Diesel was scrunched under the table now, his head on my feet. Poor kitty. I almost wished I could join him. Being the bone of contention between these two women was no fun.

"I need to speak to Mr. Harris alone." Kanesha waited, but Azalea didn't budge. "Please, Mama."

"You holler if you need anything." Azalea shot me a pointed glance before she left the kitchen. Moments later I heard her moving heavily up the stairs.

I didn't dare look at Kanesha for a few minutes. I actually felt sorry for her. Having to deal with her mother under these circumstances had to be humiliating. Azalea had, not so long ago, confided in me that she didn't think police work was a suitable job for her daughter. She had wanted Kanesha to go to medical school instead. Her daughter, however, was determined to follow her own path.

At the time I'd wondered idly whether Kanesha might have gone to medical school or even law school on her own if her mother hadn't tried to push her in a particular direction. Azalea was one of the most forceful personalities I'd ever encountered. Had she grown up under different conditions she probably would have been at the helm of a Fortune 500 company by now.

Kanesha was every bit as stubborn and opinionated as her mother from everything I'd seen. Their relationship had to be uneasy at best.

I risked a glance at Kanesha. Her expression was as stony as ever.

"Please sit down, Deputy." I gestured to a chair. "What do you need from me? Or did you come simply to inform me of Miss Vane's death?"

Kanesha sat before she answered. She pulled a notebook and pen from her pocket. "Give me a timetable of what happened here last night."

I could have refrigerated meat by putting it next to her right now, I decided. It wouldn't do to annoy her.

I nodded, then took a moment to organize my thoughts before I responded. Under the table, Diesel muttered and shifted position. I tried to reassure him by rubbing his side with my foot. He quieted.

"I went to bed before the others, except for Laura, I think. Sean went out to the porch to have a cigar and fell asleep there after he finished it." I narrated the rest of the events while Kanesha jotted notes. She didn't look at me the entire time.

When I finished, she stared at her notebook for a moment. "I still have facts to verify, but I'd say y'all are in the clear. At least in Miss Vane's death."

Did she throw that last statement in just to be spiteful? "Surely the same person is responsible for both her murder and Lawton's." It didn't make any sense otherwise.

Now she looked at me, and I didn't bother to suppress a scowl. "It's likely, but the methods were entirely different. Miss Vane's throat was cut."

A gruesome image bloomed in my mind, and I shook my head in a vain effort to dispel it. "That's horrible."

"Yes, it was." Kanesha stood.

I stared up at her. "Why do you say we're in the clear in her murder?"

"By the time the maid found her around nine this morning, she'd been dead about seven hours, give or take an hour, according to the preliminary estimate."

"While we were all in the midst of dealing with the fire department and the police," I said.

Kanesha nodded. "It's possible someone slipped away during the confusion. The hotel's only a few minutes from here, especially running. But I don't think that happened. Whoever did it would have had blood on him or would have to change clothes. Did you notice anything like that?"

"Certainly not." Even in my dazed state I would have noticed if a member of the household disappeared for that long. Besides, we were all together — and stayed together — shortly after the fire department arrived, first out in the front yard and then in the kitchen. I repeated that aloud to Kanesha.

She nodded again and turned to go, but I had a question for her. "Did your computer expert find any evidence of tampering with Lawton's thumb drive?"

Slowly she faced me, her expression unreadable. "No." She turned and left the kitchen. I didn't bother to see her to the door.

Frustrating woman. I sighed and wondered how this would all have played out had I talked to her at the sheriff's department instead. Easier on the nerves, I decided, both hers and mine.

I deplored the murder of poor Damitra Vane, but I was happy that Kanesha didn't consider any of us a suspect — and that the thumb drive was clean, so to speak.

I didn't look forward to telling Laura about the death of her erstwhile colleague and former rival. She hadn't liked the woman, but I knew she would be badly upset by the news.

I glanced at the clock. It was nearly two, and I didn't expect Laura — and Sean — home until after five. The news could wait till then. I doubted they would hear it from another source before they came home.

Before they left this morning Sean told me he had finished printing the contents of Lawton's files and left the papers in the den for me. I decided now was a good time to delve further into them for more evidence. With Damitra Vane out of the picture — I winced at the unintentional pun — Ralph and Magda Johnston were definitely center stage.

"Come on, boy." Diesel crawled out from under the table and gazed up at me. He meowed, and I patted his head. "I know, sweet boy, things were tense there for a while. But she's gone now, and we can go have some nice quiet time to ourselves."

I realized he still wore his harness, and I removed it before we headed for the den. He chirped to thank me.

The den, the room next to the living room and down the hall, was as much my personal library as anything. Bookshelves lined all the walls. A few of them were in place before I moved back to Athena. The rest I added — or rather, my contractor classmate's crew did. This room was my refuge, and I came in here when I wanted to surround myself with the warm and contented feeling my books gave me.

Diesel liked the room as much as I did. He had his special place here — an old afghan, knitted by my late wife, spread on an old leather sofa. He would stretch out and snooze at one end while I sat at the other, my feet on a hassock, and read or — increasingly often, I had to admit — napped.

While Diesel rooted around in the afghan and arranged it to his satisfaction, I turned on a couple of lamps and then went to the desk to examine the stacks of paper Sean had left.

One pile appeared to contain more letters

and probably e-mails as well. A second one was obviously the play Lawton was working on when he died. A third group, and much the smallest, seemed to be notes on various things. I glanced at them, but they didn't catch my interest.

Suddenly I recalled what Laura had revealed about Lawton's strange comment to her. "The play's the thing."

How could I have forgotten that?

I carried that stack to the sofa with me. Diesel was settled in, already stretched out, drowsing, when I got comfortable on the bit of sofa left for me and began to read. Diesel's hind feet and tail twitched against me from time to time, but I was used to this. It stopped when he fell asleep.

I read for perhaps half an hour, trying to make sense of the play. Though the scenes and acts were labeled in sequence, they seemed disconnected to me, almost as if Lawton had been writing two plays rather than one. The quality of the writing was erratic as well. In some of it I saw the brilliance that Laura kept insisting Lawton possessed. In other parts, well, the kindest word I could think of was *dull*. How Lawton got from dull to brilliant I had no idea.

The brilliant scenes captured my attention for an even more important reason than their quality. If Ralph or Magda Johnston had read any of this, they might well have killed Lawton to keep the play from ever being read, let alone produced.

THIRTY-ONE

There were echoes of *Who's Afraid of Virginia Woolf?* in Lawton's untitled play, but the characters Rafe and Maggie were distinctly their own and not pale imitations of George and Martha. This was distinctly a roman à clef, however. I easily recognized Ralph and Magda Johnston from Lawton's vicious portrayal of them and their turbulent relationship, and I hardly knew them.

Had the playwright seriously thought he would be able to produce this play? Without being sued for libel?

Lawton was arrogant, as I well knew, but this was arrant stupidity.

Plus it was a solid motive for murder.

There were unflattering portraits of minor characters as well, including Sarabeth Conley, thinly disguised as Sally Conway, but Lawton directed most of his vitriol at the main characters.

Surely once Kanesha read this she would

concentrate her investigation on the Johnstons. What more compelling motive could she find?

Then I remembered Damitra Vane.

What reason could the Johnstons have for killing her?

The obvious answer to that was that Damitra Vane either had known or seen something that could directly implicate either Ralph or Magda.

Had the Johnstons worked together on the murders? I figured Ralph would have to have killed Damitra Vane. I didn't think Magda would be strong enough to cut Damitra's throat, not without significant resistance.

Another sickening image forced itself into my head — Magda Johnston assisting her husband as he savagely wielded the knife.

For a moment I felt like I needed to throw up, but I focused on deep, centering breaths, and the feeling passed.

I pulled out my cell phone. I hesitated briefly but then speed-dialed the sheriff's department. Kanesha would probably chew me up one side and down the other for calling her, but I had to be certain she read this, and soon.

I waited for the receptionist to put me through to Kanesha. Canned music played in my ear for almost four minutes before the chief deputy answered.

"What can I do for you, Mr. Harris? I'm extremely busy right now."

Judging from her tone I was at the bottom of her list of favorite people right now, but I didn't let that intimidate me.

"Have you had time to read any of Lawton's files yet?"

Kanesha countered with "We know someone copied the contents of that drive before Miss Harris turned it over to me. I'm frankly surprised it took you this long to talk to me about it."

There was no point to feeling chagrin, I decided. "I'm surprised, Deputy, that you didn't threaten us with some kind of charge, when we talked earlier today."

"I still might bring charges, Mr. Harris. The investigation is ongoing."

The cool amusement in her tone deflated me a bit, although I should have expected her to say that. She had the upper hand and was enjoying it.

"Back to my question." I tried not to sound impatient or irritated. "Have you read any of the files?"

"Yes, I've read some of them. What is it you want to direct my attention to?"

"His play, the work in progress that the

students were workshopping."

"What about it?" She still sounded amused.

Was she deliberately trying to make me lose my temper with her? After brief reflection I decided she probably was, but I wasn't going to give her the satisfaction.

"Laura told us that, during the last conversation she had with Lawton, he muttered something. A quotation from Shakespeare, actually: 'The play's the thing.' It's from *Hamlet,* and the full quotation is: 'The play's the thing / Wherein I'll catch the conscience of the King.' "

"I've read *Hamlet,* Mr. Harris. In senior English class at Athena High School."

"Then surely you see the significance. That play has to be important. It's a clear motive for murder." My temper was beginning to fray, despite my best intentions.

"I'm well aware of what that quote might mean. Matter of fact, I've read a few pages of the play, and I'm already considering how it fits into my investigation. Now, is there anything else you wanted to tell me?"

"No, that was it." Score one for Team Berry, I decided. That's me, firmly put in my place. "Thanks for your time."

"The department is always happy to hear from the public." The phone clicked in my ear as she ended the call.

I stuck my cell phone back in my pocket and glanced over at Diesel. Head raised, eyes blinking, he meowed at me.

"I'm an idiot, boy; you might as well realize that now. I never know when to leave well enough alone." I sighed as I stroked the cat's side. He meowed again and went into languorous stretch mode, shifting until he was on his back, head twisted at what looked to me like a painful angle. I decided it was the librarian in me, the part that always wanted to help people find the information they needed. I wasn't a busybody, surely.

No point in going any further with that train of thought. I contemplated going to the kitchen for a snack, but when I considered the idea further, I knew I wasn't really hungry. It was simply a response to stress.

I picked up the pages and read further. I had to suppress more than one yawn. The dull part of the play threatened to put me to sleep. I read through the bit I had seen onstage only two days ago and marveled at the sheer banality of it. I found it hard to reconcile the staggering difference in quality between the Rafe/Maggie part and the Ferris family saga.

The plot of the Ferris story centered

around rage against the patriarch for his refusal to help his younger daughter Sadie out of trouble. The older daughter, Lisbeth, I discovered, was almost old enough to be her sister's mother. She became so angry at her father that she actually began plotting his death. She discussed different methods with Sadie, who seemed to nurse a savage hatred of her father. There was another character, whose purpose I couldn't fathom, a young child named Connie who flitted in and out. The Ferris section of the play ended before either Lisbeth or Sadie acted on one of their plans to murder old Mr. Ferris.

I laid the final piece of paper aside and leaned back on the sofa. My eyes were a bit tired from the reading, and I realized I was thirsty as well. At the moment, though, I couldn't muster the energy to get up. My lack of sufficient sleep was catching up with me. I'd sit here for a few minutes and relax, then I would take care of my thirst before I tackled the rest of Lawton's files.

I awoke some time later to the sounds of activity down the hall. I sat up and rubbed my neck, sore from having slept at an odd angle. I needed water and aspirin, in that order. Diesel still sprawled on the sofa beside me, but he stirred as I got up. He yawned, and then I couldn't resist yawning myself.

"Come on, boy, let's get something to drink."

Diesel chirped, stretched, then stepped down from the sofa to follow me out of the room.

Sean and Laura were at the table drinking iced tea when Diesel and I walked into the kitchen. Laura looked tired, but relaxed, and I realized with a pang that I would have to upset that as I remembered the events of the day.

"Hey, Dad," Sean said, half rising from the table. "Can I get you something?"

Laura greeted me as well, and I thanked Sean and said I'd take care of myself. Diesel, after pausing long enough to warble a welcome at them, disappeared in the direction of the utility room. Laura and Sean exchanged grins.

"How are you feeling, sweetheart?" I asked Laura as I poured myself a large glass of water from the pitcher we kept in the fridge. I was stalling, but the news could wait a bit longer.

"Tired, but otherwise fine." Laura smiled before she had another sip of tea. "I'm not sure I accomplished much today. All my students wanted to talk about, of course, was Connor's death." She ran a hand through her hair and left it looking artfully disheveled.

"Only natural" was Sean's comment. "Probably the most exciting thing that's happened in their lives in a while."

"That's a pretty callous way to put it." I sat down across the table from him.

"Plain fact." Sean shrugged.

"Sadly, yes." Laura rubbed her forefinger around the rim of her glass, seemingly mesmerized by the sight. "Connor didn't do much to ingratiate himself with them."

I found it hard to imagine Lawton taking the trouble to ingratiate himself with anyone — unless it was some woman he was trying to get into his bed.

I pulled up short mentally at that notion. Not a profitable train of thought, I realized, as I gazed at my daughter.

"What have you been up to today, Dad?" Sean asked.

"Dealing with the insurance agent and the contractor, to begin with." I gave them a quick summary of those conversations. Then I decided I could no longer put off telling them about Damitra Vane. "Kanesha Berry came to talk to me."

"More questions?" Laura looked up from fidgeting with her glass.

"Yes, but she also came by to share some news with me. Some pretty distressing news, in fact." I hesitated. "It's about Damitra Vane. She's dead."

Laura drew in a sharp breath and her hand jerked, knocking her glass over. There was little liquid left in it, and Sean quickly retrieved a paper towel to mop it up.

"How? How did she die?" Laura didn't even seem to notice she'd spilled her tea. Her anguished gaze was focused on me.

"She was murdered," I said as gently as I could. "Sometime last night, probably while we were in the midst of dealing with the fire." I hoped neither she nor Sean pressed me for further details. I wanted to spare Laura as much as I could, at least for now.

Laura bowed her head, and Sean and I exchanged concerned glances. I reached across the table and clasped both her hands in mine. When she looked up at me, tears shone in her eyes. "She drove me crazy sometimes, but she didn't deserve this." Laura's voice was barely above a whisper.

"No, she didn't." I squeezed her hands lightly. "I'm so sorry I had to give you such terrible news, sweetheart. It's small comfort, I know, but Kanesha will find out who did it and that person will be punished."

"She was a silly woman with not much

self-esteem." Sean's words were a sad, but probably accurate, epitaph. "Still, she deserved better."

Laura pulled her hands from mine, and Sean offered her his handkerchief. She wiped her eyes and then stood. "I think I'll go lie down for a while, if you don't mind." She offered Sean his handkerchief back but he shook his head, so she tucked it into her pocket.

"Of course not. You get some rest, and we'll call you for dinner." I heard meowing and turned to see Diesel coming back from the utility room. "And here's Diesel. Take him with you, why don't you?"

The cat didn't need any prompting. He went straight to Laura and rubbed against her legs. She smiled. "Let's go upstairs, okay?" Diesel chirped and followed her out of the kitchen.

Sean sat with one ear cocked in the direction of the hall, his eyes on me. After a moment — perhaps after he was satisfied Laura was out of earshot — he said, "Okay, Dad, what didn't you tell us? You were holding something back."

I nodded. "I didn't want to upset Laura any more than I had to. She'll find out soon enough. The killer cut Damitra Vane's throat according to Kanesha." I grimaced when the image slid back into my head.

Sean looked as sick as I felt at that moment. Neither of us spoke for a long moment.

"Maybe Laura should stay here in the house until this thing is over." Sean's hands clenched and unclenched as he spoke. "Or send her somewhere out of harm's way, like Tierra del Fuego."

"Can you imagine your sister consenting to do either of those things?" I shook my head. "As much as I agree with you, I know she'd never go along with it."

"No, she wouldn't." Sean sighed. "But one of us is going to have to stick with her every minute she's out of the house." He laughed, albeit grimly. "I even made her stand right outside the men's room today, whenever I had to go to the bathroom. She wasn't happy about that, I can tell you."

"No, I imagine not. Maybe both of us should stay with her."

"Either that, or flush out the killer somehow and end this thing as soon as possible."

THIRTY-TWO

"Not a bad idea," I said. "But I don't think it's going to be necessary."

"Why not?" Sean frowned. "Have you figured out who the killer is?"

"I believe so." I told him the gist of Lawton's play, the Rafe/Maggie story. "There's motive enough right there, even if Lawton hadn't been having an affair with Magda Johnston."

"That I'll agree with. But the play can only be considered a motive if either or both of the Johnstons were aware of its content."

"True," I said. "I've thought about that. Frankly I think there's enough motive for Ralph, in particular, even without foreknowledge of the play."

"Agreed." Sean thought for a moment. "Plus, who's to say Magda Johnston didn't snoop around on Lawton's computer at some point."

"Or Damitra Vane, for that matter. I

wonder what she knew — or saw, perhaps — that put her in danger? Maybe she had read the play and said something that alerted the Johnstons."

"Possible," Sean said. "But do you know if she ever met either of them? If she didn't meet them, I can't see them having a reason for getting rid of her. Why would they consider someone they'd never met a threat?"

"You're right." I thought for a moment. Something niggled at the back of my mind. It had to do with Damitra Vane. What was it?

Sean didn't speak, evidently aware of my effort to concentrate.

A vision of a gold earring flashed in my mind, and I had it. "Damitra Vane visited Lawton before he died. That earring of hers was found under his body."

"Yes," Sean said. "And how does that connect her to the Johnstons?"

"It might not," I had to admit. "But if she realized she'd left it behind and went back to Lawton's apartment, she could have seen or heard something then that would implicate the Johnstons. Maybe she saw one or both of them coming out of his apartment, and they saw her. She was hard to overlook."

"Again, possible." Sean frowned. "There

are still too many *maybes* in this. The dots need to be connected, and I guess Kanesha Berry will have to be the one to do it."

"No doubt she will." I shrugged. "She's read at least part of the play. I called her about it."

"Let me guess: She was thrilled to have your help." Sean quirked an eyebrow at me as he spoke.

"As much as ever." I pushed back from the table and went to the fridge. "Time to figure out dinner. I don't know about you, but I need a break from thinking about murder, plus I'm hungry."

"Sounds good to me," Sean said with a laugh. "What can I do?"

As I expected to, I found a note from Azalea on the door of the fridge. "Not much. There's a roast in the oven, with potatoes and carrots, and green beans on the stove. All it needs is warming up."

"Are you ready to have dinner now?" Sean glanced at his watch. "It's just about five-thirty. A little early."

"Yes, I suppose it is. I'm hungry, but I can wait. Let's give Laura another hour, and we'll eat around six-thirty."

"Sounds like a plan." Sean stood and stretched. "In the meantime I think I'll catch up on e-mail. I'll be on the back porch if you need me."

I nodded, and he disappeared — probably headed up to his room to fetch his laptop and a cigar from the large humidor he kept there.

My noble intentions about dinner aside, I was still hungry. I checked the cheese drawer in the fridge and found one of those small, individually wrapped cheeses that I loved. One of those would satisfy me until it was time for dinner.

I unwrapped it, removed the wax covering, and disposed of the waste. Nibbling at my cheese I wandered back to the den, intent on examining more of Lawton's files. I was pretty convinced now, perhaps against reason, that one or both of the Johnstons were guilty of double murder. There could be more evidence — although I wasn't really clear on what it might be — in Lawton's other files. I might as well have a go at them.

I popped the last bit of cheese in my mouth as I picked up the small stack of papers that appeared to be a miscellany of notes of various kinds. As I settled on the sofa, I glanced to the side, as if expecting Diesel to be there in his usual place. The spot was bare, of course, and the sofa suddenly felt much larger. I smiled. My cat managed to take up four-fifths of the space when he spread out on it, but I'd rather be crowded than not, I decided.

I figured the first two pages were random thoughts that Lawton recorded, possible ideas for other plays or scenes in the current play. One line read simply "Rolf — Rafe — Rory — Rand — Rich — Rick." Potential names for the character who ended up as Rafe in the play, I supposed. Other notes were more cryptic, like "cabinet?" or "arrest record." They meant nothing to me.

After a couple more pages of such random words — random to me, anyway — I found something that sparked a memory. Lawton had recorded "1744 Rosemary," and that, I recalled, was the address of the Johnstons' house, the scene of the party I had attended with Laura. What was the significance of that, amidst all these other notes? It seemed an odd place to record an address.

I turned the page. More cryptic notes. The capital letters "ADR," followed by strings of numbers, like "1-84321" and "1-84323." I scanned the page. There were perhaps ten numbers in all before a new heading, more capital letters, "MCA," with several strings of numbers following them.

I stared at the page for a minute or so, trying to understand what they could mean.

I couldn't come up with anything and went on to the next page. There was more of what seemed like gibberish to me, words like "bathtub," "ankles," and "bruises?" Further down the page I spotted what looked like a name, "R. Appleby," followed by numbers that translated into a local phone number after I stared at them for a moment.

Appleby, I thought. *Why is that familiar?*

Of course. That reporter for the local newspaper, Ray Appleby. Why would Lawton have his name and number? Maybe he was looking for PR for himself and his play. I could easily see him cultivating Appleby, hoping for a profile in the local paper. Anything to get some attention.

He certainly had attention now — national, perhaps even international. He was highly regarded enough as a playwright, I reckoned, to warrant media attention from all over the place.

Now that I thought about it, wasn't it odd that Appleby hadn't approached me or my family about Lawton's death? He had been pretty quick in the past to call on a hunt for news items with the other murder cases I'd been a part of.

Perhaps he didn't know yet that any of the Harris family was involved in the investigation. I hoped it would stay that way.

Appleby seemed to be a decent guy, but the less I had to do with the press, the happier I would be. I could see the headlines now, along the lines of "Local Man Thinks He's Sherlock Holmes" or some other such nonsense.

My cell phone rang, and I pulled it out of my pocket. Helen Louise was calling.

"Hello there, how are you?"

"Hi, Charlie. Taking a short break." I could hear noise in the background, the usual sounds of her bakery, with customers enjoying themselves. "Getting ready for the evening. I just wanted to call and let you know I finished my ad for the paper, and it will start running tomorrow."

"That's excellent news." I hoped she was imagining my happy smile. "Fingers crossed that you get some great applicants right away."

"That would be lovely. I'm more than ready for some time off."

I could hear the tiredness in her voice. She worked awfully hard, and I was delighted that she might soon be able to slow down a bit and have more time for us to spend together. I told her that, and she chuckled.

"If this works out as well as I hope," she said, "you might get tired of me hanging around all the time."

"Never," I assured her. And with that one word, I realized that my feelings for her were much stronger than I had been willing to admit to myself before now. I felt a sudden lump in my throat and couldn't speak.

Intuitive as always, Helen Louise was quick to respond. "The same for me, *mon petit chou.*" The warmth in her voice touched me.

My response was lighthearted. "I've never figured out how calling someone *my little cabbage* ever came to be an endearment, but it certainly sounds charming in French."

Helen Louise laughed. "French is, after all, the language of romance."

"Guess I'd better start brushing up on it, then." I did remember how to flirt, it seemed.

"There will be plenty of time to learn, I hope," she said. I could hear the smile in her voice.

"The sooner you hire some help, the better."

"If only the *Athena Daily Register* comes through the way I hope it will. Otherwise I might have to put an ad in the Memphis paper."

"Good idea," I said. I decided not to mention the fire or Damitra Vane's murder. I

321

didn't want to spoil the mood. We made tentative plans for dinner over the weekend and chatted for a few moments longer, then she had to end the call to attend to customers.

I probably had a big, goofy grin on my face as I put my cell phone away. I glanced at my watch, surprised to note that it was 6:25. Time to get up and start warming up dinner.

I put the papers back on the desk, turned out the lights, and headed for the kitchen. Thinking back over my conversation with Helen Louise, I decided I might give her ad in the *Daily Register* a boost. I would talk to Melba Gilley, my friend at the library. She would be a good source for a potential employee, because she knew practically everyone in Athena, too.

Then I pulled up short. *Athena Daily Register.* Of course.

THIRTY-THREE

I hurried back into the den and turned the lamps on again. Then I scrambled through the short stack of notes until I found the one I wanted — the page headed "ADR," with the strings of numbers.

ADR. Athena Daily Register. Why hadn't I cottoned to it sooner?

I scanned the page.

MCA. Memphis Commercial Appeal.

The name of the paper was *The Commercial Appeal,* but locals often added the *Memphis.*

The strings of digits most likely signified page numbers with dates. For example, ADR 1-84321 might mean the first page of the March 21, 1984, paper. As I scanned down the page again, I noticed that 84 was part of all the strings of digits.

What had happened in 1984 that so interested Connor Lawton? Interested him enough to make notes of newspaper dates and pages?

Back issues of the *Register* earlier than 1998 hadn't been digitized yet, and that meant I couldn't access them over the Internet. I would have to check on the *Commercial Appeal.* Offhand, I didn't know the status of its archives. Even if it were not available online back to 1984, I knew our public library had it on microfilm. Just like the *Register.*

The public library closed at six, so I would have to wait until tomorrow to check out my theory. Then I remembered that the last time I saw Lawton at the library, he wanted to look at old issues of the local paper. I had left him in the microfilm room that afternoon.

I felt increasingly certain about my theory. The library opened at nine tomorrow morning, and I planned to be there.

Time to head back to the kitchen to get dinner started — or at least heated up, I corrected myself as I replaced the page and turned off the lights.

In the kitchen I found Justin and Sean already at work on our evening meal. Sean stood at the stove, stirring the pot of green beans, while Justin set the table.

"Hi, Mr. Charlie." Justin looked up from his task with a shy smile. "How's it going?"

"Fine," I said. "Thanks for setting the table." I nodded in Sean's direction. "And for taking care of the food."

"Justin is starving, as usual, and I'm pretty hungry myself." Sean grinned when Justin made a face at him. Sean treated my boarder like a kid brother, and I had detected signs of hero worship in Justin. He had even mentioned law school a couple of times recently, and I knew Sean had been talking to him about his experiences as a law student and then as a corporate attorney in a big Houston law firm.

I didn't know if Sean had told Justin the reason he left his job in Houston and moved to Athena. I knew Sean still felt embarrassed over the situation, and we hadn't discussed it again since the time he confessed it to me several months ago.

"You feel like going to tell Laura dinner's about ready?" Sean gave the beans another stir, then replaced the lid on the pot. "If not, I'll go, and you can fix the tea."

"I'll go." I grinned. "The stairs will do me good."

"Can't argue with that." Sean favored me with a sly grin, and Justin laughed.

"Just wait till you hit fifty," I told them. "Then talk to me."

"Fifty," Justin said, his eyes widening.

"Gosh, I'm not sure I can count that high."

Sean guffawed, and I shook my head at them. "Careful, or I'll send you both to bed without any dinner."

With that I turned and headed out of the kitchen, not waiting for a reaction. Their laughter followed me.

I trod up the stairs, pretending not to feel slightly winded by the time I reached the second-floor landing. I really needed to get more exercise. Or cut down on my food intake. Or both.

Sighing, I turned down the hall toward Laura's room. The door was closed, and I knocked a couple of times and waited for an invitation to enter.

I heard a muffled "Come in." When I opened the door and stepped into the room, I found Laura in the window seat with her laptop — just barely in the seat, because of course Diesel had scrunched himself into the small space with her. The window seat was only about three feet wide and eighteen inches deep, and Diesel could easily fill the space on his own. Laura didn't appear at all uncomfortable, however.

"Dinner's about ready," I said. "Feeling any better?"

Diesel meowed at me and unfolded himself from the window seat. Once on the floor he stretched and yawned before he padded over to me for a greeting.

As I rubbed his head, Laura responded to my question. "Not a lot. I'm still really upset about Damitra. There really isn't even anyone to mourn her. I don't think she had any family left, at least not any that had anything to do with her." She sighed as she closed her laptop and set it on the floor. "It's just so sad."

I moved to the window seat and slid in beside her. She rested her head on my shoulder while I slipped an arm around her. She snuggled closer. We sat that way for a moment. Diesel stretched out on the floor in front of us, his head on his front paws like a dog. His eyes focused on us.

"Yes, it is, sweetie," I said, my voice soft. "I wish I had the words to comfort you, but when something senseless like this happens, solace can be hard to find."

"It's all such a waste, Dad." Laura sat up, pulling away from my embrace. She turned to me, her face three inches from my own. The pain in her expression hurt me, and I wanted so badly to make that pain go away. That sense of loss would remain with her, I knew, and only the distance of time could make it bearable.

I kissed her forehead, then stood. I held

out my hand, and she clasped it. "Whenever you need to talk, I'll be here for you."

"I know." Laura smiled as she got up from the window seat, her hand still in mine. Diesel pushed himself up, chirped at us, then turned and trotted out the door.

"I think he's telling us it's time to eat." Laura laughed softly. "I'm actually a bit hungry."

"Then let me escort you downstairs." I tucked her hand into the crook of my arm, and off we went.

Thanks to the interrupted sleep of last night, I was ready for bed by eight-thirty. With my stomach full of Azalea's fine meal, I soon began to feel logy and knew that my bed was calling out to me. Diesel and I settled in, and I read for a few minutes. When I dropped the book the second time, I knew it was time to turn out the lights and go to sleep.

My hand barely left the lamp switch before I fell asleep — or so it seemed when I woke the next morning to the sound of my alarm. I hadn't even had to get up during the night to go to the bathroom, and for a man just past fifty-one, that was an accomplishment. I felt much refreshed this morning, I decided. I threw back the covers and sat up on the side of the bed.

Diesel muttered at me but remained in bed while I went to the bathroom. When I emerged to dress sometime later, he was still asleep. "Come on, lazybones," I said to him. "Time to get up. You don't need any more beauty sleep."

He opened his eyes and glared at me, as if to tell me not to be so perky this early in the morning. Then he yawned and rolled over on his back to stretch. I rubbed his tummy, and he warbled for me, his good humor seemingly restored.

Diesel and I breakfasted alone this morning. I had a whole wheat bagel with low-fat cream cheese and coffee, while Diesel had to make do with only his regular food. After I finished my second cup of coffee and the paper, I sat for a moment to review my plans for the day.

Sean would again accompany Laura to campus. She didn't need to be there until ten and would be done around three. I wanted to go to the public library to check the back issues of the Athena and Memphis newspapers to test my theory about the numbers among Lawton's notes. If that proved successful and I did find something of interest, I had no idea whether it would have any bearing on Lawton's death. I had to find out, however, as any good librarian would want to do.

Depending on what I discovered, I might call Kanesha Berry again. Though I didn't look forward to another conversation with her, I hoped perhaps she might be a little more tolerant.

Right — and Diesel might start speaking French, too.

By the time Diesel and I left the house at ten minutes to nine only Justin had appeared downstairs. We left him glancing through the paper and munching some toast heavily laden with Azalea's homemade scuppernong jelly. My mouth watered at the sight of that jelly, but I steeled myself against temptation. I had work to do.

At three minutes to nine, Diesel and I stood patiently in front of the unshaded main entrance to the Athena Public Library. The morning was already steamy, and I could feel the sweat trickling down my back.

We didn't wait long, for which I was thankful. Right on the dot of nine, Teresa Farmer, the head of the reference department and second in command, unlocked the doors and ushered us in. "Good morning, gentlemen," she said in her soft voice. "What an unexpected pleasure."

"Good morning to you, too," I said, and

Diesel chirped his greeting. "We're here to do a little newspaper research this morning."

Teresa paused for a moment to scratch the cat's head, then excused herself to put away the keys in her office. Diesel and I greeted the other library staffers we saw on our way to the room that contained the microfilms and readers.

I removed Diesel's leash and put it on a table. While I did my research, he would probably go visit with his buddies among the library staff. I knew I didn't have to worry about him here where he was universally adored.

I pulled the page of notes from my pocket and unfolded it. Holding it up, I began to examine the drawers of microfilm to find the ones containing the back issues of the *Register.* I would start there and then look for the *Commercial Appeal.* After a quick online check last night, I discovered that the digital archives of the Memphis paper didn't start until sometime in June of 1990.

The first number was 1-84321 and, if I was correct in my interpretation, that meant page one of the March 21, 1984, issue. I found the appropriate drawer and then the box. Settling down at the microfilm reader, I prepared the film for reading. I was an old hand at this, and I quickly found the page I wanted.

I scanned the headlines. There was a report from the recent city council meeting and a piece on street improvements in the oldest part of town. All run-of-the-mill stuff, and I couldn't see Lawton being interested in any of it. There was one small headline near the bottom, "Former Mayor Dead at 83."

According to the brief article, only several sentences long, Hubert Norris, who had served as mayor of Athena for twelve years back in the early 1960s, had died at home at the age of eighty-three.

That didn't sound promising either, though the name Norris rang a faint bell. Where had I heard it recently?

I glanced at the article again. The survivors mentioned were his wife, a daughter, Sarabeth Conley, and a son, Levi Norris.

That's why it was familiar. Sarabeth's father.

This had to be what interested Lawton, since he'd obviously known Sarabeth. But why?

THIRTY-FOUR

There were no other details about former mayor Norris's death. The next issue indicated was two days later, the twenty-third. A Friday, as it turned out. Hoping for further information, I scrolled down the pages until I came to the first page of the issue.

Hubert Norris's death was the main headline: "Tragic Death in Norris Family." I noted with some surprise that the byline belonged to Ray Appleby. I hadn't realized he was working for the *Register* that long ago.

That explained, however, why Lawton had the reporter's name in his notes. Had he talked to Appleby about this? I would have to check with the reporter, though I wasn't keen on revealing my connections with Lawton's murder. I would have to, though, because I doubted Appleby would simply open up to me out of the goodness of his heart. He was a seasoned and shrewd reporter, accustomed to digging up information, not giving it away.

Norris's death did indeed sound tragic. He had drowned in his bath. According to Appleby, a "tearful Mrs. Norris" confided that "Hubert found it relaxing to soak in the tub with a glass or two of whisky." But "nothing like this ever happened before," Mrs. Norris went on to say.

I winced at that latter statement, knowing that people will often say nonsensical things when in shock or grieving.

Appleby didn't come right out and say it, but the inference was clear. Hubert Norris had had too much to drink, fallen asleep in the bathtub, and drowned. *Did he have a drinking problem?* I wondered.

I couldn't recall anything about the family other than Sarabeth's babysitting me when I was a child. My parents didn't socialize with the Norrises from what I could remember, nor could I recall hearing Aunt Dottie talk much about them. By the time Hubert Norris drowned in the bathtub, I was married and living in Houston, the proud father of an infant son.

I had several sources for Norris family history, however. Helen Louise was in France at the time of Norris's death, I calculated, but she still might know something. Azalea and my friend Melba Gilley could fill in any necessary blanks, as could Ray Appleby, if he were so inclined.

But why was Connor Lawton so interested in Hubert Norris's death? It seemed like an ordinary tragedy and not terribly useful to a playwright.

Unless, of course, Lawton thought there was more to the story. But what could there be? Maybe that Norris's death wasn't an accident?

Hold on, I told myself.

Before I went too far down the road of idle speculation, I decided, I should check out the rest of the page references from Lawton's notes.

I had to pull several more boxes of microfilm from the cabinets, including some of the *Commercial Appeal* issues, but once I had read through them all I had a better understanding of Lawton's interest in the Norris family.

As I read I jotted down notes on the pad I'd brought with me. My eyes were tired and my neck slightly sore by the time I finished with the microfilm. I relaxed and massaged my neck while I read through my notes.

Ray Appleby, who continued to report on

Hubert Norris's death, wrote that there was to be an official investigation of the former mayor's death. Normal procedure, I supposed, in a case of accidental death, particularly of a prominent citizen.

There were several short articles about the investigation, and one about the funeral. That event evidently attracted notables from surrounding counties, and even a former governor and several state legislators. Hubert Norris had been well known in political circles, though the highest office he ever held was the mayoralty of Athena.

The articles grew shorter and ceased by the end of June. There were sparse details of the investigation, but from what I gathered the police and the sheriff's department were eventually satisfied with the verdict of accidental death.

Why had the investigation dragged on for three months, though? That seemed odd to me. Unless the two departments were bogged down in multiple other investigations, I couldn't see this one taking three months to resolve.

So why had it? That was a question I would put to Ray Appleby for sure.

The articles mentioned little about the rest of the Norris family. The first one had listed Sarabeth under her maiden name, but subsequent ones identified her as "Sarabeth (Mrs. Jack) Conley." The son, Levi, was apparently a teenager, and that meant there was quite a gap in age between him and Sarabeth. No age was given for the widow, but after quick calculations, based on Sarabeth's probable age of thirty-two or so in 1984, I figured Mrs. Norris was a good fifteen to twenty years younger than her husband. Perhaps she was still alive — another fact I might check.

I made a note to check the obituaries in the *Register*. Not today, however. I'd had my limit of microfilm. Later I'd start with the digitized versions of the paper, and if that yielded no result, then I would tackle the microfilm again. Another of the joys of being over fifty, I had discovered to my dismay, was that my eyes tired more easily now.

Back to my notes — the final two articles from the *Register* dated from the late 1980s and concerned Levi Norris. One was simply a mention in the weekly arrest reports the paper published — much to the chagrin of the families of those arrested, I was sure. Levi had been arrested for burglary in 1988, but I couldn't find any further details on that incident.

The second, short article denoted the arrest in 1991 of Levi Norris, then aged twenty-three, for assault and battery. A small, somewhat grainy photo of Norris accompanied the article. I stared at it. His face seemed familiar. Had I seen him somewhere recently?

It took me a moment, but I placed him. I'd seen him at the cocktail party and again at the theater. Laura and I had spoken to him there, and later I saw him talking with Sarabeth in the lobby. That settled, I returned to my research.

Lawton had apparently stopped with 1991 in his survey of the *Register.* Had he found all he needed, or had he meant to do more searching but didn't have time? I pondered that while I loaded the first roll of microfilm of the *Commercial Appeal.* There were only a few references for this paper, and I soon read them. They revealed further details of Levi Norris's brushes with the law. Mostly petty thievery or assault, including one incident in Memphis that sounded like attempted rape. There was no mention of Norris's having served time for any of these offenses, and I wondered about that, too.

Levi Norris seemed to be an unsavory character. He appeared innocuous enough when I'd seen him recently, though definitely a bit seedy. Had he reformed completely? His history of assault made me uneasy. He might have been Laura's attacker, and he also could be our would-be arsonist.

But why? How could he be connected with Connor Lawton and Damitra Vane? It didn't make much sense. Ralph and Magda Johnston still seemed more likely suspects to me.

I turned off the reader and replaced the microfilm boxes in the cabinet. I could have left them in a basket provided for that purpose and one of the staff would refile them later, but I didn't see the point in making extra work for anyone.

I found Diesel at the combined circulation/reference desk with Teresa and another of the staffers. We chatted for a few minutes, until other patrons approached the service points for assistance. Diesel and I bade our friends good-bye and headed home.

I nodded to the policeman on duty in a squad car parked in front of the house as I pulled into the driveway. I was grateful to know he was there. I had done my best not to let the arson attempt rattle me, but it was there at the back of my mind, ready to unnerve me the moment I let the thought surface.

The house was quiet when Diesel and I entered the kitchen, and for the first time in my life I felt slightly spooked by the silence. This was a big house, three stories plus an attic, with many places for an intruder to hide.

Diesel picked up on my unease. He pushed against my legs and meowed, and I realized how foolish I was being. The police had been watching the house, and they wouldn't let someone sneak inside. I removed Diesel's leash and harness and hung them on the rack by the back door, all the while talking to the cat to reassure him that everything was fine. A small worm of doubt kept niggling at me, however, but I did my best to ignore it.

Obeying an impulse I pulled out my cell phone and speed-dialed Sean. He answered quickly. "Hey, Dad. What's up?"

"Just back from the library. How are you and Laura? Where are you?"

"We're fine. We're in her office. I'm reading, and she's grading some papers. Want to talk to her?"

"No, that's okay. I'm sure she's got plenty to do. I thought I'd check on you, that's all." *Stop being such an idiot,* I told myself. *Of course they're fine.*

"Are you sure you're okay? You sound a

little odd."

"I'm fine, really." I put as much conviction as I could muster into my voice, though truth be told I was still uneasy. "I'll fill you in later on what I found out at the library."

"See you around three or so," Sean said. He ended the call.

I put my cell phone away, frowning. Why couldn't I shake this feeling that something was wrong in the house?

I stood there for a moment, irresolute. Then I felt even more foolish. I couldn't stand here in the kitchen like a spooked child until someone else came home. This was ridiculous.

Forcing my feet to move, I headed for the den. I wanted to sit down with Lawton's play again, now that I knew more about the Norris family, to see what connections there were with the Ferris family in the play. I ignored the prickles at the back of my neck as I approached the den.

I paused on the threshold for a moment, willing myself to go in. I reached for the overhead light switch and flipped it on.

After glancing around the room, I reassured myself there was no intruder lurking in here.

I scooped up the stack of papers that contained the play and settled on the sofa. I had plenty of room, because Diesel hadn't come with me. He was probably busy in the utility room and would be along soon.

Soon absorbed in Lawton's play, I forgot about Diesel. It wasn't until I became aware of loud meows coming from somewhere not far away that I realized at least ten minutes had passed and he still wasn't with me.

I set the papers aside and called out his name. "I'm in here, boy. Come on."

I waited, but the meowing didn't abate. I frowned. This was unusual behavior for him. Now he started yowling, and that really spooked me. I jumped up from the sofa and hurried out into the hall.

I spotted the cat near the front door, sitting near a pile of mail. I hadn't noticed it when I came through the hall earlier, but there was obviously something in the mail that concerned Diesel.

He quieted a bit as I approached, and I squatted by him and stroked his back. "What is it, boy? What's bothering you?"

I examined the mail. There were several letters, a magazine, several circulars, and one slightly bulky manila envelope. Diesel nudged this last item with his paw and looked at me. He meowed as if to say, *This is the one.*

The address side was down, so I turned it

over, a bit gingerly, though I wasn't sure why. There was no return address, but it was for Laura. Her name and address had been cut from what looked like newspaper headlines and pasted onto the envelope. The postmark was a local one, and the amount of postage on it seemed excessive. It didn't feel very heavy, so I couldn't figure out why so many stamps were necessary.

Diesel bumped my leg with his head, and I set the envelope down again. He meowed again, and I realized with a chill what he was trying to tell me.

My hands trembling, I unlocked the front door and opened it and urged Diesel out ahead of me. I pulled the door shut and then ran down the walk, yelling and gesturing at the police car in front of the house.

Thirty-Five

The policeman on surveillance duty must have seen us the moment I opened the door, because he met us on the sidewalk a few feet from his patrol car.

"What's wrong, Mr. Harris?" He held out a steadying hand as I rocked to a stop on the concrete. His nameplate read J. PERKINS.

"Letter bomb. Maybe." I had to gasp the words out. The combination of exertion and fear had robbed me of breath. Diesel pushed hard against my legs, and I almost toppled over.

"Where is it?" The officer kept his hand on my arm, for which I was grateful.

"Just inside the front door." I tried to slow and deepen my breathing.

"Right." The officer dropped his hand from my arm and put in a call for backup. When he finished, he turned back to me. "You come with me." I followed him to the squad car. He opened the back door and indicated that I should sit.

"Okay if my cat sits here, too?" I didn't want Diesel out on the street, but I also knew the officer might object to having a cat in an official vehicle.

"Sure," the officer said with a quick smile. He moved a few feet away to answer a call on his radio.

I put Diesel in first, then collapsed onto the seat beside him, finally feeling able to relax. Diesel crowded against me, obviously freaked out by the whole episode. I did my best to calm and reassure him while the officer waited near us for backup to arrive.

"You're such a smart kitty," I told him, pulling him against me for a hug. He chirped and began to settle down. I pulled a handkerchief from my pocket to wipe the sweat from my brow and the back of my head. The air blasting from the front of the car was welcome as I began to cool down.

Moments later I heard a siren, and perhaps ten seconds after that two more squad cars arrived. Several officers got out, and Officer Perkins spoke to them. They conferred in undertones, and I couldn't make out what they were saying. As I watched, Diesel still hunched against me, they headed up the walk to the open front door.

345

I heard another car pull up, this time behind the patrol car where Diesel and I rested. I turned to see Kanesha Berry and Deputy Bates climbing out of it. Bates nodded as he passed by, but Kanesha stopped by the open door and greeted me. "What's going on, Mr. Harris?"

Her expression grimmer than usual, Kanesha listened without interruption as I related my discovery of the potential letter bomb and Diesel's role in it.

Kanesha's eyes flicked toward the cat several times as I talked. When I finished, her first comment was "He must have smelled something odd about that package."

"Thank the Lord he did. He's one smart feline." I was fervent in praise of my cat, and for once Kanesha didn't appear irritated or dismissive. "I shudder to think what could have happened if Laura had opened that thing."

"We'll soon find out if it's dangerous." Kanesha turned to watch the activity at my front door.

"What's going to happen?"

She faced me again. "There's an officer in the police department who has experience with incendiaries and bombs from when he was in the army. If it is a bomb, he'll take it somewhere and destroy it — safely, of course." She pulled out her notebook. "Tell me again what you observed about the envelope."

I gave her the description again, and she jotted down the details. There was activity nearby, but it wasn't until I finished talking that I realized that two of the squad cars were gone, and Officer Perkins waited nearby to speak to Kanesha.

She turned to Perkins as she put her notebook away. "You wanted me, Officer?"

"Yes, ma'am." Perkins nodded respectfully. "The suspicious parcel has been removed, and it's okay for Mr. Harris to go back in his house, if he's ready."

"Thank you, Perkins." Kanesha dismissed him with a curt nod before she spoke to me. "You feel like going back inside?"

"Yes," I said, and Diesel added a meow to that.

A smile came and went quickly on Kanesha's face as she stood aside to allow me room to get out of the squad car.

"Come on, boy," I said, and Diesel hopped out.

Kanesha escorted us up the walk, and I decided to risk a question. "How is the investigation going?"

"About as well as could be expected." Kanesha paused on the doorstep as Diesel

347

and I entered the house.

When I realized the deputy hadn't followed me inside, I turned back. "Won't you come in for a minute?"

"Sorry, too much to do." Kanesha regarded me with what I thought could actually be sympathy. "Be careful, Mr. Harris. You and your whole family. We're going to keep a watch on your house, but if anything or anyone seems at all suspicious to you, call 911 immediately."

"You *will* catch whoever is doing this, won't you?" Those knots in my stomach were making a comeback.

"Yes, we will. I'm not going to tolerate this kind of crap in *my* county." Kanesha's firm certainty made me feel better. For a moment she reminded me of her mother. I had seen Azalea with that fierce expression numerous times, and I realized how much alike mother and daughter really were. That probably explained why they seemed to butt heads so often.

I doubted Kanesha would appreciate my pointing that out, however.

"Now, you'll have to excuse me," Kanesha said with a quick nod. "I've got to get back to the office. I'll let you know about the package as soon as I have more information." She turned and headed down the walk.

"Of course. Thanks, Deputy." I spoke to her rapidly retreating back. With a shake of the head, I stepped inside and shut the door.

Diesel rubbed against me, and I scratched his head. I told him again what a smart kitty he was. I told myself I'd feel foolish if the package turned out to be harmless, but I couldn't forget Diesel's behavior. That had to mean something was odd about the package. I prayed that no one was injured when they examined it further.

My head had begun to throb, and I figured I was a bit dehydrated. In the kitchen I poured myself a large glass of chilled water from the fridge, and after downing that I started to feel better. Diesel came back from a visit to the utility room as I was finishing my second glass. I decided he deserved a treat for his cleverness, and I rewarded him with a handful of the tidbits I stocked for that purpose. The moment he saw the package in my hand he started warbling, because he knew exactly what I was doing. He placed a large paw on my hand and pushed down as I bent over to put the treats on the floor for him.

I watched until he finished, and when he looked up, hopeful for more, I gave him a second handful. I made sure he saw me put the package away in the cabinet, however, when he finished his second round.

"That's all for now, boy," I told him. He gazed at me for a moment before he commenced washing his right front paw.

Time to get back to work, I decided. What had I been doing before Diesel alerted me to the presence of the strange envelope?

Ah, yes, I was reading the draft of Lawton's play. I headed back to the den, this time with Diesel on my heels. We settled down on the sofa, me confined to a small portion of it on one end while Diesel stretched out to occupy the rest. He soon dozed off, curled on his back with his front paws in the air. I resumed my reading.

I didn't spend much time on the portion of the play I thought was based on Ralph and Magda Johnston. There didn't seem to be much new that I could glean from those pages. Instead I focused on the sections that featured the Ferris family. The more I thought about it, the more I figured it was obvious that the "Ferrises" were really the Norrises.

Based on Lawton's notes and the articles from the two newspapers, I had to conclude that Lawton was deliberately writing about the real family, thinly disguised. But why? I kept coming back to that question.

How did Lawton know so much about the history of the Norrises? He had spent his early years in Athena, I knew, but hadn't he left when he was only four or five? I thought that was what someone told me. So what was the connection?

Pictures of Connor Lawton flashed in my head — Lawton at the Theater Department party, both inside and outside the house. I had puzzled over his behavior at the time, and that might be the clue I needed.

On a hunch I got up and went to the desk and fired up my computer. I waited, not very patiently, for it to finish all the preliminary gyrations it had to go through before I could use it.

When it was ready I opened my browser and typed in the address to the public library website. From there I could link to the information I wanted: Athena County property tax records.

I wanted to follow a hunch to find out what, if any, property the Norris family might still own in Athena. Then I would try to find out where the Lawtons had lived in Athena when Connor Lawton was a child. The answer might be that simple, that the Norrises and the Lawtons were neighbors back then.

After I found the link I wanted, I clicked and was taken to the property tax database. I could search by parcel number or by name. Since I had no idea what the parcel number in question was, I put in the name Norris.

There were eight results, but none of the Norrises was Hubert or Levi or even Sarabeth. Nor were the addresses ones I expected.

Now what? I thought for a moment, then typed in Conley, Sarabeth's married name.

This time there were seventeen results, Conley apparently being a more common name than Norris, at least in Athena.

I scanned the listings and then stopped at one for a Joseph Conley. The address was *1744 Rosemary Street.* Why did that sound familiar?

I puzzled over it for a moment, then I had it — Ralph Johnston's house, the site of the Theater Department party.

At least I had thought it was his house, but evidently it belonged to Sarabeth and her husband instead.

Lawton also had it in his notes, so it meant something to him.

I decided to follow my hunch further. I pulled out my cell phone and punched in the number for the public library. The very person I wanted to speak to answered. "Hi, Teresa, this is Charlie. How are you?"

We exchanged pleasantries, then I asked, "Are you really busy right now?"

"No, not terribly," Teresa replied. "What can I do for you?"

"I need to check something in one of the old phone books, if you wouldn't mind. I could come down there and do it myself, but I'm too impatient." I laughed.

"Not a problem. What year or years do you need?"

I did a quick calculation. "1982 or 1983 should do it."

"I'm going to put you on hold while I go pull them. Be right back." Soft music played in my ear.

The old phone books resided in cabinets in the same room with the microfilm, so I knew it would take Teresa a minute or two to retrieve the requested items.

I glanced over at the sofa. Diesel was still asleep. I smiled as I turned back to the computer.

Teresa came back on the line. "Got them both. What are you looking for?"

"A family named Lawton who might have lived on Rosemary Street back then."

"Okay, I'll check." I heard Teresa put the

phone down and begin to riffle through the pages.

Would my hunch pan out?

THIRTY-SIX

While I waited for Teresa to give me an answer, I drummed the fingers of my free hand on the desk. The habit used to drive my late wife crazy, and I gradually trained myself not to do it anymore. I frowned and stilled my hand. When had I started doing it again?

Probably nerves, I decided. Before I could ponder it any further, Teresa spoke in my ear.

"Here it is, Charlie. Declan Lawton, 1742 Rosemary Street. He's the only Lawton in the book. Is that what you were expecting?"

"Yes. Thank you so much, Teresa." We chatted a moment longer, then I ended the call and stuck the phone back in my pocket.

Since there was only one listing for a Lawton in the phone book of the time, Declan had to be Connor's father. That meant the Lawtons lived right next door to the Norrises when Connor was a child.

I found a blank piece of paper and a pencil and jotted down the name and address. I stared at the page for a moment before I put the pencil down.

Okay, so I proved that the Lawtons and the Norrises were neighbors at one time. Also that Sarabeth still owned her parents' house. What did that do for me?

I flashed on Connor, the night of the party, standing on the sidewalk in front of 1742 Rosemary Street and staring at it. Was he remembering the early years of his life? Or puzzled by a house that seemed strangely familiar?

Then I recalled his odd actions in the kitchen of Sarabeth's house, how he had stared at the cabinet and then gone to open it and peer inside. Was that another memory surfacing? A sense of déjà vu on Connor's part would explain that episode, I now realized.

How much had he remembered of his childhood in Athena? He had been four or five when his family left. Someone told me that, but now I couldn't recall whom.

Laura was the only person I could ask about Connor's memories, and I hoped like anything he had talked to her about them. Otherwise I couldn't go much further with my theory.

Well, not really a theory, I had to admit to myself. I still hadn't figured out the point of this. Connor's early childhood in Athena might have nothing to do with his murder.

But I guess I'd read too many mysteries — like every one of Ross Macdonald's books for a start — in which the semi-distant past weighed heavily on the present. What if that were the case here?

I glanced at my watch. A few minutes before three. Sean said he and Laura would be home around three. I debated calling Laura now because I was in such a hurry to ask my questions.

Sean and Laura's arrival home moments later saved me the trouble. I noticed Diesel perk up on the sofa just before I heard Sean calling out from the hallway, "Yoo-hoo, Dad, we're home. Where are you?"

"Come on, boy," I told the cat, but I could have saved my breath. He was off the sofa and out the door practically before the final syllable was out of my mouth.

When I stepped into the hallway, I raised my voice and responded to Sean. "Here I am. I was in the den working."

"We'll be in the kitchen." Sean's voice echoed down the hallway.

Laura sat at the table, Diesel already beside her, warbling away, and Sean had the fridge door open, head inside. He pulled out two beers and popped the caps before handing one to his sister. Spotting me, he asked, "Something to drink, Dad?"

"Some iced tea, I think, but I'll fix it." I waved him away, and he sat in his usual place at the table.

While I poured my tea and sweetened it, I said, "I have some rather unpleasant news for you, I'm afraid. Diesel and I had quite a bit of excitement this afternoon."

Laura's expression was apprehensive, and Sean's was wary as I took my own place across from Sean.

As calmly and clinically as I could, I related to them the events of the afternoon. Neither of them spoke until I finished, and then Laura erupted into speech.

"What the devil is going on here? Who hates me enough to want to kill me? Damitra is dead, but even if she was still alive, she'd never do something like this." Laura paused as she wrapped her arms across her chest and began to rock slightly in her chair.

Diesel knew she was upset, and he put his paws on her leg and rubbed his head against her side. She was so distressed, however, she appeared not to notice him. Sean and I both got up and went to her. I had to lean over the cat to do it, but I wrapped my arms

358

around her.

"It's going to be all right, sweetheart. Kanesha is really angry over this, and she'll put a stop to it. Nothing's going to happen to you. Whatever nutcase did this will be behind bars soon." Outwardly calm and soothing, I did my best to reassure her. But inside I could feel my guts roiling and my temper flaring. These threats against my daughter were causing me to have thoughts of violence I normally shied away from completely.

The glint in Sean's eyes told me he was as furious as I was. The sender of that package had better hope neither Sean nor I got to him before the police did.

Laura soon calmed down, and Sean and I resumed our places.

"Sorry, Dad," she said. "For a moment there it was all just too much."

"You've been under a tremendous strain." I regarded her with loving sympathy. "I hate that all this has happened, because you were so looking forward to the semester."

Laura nodded. "I really wanted to see what teaching was like. It's something I've been thinking about, but with all the craziness, I'm not sure I'm doing a very good job."

"I'm sure you're doing great." Sean patted his sister's shoulder. "As soon as this is all settled, you'll be able to focus and maybe even enjoy the rest of the semester."

"Wouldn't that be nice?" Laura's wistful tone tugged at my emotions.

"I've been doing research today, and it's possible that what I've found out could have some bearing on the murders." I didn't want to upset Laura any further, but I needed to talk to her about Connor. I hoped Lawton had talked to her at some point about his childhood here in Athena and about his play.

"What have you found out?" Sean followed my lead well. He cut his eyes sideways at his sister, and I knew he was concerned about upsetting her, just as I was.

"Before I get to that," I said, addressing Laura, "I need to ask you some questions, sweetheart. I know this could be upsetting to you, but I need to talk to you about Connor."

Laura had a couple of sips of her beer before she responded to me. "It's okay, Dad. I don't mind. What do you want to know?"

I decided to start with his childhood, then move on to the play, because that seemed the logical sequence. Accordingly, I asked her, "Did he ever tell you anything about his living in Athena as a child?"

"Sort of," Laura said with a frown. "When I first started seeing him, we had one of those talks where we discussed our families, you know, the kinds of things you always talk about at some point early in a relationship."

Sean and I nodded encouragement, and she continued.

"He told me that his parents were dead — they were kind of older when he was born, in their forties, I think, and he wasn't really planned. Anyway, he grew up in Vermont. His dad was an English professor there, and his mother taught piano. When I told him my father lived in Mississippi, he asked where. He laughed when I said Athena."

She paused for more beer. "I asked him what was so funny about that, figuring he was going to say something smart-ass about the South, but instead he said he'd actually been born in Athena. His dad was a professor at the college, but they left when he was five or something."

"That was an odd coincidence." Sean drained his beer and retrieved another from the fridge. He checked to see if Laura wanted another, but she shook her head.

"Yeah, it was pretty weird," Laura said.

"He told me, though, that he had no clear memories of Athena, just some vague impressions of his room and the backyard where he played a lot. There was a family next door that he'd stay with sometimes when his parents went out of town. That was about it."

That was disappointing. I was counting on the fact that he remembered much more about those years in Athena. I wasn't actually sure why, though. The idea was still trying to form itself in the dim recesses of my brain. I'd have to let my subconscious do its work and then hope I figured it all out.

"Even when he came back here and started living here again? Surely that stimulated his memory?" Sean expressed my thoughts more quickly than I could.

"I was talking about that conversation, months ago in LA, when we first discussed that stuff." Laura sounded impatient. "I hadn't gotten to things he told me more recently."

I was relieved to hear that. "Like what?"

Laura turned to me. "Once he was back here, little things started coming back to him. There were some places that were vaguely familiar, like that old toy store on the square and a couple of buildings on campus." She smiled sadly, and for a moment I thought tears were in the offing. She took a deep breath, however, and continued steadily. "He also made a comment or two about a house, but I wasn't sure which house he was talking about. I think, though, it was the house they lived in here."

"That doesn't sound very specific." Sean picked at the label on his beer bottle. "Couldn't he tell you where the house was?"

Laura looked uncomfortable as she glanced at me. "He was drinking a lot." She shrugged. "He always did when he was really into a new play. At least that's what he told me when I complained about it."

"I know the house he lived in," I said, startling them both.

"How did you find that out?" Sean sounded incredulous.

"Well, I am a librarian, you know." I grinned at them. "We know how to find things out."

Sean laughed, and Laura smiled at me. I went into mini-lecture mode as I recounted the process by which I figured it all out. While I talked, Diesel left Laura's side and came to sit by me. He butted his head against my leg to gain my attention, and I scratched his head as I continued my story.

"Pretty clever," Sean commented when I finished.

"I'll say," Laura added. "So Connor lived in the house next door to Sarabeth and her family." She paused, looking thoughtful. "That may explain something he said to me on the phone the other day."

When she didn't continue, I prompted her. "What was that?"

Laura blushed. "It wasn't very nice, I'm afraid. I don't want to repeat his exact words, Dad, because you wouldn't like it."

I grimaced. "At this point I doubt anything he said could shock me. Go ahead."

"Me either," Sean said. "Spill."

"Well, okay then. He was angry about something, and when I tried to get him to tell me what happened, he wouldn't. All he said was, 'That fat witch' — except he didn't say *witch* — 'may think she can shut me in like she used to, but I'm too big now.'"

THIRTY-SEVEN

I frowned. There was something odd about what Laura said, but for a moment I couldn't quite isolate it.

Then I had it. "You said just now 'may think she can shut me in like she used to.' Are you sure he said 'shut in' and not 'shut up'?"

Laura nodded while Sean looked on, obviously curious. "Yes, I thought it was odd, too. I tried to ask him what he meant, but he'd obviously had a lot to drink. Getting him to focus when he was drunk was difficult."

"So who was the fat witch" — Sean grinned slightly at the euphemism — "he was talking about?"

"Sarabeth Conley," Laura and I said in unison.

"Had to be," I continued on my own. "She's tall and heavy, and she gave him a dressing-down on Monday, right there on stage. He seemed a little intimidated by her, too. Plus, her family was probably the one he stayed with."

"She did act like she knew him," Laura said. "I wasn't around the two of them together, except maybe twice, but she wasn't intimidated by him like everyone else seemed to be."

"If she used to babysit him when he lived here, she probably wasn't." Sean laughed. "Like Azalea, for example. Remember that summer you and I came and stayed with Aunt Dottie for two weeks while Mom and Dad went to England? I was, what, eleven? And you would have been nine."

A shadow passed over Laura's face at the mention of her mother, but she managed a smile. "I'd forgotten about that, but you're right. Once someone's cleaned your snotty nose and supervised your bath, I guess they don't always see you as an adult."

I cleared my throat to get rid of a sudden lump. "Another question, sweetheart. Do you remember the context of that statement Connor made?"

"You mean what prompted him to say that about Sarabeth?" Laura asked.

"Exactly." I of course couldn't prove it, but I was sure now that it was Sarabeth Connor had been referring to with his rude comment.

"He was talking about the new direction he was going with the play. He had started with one set of characters, but then he decided to switch and write about different ones instead." Laura shook her head. "I asked him why, and all he could tell me was that he felt like he had to. This story was coming to him, kind of like memories, and he just had to write about them. He wasn't sure why."

Sean snorted. "Probably just the bourbon talking."

Laura looked thoughtful. "I was inclined to think that at first. But Connor said that, whenever he sat down to write, these things kind of poured out. It was slow at first, but the longer he was in Athena, the more often it happened." She glanced at me. "Does that make sense to you?"

"It's starting to," I said. My amorphous idea was finally beginning to coalesce into something substantive. "Repressed memories."

Sean and Laura looked at each other, then at me. Sean spoke first. "So you think he was writing about things that really happened? To him?"

I nodded. "I read through the play, and I thought the two sets of characters — I mean

the fact that there *were* two sets of characters — was odd. It seemed like a very
disjointed way to tell a story, because there
was no indication that the story lines would
connect. Then, once I found out that Connor lived next door to Sarabeth and her
family as a child, I had this vague notion
that the second set of characters might be
connected to the Norrises. Norris was Sarabeth's maiden name."

"And the family in play is named Ferris."
Laura nodded. "And the older daughter in
the family is named Lisbeth. Sarabeth,
Lisbeth. Norris, Ferris."

"That makes sense," Sean said. "The
similarity of those names can't be simple
coincidence."

"I don't think they are," I said.

"Does Sarabeth have a younger sister?"
Laura asked.

"No, a younger brother, Levi Norris. He's
the man you and I spoke to briefly on
Monday. Remember the man who came
from backstage and asked us if we'd seen
Sarabeth?"

Laura nodded at me, and I continued.
"The younger daughter in the play is in
trouble, about to go to jail because of
something she did. The father refuses to
shell out any money to help her, and the

older sister is very angry about it."

"Do you know anything about Levi Norris?" I could see that Sean was intrigued by this, and with his lawyer's brain he was quickly making the connections.

"He's been in trouble with the law numerous times," I said. "I found some odd notations among Connor's notes, and eventually I figured out they were references to newspaper articles." I offered them a brief rundown of my search through the newspaper archives at the library. At mention of the library, Diesel head-butted my thigh again, and I responded with some scratching of his head. He rewarded me with contented rumbling.

"Then Connor was writing about an incident that happened in the Norris family." Sean drained the last of his beer and set the bottle aside. "An embarrassing incident it sounds like, but surely old news. People in Athena already know about the son's brushes with the law."

"Of course they do. In a town like this, everyone always knows." I could see the point Sean was attempting to make.

Evidently Laura did, too. "Even if it is old news that everybody knows, that doesn't mean the family would want to see it brought up again. Particularly onstage in

369

front of the whole town."

"Yeah, I see your point," Sean said. "But surely, Dad, you're not thinking that's a motive for murder, just to stop the play from being performed."

"That's only because you haven't read the play." Laura rubbed her nose. "Dad and I have. Lisbeth in the play is pretty angry with her father because he has the money to solve the problem but refuses. She says at some point that if he was dead, there wouldn't be a problem."

I ran quickly through my memories of what I'd read. "Furthermore, in one scene Lisbeth tells her sister not to worry, she's figured out how to solve all their problems. Then she says something to the effect that their father won't ever say no to them again."

"Is Mr. Norris still living?" Sean leaned forward eagerly. "I bet he's not."

"He's not. I found his obituary. It was one of the pages Connor had listed."

"When did he die?" Laura asked.

"March of 1984. He had been mayor of Athena at one time, and he died at home. There was an investigation, and the eventual conclusion was that it was an accident. He drowned in the bathtub. According to his wife, he liked to soak in the tub and drink whisky."

"The inference being that he had too much to drink, passed out, and drowned." Sean shrugged. "What's so mysterious about that? It's not very smart to get drunk and soak in the tub."

"No, it's not," I said. "The strange thing was, the investigation into his death went on for three months."

"There must have been something about it, then, that made the police think it wasn't a simple accident." Laura frowned. "There was nothing in Connor's play about the father's actual death."

"No, but there were some cryptic notes." I tried to recall what I'd read. "Oh, yes, Connor had the words *bathtub, ankles,* and *bruises* in his notes, along with question marks."

"I don't see the significance," Laura said. "Well, *bathtub,* of course, since Mr. Norris died in the bathtub."

"I think I may have the answer to that," I said. A picture was slowly forming in my mind. I knew I had read about a similar situation in a murder mystery at some point.

"What is it?" Sean's impatient question brought me out of my reverie.

"A way to murder someone and probably

get away with it, because it would look like an accident."

THIRTY-EIGHT

"What *is* this method?"

Once again I'd fallen silent, picturing what I'd read in my mind, and Sean's question prompted me to explain aloud.

"I can't remember which book I read it in," I said. "But what you do if you want to kill someone in the bathtub is grab him or her by the ankles and pull up until the victim's head is underwater."

Laura frowned. "That sounds horrible, but surely the person in the tub can lift himself up or jerk his legs loose."

I shook my head. "That's what I would have thought too, but evidently it's not the case. Particularly if the person pulling the legs up is strong."

"And in this case we're talking about an elderly man who'd been drinking." Sean shrugged. "He probably didn't have much upper body strength anyway. Pretty quick method to get rid of someone in your way."

"Definitely," I said. Visualizing it, however, made me a little sick to my stomach.

"But how can you find out more about the Norris case?" Sean pointed out an obstacle. "Unless you can convince Kanesha Berry to open the files and let you see the autopsy."

"She might end up having to do that," I said. "Not necessarily letting me see it, of course, but reopening the case." I shook my head as I pictured telling all this to Kanesha. "I have another way to find out about the case. Ray Appleby."

"Who's that?" Laura asked. "The name sounds vaguely familiar."

"Reporter for the local paper," Sean explained to her. "Thanks to Dad's so-called career as an amateur sleuth, he's encountered Appleby a few times." He turned to me. "Was he a reporter back then?"

"He was," I confirmed. "His name was in Connor's notes, and I'm willing to bet Connor talked to him about the Norris case. I'm going to call him myself and probably ask him some of the same questions."

"Will he talk to you?" Laura asked.

"Yes," I said with confidence. "Particularly if it's connected to the other murders. He'd be the first person to break the story, and any reporter worth his beans would go for it." I stood and glanced at my watch — almost five-fifteen. "Even though he might have gone home for the day, I'm going to call the *Register* offices. I'll ask them to get a message to him, and I bet he'll call back right away."

I pulled the local phone book out of a cabinet drawer and looked up the number. Before I could punch it in, however, Laura stopped me with a question.

"Dad, how did Connor die, do you think?"

I thought about that for a moment as I regarded her. I remembered the red splotches I had noticed on Connor's face and neck. Splotches that indicated he could have been suffocated.

Reluctantly, because I didn't want to cause her further pain, I offered my conclusion.

She averted her eyes for a moment when I finished, but then she met my gaze again. "Suffocated. Drowning is a form of suffocation, isn't it?"

I nodded.

"Good point." Sean shot his sister an approving look. "So both old Mr. Norris and Connor died from being suffocated to death."

When Laura winced, Sean immediately

appeared contrite. "Sorry, sis. I didn't mean it to sound so clinical."

Laura responded with a wan smile. "I know you didn't. I'm okay."

"Kanesha will have to confirm all of this," I said.

"It could simply be coincidence," Laura pointed out.

"Yeah, it could," Sean said with obvious reluctance. "But both victims liked to drink. We don't know that Mr. Norris was a heavy drinker, but that might be something Ray Appleby can tell us."

I nodded. "I'll certainly ask him." I turned back to the phone book, located the number again, and punched it into the phone.

When a woman answered, I asked for Ray Appleby and was told I had just missed him. "I have something urgent to talk to him about. Could be a big story," I said, laying it on thick. "I know he'll want to talk to me, so can you get a message to him right away?" I gave her my name and number. "Remember, this is really big."

She assured me she'd see that Appleby received my message as soon as possible, and I hung up and leaned against the counter.

Sean and Laura watched me while I kept my eyes on my watch. *Be available,* I thought. *Be available.*

One minute and twenty-three seconds after I hung up the phone, it rang.

I snatched it up and said hello.

"Mr. Harris? Ray Appleby here. You have a big story for me?"

I heard a touch of skepticism in his tone, but he knew I'd been involved in two previous murder cases. "Yes, I'm pretty sure I do. It has to do with the death of the playwright Connor Lawton."

"Got you," Appleby said, and by those two syllables I knew I'd captured his interest. "Can I come over and talk to you right now?"

"Please do," I said. "You remember the address?"

After assuring me he did, he concluded with, "Be there in ten or less." The phone clicked in my ear, and I hung up.

I repeated the reporter's side of the conversation for Laura and Sean. While we were discussing the questions we wanted to ask Appleby, I heard the front door open and steps in the hallway. For a moment I tensed, then I remembered the front door was locked, and whoever just came in had a key.

Moments later Dante bounced into the room, barking to announce his arrival. He made a beeline for Diesel, still at my side, while Stewart entered the room in more leisurely fashion.

"Howdy, everyone," he drawled. "How nice of you all to be here to greet me." He grinned. "So what kind of family confab are you having?"

Sean spoke first. "We're waiting for that reporter, Ray Appleby. He's on his way over."

"Dante, calm down," Stewart said as his eyes glinted with interest. The poodle was still barking at Diesel, who was studiously ignoring him. At Stewart's command, however, the dog shut up and trotted over to his master. "Good boy. Now, what's Ray coming here for?" He pulled out a chair next to Laura and sat, and Dante hopped into his lap and snuggled down.

I explained the situation to him as briefly as I could. The doorbell rang as I was finishing. Sean went to answer it.

He walked into the kitchen with our visitor moments later. He introduced Laura and was about to introduce Stewart, when Stewart interrupted him.

"Oh, Ray and I go way back, don't we, Ray?" Stewart arched one eyebrow as he regarded the reporter.

Appleby, who appeared to be about my age, reddened slightly at Stewart's flirtatious tone. "Unfortunately, yes."

"Now, Ray, is that any way to talk about me?" Stewart grinned.

This was intriguing. From Stewart's behavior I gathered that he and Appleby knew each other in a way I hadn't expected. Laura and I exchanged bemused glances. Stewart rarely spoke about the men he dated, at least to me, and here was one in the flesh.

"You're a pain in the derriere, Stewart, and you know it." The reporter flashed a quick grin. "What the heck are you doing here?"

"I live here," Stewart said.

Appleby glanced at Sean and back again at Stewart, and the meaning of his gesture was obvious. Stewart laughed. "I only wish," he said. "No, I'm a boarder, plain and simple."

"Nothing plain and simple about you," Appleby retorted.

"Why, Ray, what a sweet thing to say." Stewart batted his eyelashes, and Laura and Sean burst out laughing. I had to join in.

Appleby rolled his eyes. "I didn't drop everything and come over here to rake up the past with you." He turned to me. "What is it you have to tell me about Connor Lawton, Mr. Harris?"

"Have a seat, why don't you?" I gestured

to an empty chair across from Laura and Stewart.

Appleby complied as Sean resumed his own seat.

"Can I offer you something to drink?" I asked.

The reporter shook his head. "I'm fine, thanks." He was clearly impatient for me to get on with it. He kept darting glances across the table at Stewart, but I pretended not to notice.

"This is all related to the death of Connor Lawton," I began. "But we think the roots of it may go back to 1984."

Appleby appeared intrigued. He pulled a small notebook and pen from his shirt pocket. "What happened in 1984 that's possibly relevant?"

"The death of former mayor Hubert Norris." I paused to gauge the effect. Appleby was definitely surprised.

"How are the two connected?" he asked.

"Connor was born here in Athena, Mr. Appleby," Laura said. "He lived here with his parents until he was about five, I think. That would have been in 1984."

"Call me Ray." Appleby nodded. "Yeah, I knew Lawton was born here, but I still don't see the connection."

"The Lawtons lived next door to the Norris family," Sean said.

"Okay," Appleby said. "But what's the connection?"

I realized then that I had never fully articulated my idea. Mainly because there was a piece still missing, one last, vital link that needed to be uncovered. But what was it? There was something I wasn't getting. But what?

Then I had it. The kitchen cabinet.

But Appleby and the others were staring at me, waiting for an answer to the question.

"I'll get to that," I said. "First, let me ask you some questions, Mr. Appleby."

"Ray," he said. "Shoot."

"Okay, Ray." I nodded. "You covered Hubert Norris's death and the investigation into it for the *Register*."

"Yeah, it was my first big assignment," the reporter said. "I'd been with the paper about a year then."

"Why did the investigation drag on for three months?" I asked. "It sounded pretty straightforward to me. Accidental death of an elderly man in his bathtub."

"On the surface, that's exactly what it seemed like." Ray nodded. "Old man Norris was a pretty heavy drinker, and his wife swore up and down that he liked to soak in the tub and drink."

"That much was in the paper, more or less." I said. "Is there more to it, then?"

"I always thought so. Norris had a lot of money, and he was notoriously tightfisted with it. There was a son, a teenager. Yeah, Levi, that's his name. Anyway, he was always in trouble of some kind. Shoplifting, joyriding, you name it, and the old man was always paying someone off to keep the brat out of jail." The reporter paused. "A couple of weeks before Norris died, Levi had finally landed in jail. A hit-and-run in which a child was badly injured. Norris refused to post bail, from what I recall."

"What happened to his money when he died?" Sean asked.

"The wife got it all," Ray replied. "And not long after the old man died, his wife posted bail for Levi. She must have paid off the family whose child was injured, because it never went to court."

"This child who was injured," Laura said slowly. "It wasn't Connor, was it?"

"No," Ray said. "I forget the name, but it wasn't Lawton."

"Hubert Norris's death turned out to be pretty convenient for his son, wouldn't you say?" Stewart regarded Ray with a knowing expression.

"Sure did," Ray replied. "I believe the police thought so, too. Norris had soaked in the tub, drinking, hundreds of times before, so why did he fall asleep and allegedly drown this time? Too convenient."

I remembered Connor's notes and the word *bruises*. "Was there anything to indicate that it might not have been an accident?"

Ray frowned. "The only thing I can recall is that Norris apparently had a bruise on one ankle. The family couldn't explain it, and I think the police eventually just had to drop it and let it go as an accident."

"But you think there was more to it." I felt certain I was right about that.

"The whole thing was odd," Ray said. "I spoke to the widow and the daughter a couple of times. I never got the impression that anyone was grieving over the old man's death. The daughter seemed almost happy, frankly."

"That's really sad." Laura frowned.

"Back to my original question." Ray tapped his notebook with his pen. "What's the connection with Lawton?"

All eyes turned to me, and even Diesel — who had been unusually quiet until now — sat up and warbled.

I took a deep breath and hoped what I

was about to tell them didn't sound completely far-fetched.

"It all has to do with a little boy and a
kitchen cabinet."

THIRTY-NINE

As I expected, they all looked puzzled by my statement. Even Diesel meowed.

"Bear with me," I said. "This is going to take a few minutes to explain. First off, we know that Sarabeth Norris, now Conley, used to babysit Connor. Evidently he would stay with the Norrises when his parents went out of town."

Ray was scribbling in his notebook.

"In fact," I continued, "Sarabeth was my babysitter too, although quite a few years earlier."

Sean and Laura smiled at that.

"Now, jump forward almost thirty years, to a party held not long ago in Sarabeth's house, the house that belonged to her parents. I was sitting alone in the kitchen, not feeling much inclined to rejoin the party. I was over in the corner, out of sight, when Connor came in to get something to drink."

"I sort of abandoned you, didn't I?" Laura frowned. "Sorry about that, Dad."

"I was fine." I smiled. "Anyway, there I sat, drinking my wine, when Connor came in and got himself a beer. He leaned against the counter and lit a cigarette. While he drank and smoked, he was staring at something in the kitchen. Then he went over and squatted in front of a cabinet in the wall and opened the door. He looked inside, and then he said, 'Not so nuts after all.'"

"What a strange thing to say." Stewart scratched Dante's back, and the poodle whimpered with pleasure. "What the heck did it mean, though?"

"That cabinet obviously held some kind of memory for him. In his notes he even wrote the word *cabinet*. All kind of strange, but then when you add to it another odd remark he made to Laura, it starts to make more sense." I paused to let Laura speak.

She looked puzzled for a moment, and then I could see that she figured out what I was talking about. "Yes, he said something about a fat woman. That she 'may think she can shut me in like she used to, but I'm too big now.' Do you think he was talking about someone who shut him up inside a cabinet?"

I nodded. "I think he was. I think Sarabeth might have put him inside that cabinet, probably to punish him. I imagine he was a pretty rambunctious child."

"He was also a little claustrophobic," Laura said. "Maybe that's why."

"That's all interesting speculation," Ray said. "But how does that connect with Norris's death?"

Stewart snorted. "Come on, Ray, don't be so dense. Remember the old saying, 'Little pitchers have big ears'?" He shook his head. "They probably locked the kid in the cabinet and forgot he was there. No telling what he might have heard."

"There was a child in the play," Laura said. "A child named Connie. I thought Connie was a girl."

"But Connie *could* be a nickname for Connor," Sean said. "He could have called himself that, or something close to it. I remember I had trouble with *Laura* when I was small." He smiled at his sister. "I called you Lah-wuh until I was five or six."

"What's this about the play?" Ray looked puzzled, and I couldn't really blame him. He didn't have all the details that we did.

I hastened to explain. "There are scenes in the play that are reminiscent of what happened in the Norris family. In fact, the family in the play is named Ferris. Not that different from Norris."

"So you think the play Lawton was writing was based on his childhood memories?" Ray scribbled some more in his notebook. "Fascinating."

"Repressed memory, isn't that what it's called?" Stewart asked.

"Yes," I said. "According to Laura, Connor didn't remember much about his life in Athena until he came back here. Then, slowly, memories started to surface."

"That's when he totally changed the focus of the play." Laura ran a hand through her hair a couple of times. "At first he probably wasn't aware of what he was doing. The story was just there, in his subconscious, and out it came. The more he wrote, the more he saw of people and places here, the more memories that surfaced."

"That's exactly what I think happened." I nodded approvingly at my daughter.

"So, basically what you're telling me is this." Ray fixed his gaze on me. "Sarabeth Norris drowned her father in the bathtub because the old man refused to help her brother. Lawton overheard something potentially incriminating when he was possibly locked inside the kitchen cabinet. Then, nearly thirty years later, he comes back to Athena and starts writing a play, and that play is about what happened to the Norris family."

"Yeah, that's pretty much it." Sean nodded. "Then Sarabeth, or maybe her brother, killed Lawton because they wanted to stop the play. They were probably afraid that people would remember their father's death once they saw the play and start connecting the two."

"Seems kind of far-fetched to me," Appleby said. "Like something out of Agatha Christie." He shook his head. "But it's just oddball enough to be true. What do you expect me to do?"

"Nothing, for the moment," I said. "This is all speculative. The only thing to do is to lay all this in front of Kanesha Berry and let her handle it."

"Are there any other suspects? She hasn't had much to say to the press about the investigation so far, simply the standard comments about following up leads." Ray sounded disgruntled.

I'd been so caught up in developing my hazy, unformed idea into a full-blown theory that I'd forgotten all about Ralph and Magda Johnston. We had all spoken freely with Ray about Sarabeth's alleged involvement in Connor's death, mainly because I needed information that only Ray could supply. But could I justify telling the reporter about the Johnstons' dirty laundry?

I realized that Laura, Sean, and Stewart were watching me expectantly, waiting for me to respond to the question.

"Guess there must be," Ray said with a slight smirk. "Otherwise you would have denied it already. So who is it?"

"I'm on the proverbial horns of a dilemma," I said in an effort to stall. I continued to think. I could tell him what Helen Louise told me, because evidently the Johnstons' marriage woes were widely known in town. But I didn't think I should say anything about the letter Connor wrote concerning Ralph's play.

"Okay, here goes," I said, and four pairs of eyes stared at me. "Connor was having an affair with a married woman, one who's apparently notorious for sleeping around."

"You mean Magda Johnston." Ray's statement didn't really surprise me.

"Yes. I had it from a very reliable source that she and Connor were seen together on several occasions, and their behavior with each other made it clear they were having an affair." This was all so sordid, just as the story of the Norris family was. But somewhere in all the sordidness lay the answer to Connor's death — and perhaps to Hubert

Norris's and Damitra Vane's deaths as well.

"Johnston did try to beat up that athlete his wife was screwing around with." Ray cocked his head to one side as he regarded me. "So maybe Johnston finally went postal and offed the guy his wife was sleeping with?" He nodded. "That doesn't sound nearly so far-fetched to me. There are all kinds of stories about those two nuts."

"There's another motive as well, but one that I really can't go into detail about," I said, feeling somewhat foolish. "But it has to do with a professional matter."

"Let me guess," Ray said, a speculative gleam in his eye. "Ralph Johnston — excuse me, *Montana* Johnston — fancies himself as a playwright." He snorted derisively. "But I saw that play of his, and it was horrendously bad. Your cat could probably write something better."

I smiled fondly at Diesel, who lay by my chair, his head on his front paws. "I can't argue with that. I saw the play, too."

"Then I'll bet Lawton mouthed off about Johnston's play." Ray grinned. "I interviewed Lawton right after he first got to town, and he was pretty full of himself. I left out some of the less-than-polite things he had to say about the Theater Department at the college."

"I can neither confirm nor deny your conclusion." I smiled. Ray Appleby was sharp, I had to admit.

"No need to." Ray nodded. "I've also interviewed Johnston a couple of times. He's his own biggest fan, believe you me, and I know he wouldn't take it too well to have someone like Lawton come in here and tell him he's an idiot."

"What do we do now? Invite them all over for tea in the library where you do your best Hercule Poirot imitation and reveal all?" Stewart's facetious question was directed at me.

"That's not exactly what I had in mind," I said in a mild tone. "My plan is to lay it all in front of Kanesha and let her handle it from there. I don't want any more incidents —" I broke off, remembering too late that I didn't want to bring up the attacks aimed at Laura in front of a reporter.

Ray was quick to seize on my gaffe. "Incidents? Like what?" He paused for an answer, but when none of us responded, he continued. "That must be why the police are watching your house. Unless, of course, one of *you* is a suspect." He eyed each of us in turn, then fixed his attention on Laura. "You knew Lawton pretty well, didn't you?"

"Yes, I did," Laura said. "But I didn't have

anything to do with his murder. And neither did anybody else in this room."

Ray focused his gaze on me. "I really don't think one of you is a murderer, although *you* do seem to have a knack for getting involved in murders. Tell me, then, why are the police watching your house?"

I figured I couldn't hold out any longer. "There have a couple of attacks aimed at Laura. She was assaulted in her office on campus, and earlier today there was an envelope in the mail, addressed to her, that might have been a letter bomb." I left out the attempted arson.

Ray whistled and looked at Laura. "Somebody's sure got it in for you. Why?"

"We don't know," Sean said curtly. "Whoever's behind it must think she knows something incriminating."

"Something that Lawton told you and no one else." Ray was still focused on Laura.

Laura shrugged. "I have no clue what that could be. Anything that seems pertinent I've already discussed with my father and my brother."

Ray turned back to me. "You know, the more I think about it, the odder it seems. You've got old man Norris, death by drowning in a bathtub, right? And then Lawton, how did he die?"

"Suffocation, I think." I wondered where Ray was going with this.

Ray nodded. "Okay. Then there's this Damitra Vane woman. She has to be connected, right, because the only reason she was in town was because of Lawton, correct?"

I nodded.

"She had her throat cut." Ray looked thoughtful as he continued. "Then your daughter was attacked in her office. You also tell me that she got sent what could have been a letter bomb."

Again I nodded. There was also the arson, but I still didn't bring it up. I was beginning to see the point he was trying to make.

"Two men suffocated to death. Nasty, but not really violent, right?" Ray gazed at us each in turn, and we all nodded. "Then you have a stabbing, an assault, and a bomb. All really violent."

He paused, and again we nodded.

"Don't you see?" Ray asked. "Looks to me like we're talking about two very different people committing these crimes."

FORTY

I wasn't as surprised at Ray's assessment of the murders as the others appeared to be. I had no idea whether he was right, of course, but he had picked up on something that had been bothering me.

"I believe that's a valid point, Ray," Sean said. "Murder is a violent crime, but there are levels of violence. I wonder what a profiler would make of the three murders, an assault, and a letter bomb?"

"A profiler might look for someone with a history of violence," Ray replied. "Like Levi Norris. He's been in and out of trouble since he was a kid. Increasingly violent trouble, including attempted rape."

"We know about some of that," Laura said. "Dad found references to it in the newspapers."

"The police and the sheriff's department know all about Levi's history. He's been pretty clean, as far as I know, for the past ten years or so. But it wouldn't surprise me a bit if he was behind the stabbing, the assault, and the letter bomb."

"I want to put a stop to any more violence and protect my family." I spoke in a fiercer tone that I intended, but I supposed my subconscious feelings of fear for my family's safety came through. "Kanesha's going to have to listen to me about all this."

"That's probably my cue to leave." Ray Appleby stood and put his notebook and pen away. "She wouldn't allow me to hang around anyway, even if she does agree to talk to you." He glanced at Stewart in what I thought was a studiously casual manner. "Besides, dinner's waiting for me at home."

"How sweet." Stewart arched both eyebrows and tilted his head slightly. "Who is it *this* week, Ray?"

The reporter's face turned fiery red, and I thought he might stroke out right in front of us. Stewart offered an angelic smile, while Laura and Sean both turned their heads away. Ray stood there, silent a moment longer, and then the red faded away. He nodded to me. "I'll check in with you later, after the sheriff's department has issued some kind of statement. I really think you're on to something with Sarabeth and Levi Norris."

I escorted him to the front door, and when I returned to the kitchen the others were laughing. "I can't believe how bratty you can be." Laura shook her finger at Stewart. "That wasn't a nice thing to do." She grinned.

"A queen's prerogative," Stewart said with a smirk. "Sometime I'll tell you the whole, boring story, darlin', but let me just say that I have my reasons." He batted his eyelashes at my daughter. "And they are *good.*" He drew the last word out until it sounded like it had five syllables.

Sean snorted. "Promise me you'll give up the Jack McFarland routine one of these days before you drive us all nuts, okay?"

Stewart and Laura both sputtered with laughter in response.

I stood patiently until the hilarity died down, trying not to smile. When the three of them sobered enough to focus on me, I said, "Time to get serious, gang. I'm going to call Kanesha and try to get her to listen to me. We've put together an interesting scenario, but we have no idea what kind of evidence she has. Maybe all she needs is some of the information we have, maybe not. But I want this resolved as soon as possible, because I don't like the notion of my family being under a threat of more violence."

Diesel came up to me and rubbed against my legs, meowing as he did so. I knew he had picked up on the turmoil I was feeling, a mixture of excitement and dread. I scratched his head and murmured to him that everything was all right, and he stopped talking and relaxed against me.

"Of course, Dad," Sean said. "Whatever you want us to do, just tell us."

"Thanks, son. I know I can count on you." I paused. "The main thing is to stick together and not let Levi or Sarabeth get close to any of us until this is over."

"Are you convinced it's them, and not the Johnstons?" Stewart put a restless Dante on the floor, and the dog ran toward the utility room and his water bowl.

"Yes, I am." I scratched Diesel's head because I could feel him getting skittish again. "Because of Hubert Norris, primarily. His death was too convenient. It has to be linked to the present."

"I think you're right," Stewart said. "I don't know about y'all, but I'm hungry. That I can do something about. How about I get dinner started while Charlie calls Wonder Woman?"

"Good idea," Laura said. "I'm hungry,

too. I'll help."

"Me, too," Sean said. "Unless you need me for something, Dad."

"No, go ahead. I'm going to the den and call Kanesha from there."

Diesel came along with me to the den. I sat at the desk, and he climbed onto the sofa and nestled into his afghan. He meowed a couple of times, as if inviting me to join him. I knew what he wanted, of course — back scratches and belly rubs, for which he would reward me with purring and warbling.

"In a minute, boy," I said. "Have to make this phone call first."

I didn't relish the forthcoming talk with Kanesha. She might still be aggravated over the scene with her mother the other day. I couldn't help being in the middle of it, but Kanesha wasn't quite rational when it came to her mother. I wasn't afraid of her. I simply didn't like confrontation that much. Talking to her always felt more like confrontation than conversation.

Still, I had provided helpful information in two previous investigations, so maybe she'd be willing to listen to me this time.

I punched in the number that I knew all too well these days and waited for a response. "Could I speak to Chief Deputy

Berry, please? It's Charlie Harris, and I have some urgent news for her."

The voice on the other end expressed regret that the chief deputy wasn't available and I was welcome to leave a message and a callback number. With a distinct feeling of anticlimax, I repeated that my need to speak with her was urgent and gave my cell number. "She can call me at any time."

I received further assurances that the message would be delivered, and that was that. I set my cell phone down and stared at the papers on the desk.

I didn't know how long it would be before Kanesha returned my call. Minutes? Hours? It was frustrating not being able to unburden myself and turn it all over to her.

Sean interrupted my mental stewing. "Dad, can we talk a minute?"

I turned to see him entering the den. I nodded. "What is it?"

"Just got off the phone with Alexandra," he said as he perched on the edge of the sofa. Diesel shifted position and pushed his hind paws against Sean's leg — a clear signal that Sean was supposed to give him attention. Sean grinned and started rubbing the cat's tummy. "She really needs me tomorrow morning. She has to take a deposition in Tupelo and wants me to go with her. Can you be Laura's bodyguard until I get back, probably sometime after lunch?"

"Of course. I'll call Melba first thing in the morning and let her know I won't be in."

"Sorry you have to miss work again." Sean stood, and Diesel grumbled at the removal of the attentive hand on his stomach. "Have you talked to Kanesha yet?"

"Missing work isn't a problem," I said. "And no, I haven't talked to Kanesha. She wasn't available, and I had to leave a message."

"Irritating," Sean said with a sympathetic smile. He knew how impatient I could be in situations like this. "Dinner won't be long. I'll give you a holler when it's ready."

"Thanks." As he left I turned back to the papers on my desk. Perhaps I should go through them and make my own set of notes, help me organize my thoughts for when I did talk to Kanesha.

I found a pen and a legal pad and started to work. A few minutes later I felt a large paw on my thigh, and then Diesel thrust his head under my right arm and pushed. I put down the pen and rubbed his head. "Sorry, boy, I know you want some attention. I'm distracted right now, so you'll have to forgive me."

Diesel responded with some plaintive meows, but continued attention to the area behind his ears turned the meows into happy warbles.

Sean called me for dinner before I could get back to my notes, and Diesel and I headed for the kitchen.

I had a hard time getting to sleep that night. Kanesha had yet to return my call, and I had to use every ounce of self-restraint I possessed not to call the sheriff's department every half hour. I could have tried to talk to someone else, at least to assuage some of my growing need to share this theory. But I knew that Kanesha was the one who would have to decide what to do with my information, so I might as well wait until I could tell her.

Sleep, when it came, was not particularly restful, and I wanted to take a baseball bat to my alarm when it went off the next morning. Diesel, who had been sleeping next to me, picked up on my grumpy mood and did what I referred to as his "adorable kitty routine." Winsome looks and sympathetic chirps added to languorous stretches were all designed to soften me and make me say, "What a sweet/cute/adorable boy you are," and thereby improve my mood.

Naturally I couldn't resist this and did feel better by the time I went downstairs for breakfast. Thinking about the morning ahead and fretting over the lack of a return call from Kanesha, however, pushed my level of grumpiness right back up. I considered insisting that Laura stay home today, but I knew she would argue with me.

We made it to her office on campus a few minutes before nine, with Diesel in tow. He inspected her office while I settled in the only visitor's chair. Laura booted her computer and prepared to read e-mail.

"There's coffee down in the staff commons area," Laura said.

"I'm fine." I'd had my requisite two cups before we left home. "Don't worry about me. You focus on your work, and I'll sit here and read. Diesel will settle down in a few minutes after he's smelled everything there is to smell in here."

Laura smiled as she watched the cat for a moment. "He is definitely curious, isn't he?" She turned back to her computer screen and soon became absorbed in her task.

I pulled a book out of my briefcase and settled down to read. In times of stress I tended to reread old favorites, and this morning I had pulled an old favorite off the shelf, Georgette Heyer's *The Grand Sophy*. I was soon immersed in it and barely noticed when Diesel came to stretch out under my chair.

I'd read about twenty pages when the entrance of a visitor startled me.

"Good morning." Sarabeth Conley stood in the doorway. "May I come in?"

FORTY-ONE

I'd hoped we could avoid Sarabeth today, at least until I'd had a chance to talk to Kanesha. But here she was in the doorway, offering a tentative smile as she peered around the door at Laura.

I stood and forced a smile. "Good morning. Would you like to sit down?"

Sarabeth spotted Diesel under the chair. "Goodness, what a big cat. He won't bite, will he?"

"Not unless you're mean to him." Laura, her expression neutral, looked up at Sarabeth. "Then he might gnaw your leg off."

Sarabeth tittered nervously and darted glances back and forth between Laura and Diesel.

"It's okay," I said. "Sit down. He won't bother you."

When Sarabeth made a tentative move toward him, Diesel crawled from under the chair and moved around the desk to sit by

Laura. Sarabeth occupied the chair, and I took up position against the wall between her and Laura. If she attempted anything, I could block her before she could reach my daughter.

"What can we do for you?" Laura's tone was cool but professional.

"I just wanted to see how you're doing," Sarabeth said. "After that nasty bump on the head. I hope you're feeling a lot better."

Sarabeth sounded completely sincere, and I wondered whether she had any acting experience. I knew I'd have to call upon every bit of acting ability I might possess to keep from letting her realize I was suspicious of her.

"I'm feeling fine," Laura said. "Luckily I have a hard head." She darted a mischievous glance at me before gazing solemnly at Sarabeth again. "I'm pretty hard to kill, as it turns out."

Sarabeth frowned. "What are you talking about? You don't think whoever assaulted you here was trying to kill you, do you?"

She was playing this to the hilt. In a way, I couldn't help admire her nerve. I felt fairly certain her brother Levi was the one who hit Laura, and she must have known that, if not condoned it.

"Oh, that bump on the head wasn't

much." Laura's airy tone alerted me that she was up to something. I tried to catch her eye but she studiously avoided my gaze. "But add to that an attempt to burn down our house while we were all asleep, and then a letter bomb delivered to the house with my name on it, and I think that adds up to attempted murder. Don't you?"

Sarabeth paled, and she clutched at her heart. For a moment I was afraid she was going to topple over in a faint. She held on to the chair for dear life with her other hand. "Burn down your house?" Her voice came out in a strained whisper. "Letter bomb?"

Laura nodded. "Pretty nasty, isn't it?"

"Was — was anyone hurt?" Sarabeth still had a hand over her heart. The color had yet to return to her face, and her breathing was labored.

Did I need to call 911? Was she going to have a heart attack? If she was acting, she was carrying it way too far.

"Are you okay, Sarabeth?" I moved nearer. "You don't look so good."

She shook her head. "I'll be okay in a minute. Just the shock, I guess. I had no idea any of these things happened. I never dreamed —" She broke off, appearing confused.

"Sorry, what was that?" Laura asked, her expression hard.

"Nothing," Sarabeth said. She pushed herself to her feet. "Nothing really. I'm glad you're safe, but I really have to get back to my desk. Something urgent to deal with that I just remembered."

"Of course," Laura said, and we both watched her go.

The moment I thought she was safely out of earshot, I spoke. "That was truly bizarre. If she was telling the truth, she didn't know anything about the arson attempt or the letter bomb. Was she acting, do you think?"

"Hard to say." Laura bit her lower lip for a moment as she considered further. "If she was acting, she ought to be on Broadway right now, because she's brilliant." She paused, then shook her head. "But you know, somehow I don't think she was acting. I think she really was surprised and upset."

Before I could follow up on that, a knock sounded at the door. I jerked to attention, suddenly aware I'd let my guard down completely. Diesel, however, was meowing as he walked around the desk to greet the new visitor.

Kanesha Berry stood in the doorway. "Morning, Mr. Harris, Miss Harris. I stopped by your house, and Mr. Delacorte told me you'd be here." She glanced down at the cat, now standing in front of her and gazing up. "Hello, cat." Diesel meowed again.

"Come in, Deputy," I said. "Am I ever glad to see you."

Kanesha stepped around Diesel, but the cat followed her for the few steps she took. I motioned toward the chair. "Please, have a seat."

"Thanks," Kanesha said. She started to sit, but stopped abruptly and pointed to something in the chair. "What's that? Where did it come from?"

I moved closer to see what she was talking about. In the middle of the seat lay a purple sequin and two small beads.

"They probably came off Sarabeth's dress," I said. "Or caftan, really. She wears these highly decorated ones. They have beads and sequins and things all over them." I made a move to sweep them out of the chair, but Kanesha stopped me.

"Sarabeth Conley?" she said. "These came from her clothes?"

Her sharp tone told me that there was something significant about these little objects. "Yes, she was just here talking to us and sat in the chair. I was sitting there before she came in, and they weren't in the chair then."

Kanesha pulled out her cell phone. "Bates, come on in and bring the kit." She ended the call. "You have something urgent to talk to me about. What is it?"

I glanced down at the seat of the chair and back at her. Her expression didn't change. I was burning with curiosity, and from one quick glance at my daughter I knew Laura was, too.

"Yes, I do. It's about the murders. We've come across some information you should have, if you don't already."

Kanesha didn't change expression, but somehow I could feel her irritation. "Well, go on. What is it?"

"It's about the Norris family. I don't know whether you remember when Sarabeth's father, Hubert, died, almost thirty years ago."

Her expression altered to one of minimal interest. "I was in junior high. I vaguely recall it."

"His death was ruled an accident. He drowned in the bathtub after drinking whisky. There was an investigation that lasted three months, but the final verdict was accidental death."

"But you obviously think there was more

to it." Kanesha crossed her arms over her chest and leaned against the door frame.

"I think he might have been murdered." I hurried through the explanation of the method, but before I could get into the motive, Deputy Bates appeared.

"Excuse me." Kanesha pointed to the seat of the chair. "Bag that and label it 'Sarabeth Norris.' "

Bates got to work, and Kanesha focused her attention on me again. "Please continue."

I complied with her request, and it took me several minutes to outline the main points I wanted to make. Bates finished his task while I talked, and Kanesha motioned for him to wait in the hall. Laura kept Diesel by her side and hushed him a couple of times when he tried to contribute to my narrative. Kanesha didn't appear amused by that, though I had to suppress a smile.

When I finally ran down, I thought I spotted a ghost of a smile hovering around Kanesha's lips.

"Interesting." She nodded. "Anything else?"

I decided to tell her about Sarabeth's odd behavior during her visit just now. "What do you think?" I asked when I finished.

"Also interesting. It's all beginning to fit

411

together." Kanesha nodded. "I appreciate your information, Mr. Harris." She turned as if to leave.

"Come on, now," I said. "You can't just go and not say more than that."

She turned back with an actual smile. "No, I guess not." She glanced at Laura, then back at me. "Thanks to those little doodads in the chair, I now have pretty conclusive evidence that Sarabeth Conley murdered Connor Lawton."

FORTY-TWO

"A sequin and two beads conclusive evidence? How?" Had they found similar items in Connor's apartment?

"Okay, what I'm about to tell you hasn't officially been released yet, but as the closest thing Lawton had to family, I think you should know." Kanesha paused to stick her head out the door and confer briefly with Bates. When she finished she pushed the door closed and leaned against it.

"Why don't you sit?" She nodded at the chair.

"Okay." I sat, wishing she'd hurry up and start talking.

"The autopsy on Lawton hasn't been finalized, but we do know that he was suffocated. He had a high blood alcohol content, so more than likely he was passed out when it happened, and may have died without ever waking up."

I checked Laura and, although she had

paled, she seemed composed. My heart went out to her, because I knew this was difficult for her. Having to hear the details of how a friend died is never easy.

When neither Laura nor I commented, Kanesha continued. "The pathologist at first couldn't figure out how it was done, but she did find some odd things lodged in his nasal passages and in his beard. I had no idea where they came from until today."

"Beads and sequins," I said, dumbfounded. "From one of Sarabeth's caftans. But how?"

Kanesha shrugged. "I think she maybe just wadded up part of her caftan and covered his nose and mouth with it. She was strong enough to hold him down if he roused and started to struggle."

Laura cried out at that, and I couldn't blame her. The image conjured by Kanesha's words was disturbing. I got up from my chair and went to comfort Laura. "I'm so sorry, sweetheart," I said softly as I squatted by her chair. I put my arms around her, and she laid her head on my shoulder for a moment. Then she pulled away to find a tissue and dab at her eyes.

"Sorry," Kanesha said. "I know it's upsetting, but I think that has to be the way it happened."

"You're right." I shook my head as I stood. I remained beside Laura. "It's all too easy to visualize, unfortunately. In both cases, she took the most expedient means, and the fact that she's tall and strong made it so much easier." Diesel rubbed hard against my legs, seeking comfort, and I rubbed his head.

"Yes. I'm going to be arresting her shortly, as soon as I can get the warrant, and you won't have to worry about her anymore." Kanesha smiled grimly.

"That's wonderful," I said. "But what about Levi Norris? Do you think he's responsible for Damitra Vane's murder and the rest?"

"That's one reason I wanted to talk to you too this morning." Kanesha sounded smug. "By the way, that was a letter bomb, and you were smart to do exactly what you did. It could have killed whoever opened it and anyone standing nearby."

For a moment I felt like I was going to pass out, and I leaned against Laura's chair. I managed to collect myself when I heard Laura saying "Dad! Daddy, are you okay?"

"I'm okay," I said, though my voice sounded strained, even to me. Laura got up and insisted that I take her chair. Since my knees were still wobbly, I did, and she stood by me with an arm across my shoulders.

Kanesha, with a guilty expression, apologized. "Didn't think you'd react that way. I shouldn't be so blunt sometimes."

I nodded but didn't comment.

After a moment she continued. "You won't have to worry about Levi Norris either. The police picked him up about an hour ago, and he's in jail, pending charges."

"For what?" Laura asked.

"Murder, specifically the murder of Damitra Vane," Kanesha said. She paused for a moment. "I won't go into the details, but Norris left evidence at the scene that I'm confident we'll be able to link to him."

I wanted to ask what kind of evidence, but I doubted Kanesha would answer.

"I'm sorry that you and your family had to go through all this." Kanesha's expression of sympathy touched me. For once I truly believed she empathized. "I'm sure Norris was responsible for both the letter bomb and the arson. But it's over now. You're safe."

"Thank you, Deputy," I said. "I'm so relieved, I don't know what to do."

"Me, too," Laura said.

Diesel had to add his few cents' worth, and that eased the tension. Even Kanesha laughed. She bade us good-bye and disappeared out the door.

I looked up at Laura, still leaning against me, and smiled. "Let's go home and share the good news."

The following weekend, we were all gathered in the kitchen, along with Frank Salisbury and Helen Louise Brady. Sean had invited Alexandra Pendergrast, but she couldn't join us. Helen Louise provided the dessert, Stewart outdid himself with dinner, and Frank brought the wine. The mood was festive, and we celebrated heartily.

Conversation as we finished our dessert inevitably centered on the arrests of Sarabeth Conley and Levi Norris.

"It was all rather anticlimactic, as it turned out." I sipped at the excellent pinot noir Frank supplied. "I was all geared up to argue with Kanesha and make her listen to me. I just knew she was going to argue, but the way it turned out, I didn't have to."

"As long as it's over, who needs a tense confrontation with the murderer?" Helen Louise laughed. "They always seem a bit contrived in some of the books I read."

"I know what you mean." Stewart shook his head. "I've seen every episode of *Murder, She Wrote,* and I adore Angela Lansbury to pieces. But you'd have to be insane to let

Jessica Fletcher within ten yards of your house. Talk about harbingers of death. And the way she was always rounding everybody up and then *Revealing All*." He treated us to a theatrical shudder.

"That's television." Sean snorted. "We all know it doesn't have a lot to do with real life."

"I've had enough of *real life* to do me for a while," Laura said. "It's so nice just to settle into a routine with my classes."

"What about the play your students were going to be doing?" Justin asked. "With all that's happened, are you just going to forget about it?"

"No, we're going on with the project, just a different play. I suggested several, but" — Laura rolled her eyes — "Montana Johnston insisted we do his new play. Of course I can't say no."

Frank snickered. "Maybe another rousing failure will finally convince him to stop writing plays. He obviously has no talent whatsoever for it."

"Without Connor here to insult him, he can pretty much ignore anyone else." Laura frowned, and I knew she still grieved over the death of her friend, though she seemed to be the only person who did.

Frank clasped her hand in his, and she

smiled. The adoring glance he bestowed upon Laura surprised no one. The two were now practically inseparable, and I kept expecting to find that he'd moved into my house.

They hadn't gone that far, however, for which I was thankful. I'm rather old fashioned about some things, and that was one of them. If their relationship continued and they wanted to move in together, I'd have to live with that. But as long as Laura was here, under my roof, well, there were limits.

The conversation drifted onto other topics, and I sat and observed the interactions among my family and friends. Helen Louise chatted easily with Sean and Justin, while Frank, Laura, and Stewart discussed plays they'd seen in New York.

The four-legged members of the family were sound asleep under the table, their tummies full, worn out by more attention than they knew what to do with. Dante snored lightly, while Diesel occasionally woke to stretch and yawn. He then went right back to sleep. I smiled at the sight and enjoyed the general air of contentment and relaxation. This was how it should be, family and friends happy and enjoying one another.

I thought briefly of Sarabeth Conley and

Levi Norris and their sad story. Sarabeth apparently continued to insist that her father's death was an accident, but she had admitted her guilt in Connor's murder. She simply refused to say why she'd done it.

I believed I knew why. When Sarabeth saw Lawton's play being workshopped, she realized the scenes were too close to reality. I was sure Lawton was present, hiding in the kitchen cabinet, and overheard Sarabeth planning her father's death. He was too young to understand the implications at the time, but the repressed memories were there, waiting for some stimulus to revive them. The memories of the people and their actions seeped into his writing, and Sarabeth must have feared that the playwright would eventually realize that his work wasn't simply fiction. She stole the laptop and killed Lawton to keep the truth behind her father's death from ever being revealed.

That solution seemed reasonable to me. Perhaps the full details would come out during the trial.

Yesterday I had received a letter from her, and the moment I realized the source I was tempted to throw it away unread. But curiosity got the better of me, and I read it.

The letter contained an apology, of sorts. Sarabeth talked about family and how important it was, particularly the relation-ship between parents and children. "Some-times," she wrote, "parents will do anything — even kill — for the sake of their children. Surely you can understand that, Charlie?"

I did, but I had to deplore what she had done on her brother's behalf.

But there was more to the letter, and my eyes widened with shock when I realized what Sarabeth was telling me.

"Having a child is a terrible responsibility, and we don't always raise them very well. My parents didn't do too well by me, but that's life. Mistakes happen and can't be fixed, but he's my son, though he doesn't know that, and I had to protect him. I hope you can understand that."

She signed it with only her name, Sara-beth.

Levi was her son. The revelation stunned me.

I hadn't shared that with anyone yet. I wasn't sure if I would. Sarabeth had en-trusted me with a secret, and I thought I should respect her confidence, despite all that had happened.

I focused gratefully once more on my fam-ily and friends and let the warmth and joy of their presence envelop me, thinking all the time how lucky I was.

The employees of Thorndike Press hope you have enjoyed this Large Print book. All our Thorndike, Wheeler, and Kennebec Large Print titles are designed for easy reading, and all our books are made to last. Other Thorndike Press Large Print books are available at your library, through selected bookstores, or directly from us.

For information about titles, please call:
   (800) 223-1244

or visit our Web site at:
   http://gale.cengage.com/thorndike

To share your comments, please write:
   Publisher
   Thorndike Press
   10 Water St., Suite 310
   Waterville, ME 04901